NIGHT WAVES

A Science Fiction Story

22-23
31 —
110 — 114

IZZY DOROSKI

www.izzydoroski.com

ISBN 978-0-9908045-2-9 (pbk.)
ISBN 978-0-9908045-3-6 (ebk.)

Line Editor: Crystal Watanabe
Book Editor: Lourdes Venard
Cover Art & Book Design: Lia Rees

Image Credits

Chapter 2: Cueva © kikofjl 2007
License: CC-BY

Chapter 21: Gough Island © Prof. Peter Ryan,
FitzPatrick Institute of African Ornithology

Chapter 30: Mosasaurus © N.Tamura 2009
License: CC-BY-SA

Chapter 35: © Sailko
License: CC-BY

Images have been adapted slightly to improve
print results in this monochrome paperback.

" We expect more discoveries like this in the future, so don't be surprised if we find more unimaginable creatures deep below the ocean. "

Visit the official website at:

IZZYDOROSKI.COM

for information, updates,
preview, reviews, where to
purchase, contact the author,
blog and media

It's a complex and time-consuming process writing a book, a true labor of love, from the initial step of thinking up an interesting story to the process of getting it down on paper and refining it into a beautifully crafted novel. All this would not have been possible without the help and services of several people who assisted me along the way. Some of these people deserve to be noted.

Having a good line editor go over the story, making it the best it can be, is always a good idea and I was lucky to get a real professional with Crystal Watanabe. She skillfully adjusted the grammar and enhanced the flow of the story, getting the verbiage to read as easy as possible. I am totally in gratitude for Crystal's assistance.

As good as the manuscript was, I knew I had to find a great final review editor to look over the completed draft to see what was then needed to make the story complete and perfect. I again went with Lourdes Venard as my book editor. Lourdes had been the book editor of my first book, *The Inverted Mask*, and I was very happy with the job she had done on that project. She truly helped me refine and sculpt the manuscript into a professionally laid out sci-fi novel that everyone would enjoy reading.

I wanted the cover design to reflect the image and feeling of the story. Luckily, I discovered Lia Rees, a graphics designer from England. Lia created a stunning bold concept that projected the adventure of the story as soon as you set eyes on the cover. She also assisted in creating the website for this book and the interior pictures and graphics inside the book. Lia also assisted me in getting my final manuscript formatted into the printing company's required setup.

A special thanks must be given to David De Ridder for his expert proofreading and examination of the manuscript. He assisted significantly in getting it into a nice sparkling easy read.

Lastly, I would like to thank the family members and friends who encouraged me during the entire process of the book development. That always helped me continue on the long adventure of getting my second book published. Thanks to you all!

To my wife Jeanne,
who helped me in every way
possible in creating this book.

USS *Scorpion* (SSN-589) was a
Skipjack-class nuclear submarine
of the United States Navy that
entered into service December of
1959. During her years of service,
the *Scorpion* participated in
exercises with 6th Fleet units and
NATO-member navies patrolling
the Atlantic Ocean.

The *Scorpion* transmitted its last message just before midnight on May 21, 1968, and was classified as *presumed lost* on June 5, 1968. After an extensive search and investigation, the US Navy determined the wreck of the *Scorpion* to be on the bottom of the Atlantic Ocean. A court of inquiry stated that "The certain cause of the loss of the *Scorpion* cannot be ascertained from evidence now available."

To this day, the loss of the *Scorpion*, with ninety-nine crewmen dying in the incident, cannot be fully explained. Let us remember their lives and not forget the service and courage that they provided. They are on eternal patrol and will always be remembered.

CONTENTS

Prelude...................................xiii

Chapter 1: Sounds from the Deep...............1

Chapter 2: Exploring the Blue Hole...........7

Chapter 3: Cruising to the Airport...........16

Chapter 4: Ocean Engineering Corporation International (OECI)...........................20

Chapter 5: The Submarine Launch..............28

Chapter 6: An Unusual Request................42

Chapter 7: Aboard the *Aquatarus*............56

Chapter 8: Located on Radar..................64

Chapter 9: Launch............................73

Chapter 10: The Mysterious Discovery.........84

Chapter 11: Nighttime Alert..................97

Chapter 12: From the Bottom.................106

Chapter 13: Rendezvous with the *Pemaquid*.....116

Chapter 14: Arrival at Port Jefferson Harbor.126

Chapter 15: The Ocean Science Symposium......129

Chapter 16: A Strange Call..................144

Chapter 17: Enjoying the Night Out..........153

Chapter 18: Journey to Gough Island..........160

Chapter 19: Deep Sea Marine Creatures........168

Chapter 20: Celebrating the Contract.........176

Chapter 21: Deep Dive off Gough Island.......186

Chapter 22: Descending in the Moon Pool......196

Chapter 23: Flying to the *Ososcelos*..........207

Chapter 24: Escape from the Deep.............217

Chapter 25: South Africa.....................229

Chapter 26: Cape Town........................238

Chapter 27: Zepheron Corporation.............245

Chapter 28: Into the Desert..................259

Chapter 29: West of Africa...................272

Chapter 30: Creatures of the Deep............283

Chapter 31: The ITUS Project.................295

Chapter 32: Tunnel 19........................307

Chapter 33: Controlled Demolition...........315

Chapter 34: A Celebration....................325

Chapter 35: Revisiting the Atlantic..........332

About the Author.............................

Prelude

Throughout the ages, ancient people have gazed out from the shoreline, peering into the vastness of the ocean, wondering what lies out there beyond the immense horizon. They walked the beaches, climbed the cliffs, felt the spray of the surf on their faces, and thought about the wonders and mysteries below the ocean depths. Sailors and fishermen ventured out into the sea to gather its bounty and riches and came back influenced by its strangeness and energy. They told tales of weird and wonderful sightings they encountered while at sea, tales of ghost ships, unusual fog, huge waves, and of unknown monsters from the deep.

Even today in our advanced technological world, we still enjoy our special moments with the sea. We contemplate its beauty and mystery. We walk its shores, feel inner peace, and ponder its unknown depths and power. For years, scientists have studied the oceans and have made many surprising discoveries about its inner workings, but they have also come to recognize that its endless depths still conceal much mystery. They have come to realize that the spirits of the ocean have kept their most treasured secrets from us.

[1]

Sounds from the Deep

May 21, 1968
Time: 23:37

The USS *Scorpion*, a Skipjack-class nuclear-powered submarine with a crew of ninety-nine crewmen and officers on board, was headed on a course northeast at nineteen knots. She was three hundred and fifty feet deep in the Atlantic Ocean and four hundred nautical miles southwest of the Azores. Their mission was highly classified and extremely important.

Captain Bryant lay in his bunk. He was still half asleep, but the footsteps outside his door intruded on his dreams. His mind cleared and his eyes opened when he heard the knock on his door. He stirred for a moment, then slowly got up as the knock became more insistent. Upon opening the door, he was greeted by Chief Petty Officer Clarence Randall.

"Sir, sorry to disturb you, but your assistance is needed in the control room immediately, sir."

Bryant raised an eyebrow and scowled. "What's the issue, Randall?"

"Lieutenant Lane asked me to get you, sir. An unidentified potential threat has been detected, and they request your assistance."

A surge of adrenaline pushed away the last of Bryant's sleepy haze. "Very well, Randall. I'm coming."

Bryant grabbed his navy-blue cap, which was emblazoned with the official US Navy seal, tugged it firmly into place, and followed CPO Randall toward the control room. They passed through an interior hatchway, turned left, headed up a flight of stairs, and proceeded forward into the hallway. As they passed the radio room, a loud general quarters alarm sounded several times. The alarm was accompanied by flashing red lights that lit up the area around the well-illuminated control room.

"Battle stations! All hands on deck!"

Bryant's heart rate picked up as he raced into the room where Lt. Lane was leaning in to examine the sonar displays with the chief sonar technician. Looking up, Lane noticed Bryant and blurted, "Captain, we've got an NFG! No frigging good at all. It's an unidentified target, sir."

Bryant's brows pulled together in confusion. "Lieutenant, what's going on out there?"

"Sir, we've been following a Soviet supply surface vessel for the last several hours. It's heading northeast toward their convoy. Then a short while ago we also detected something that seems to be a Soviet Delta 3 class sub."

"Are you sure, Lieutenant?"

"Well, that's the problem, Captain. We were tracking it for some time, but then we lost the signal. Some minutes later the signal reappeared again suddenly, but we're picking up something else very close to it as well."

"So there are now two separate signals?"

Lane's voice cracked. "We heard a robust echo from the Delta 3. Then we detected another sound not associated with the sub. That one has us completely baffled. What the hell could it be, sir?"

***

Three nautical miles southeast of the USS *Scorpion*, on the surface of the Atlantic Ocean, the USS *Midland*, a Bainbridge-class destroyer, was tracking the undersea activity of the USS *Scorpion* as well as the nearby Soviet surface and subsurface vessels.

The hull of the elegant, powerful ship was cold and dark. No light was visible from the deck other than the stars high in the pitch-black sky. A breeze blew across the deck as white-capped waves pounded the ship. It sped along at seventeen knots in a northeasterly direction toward the Soviet convoy.

Three levels below the deck of the sleek destroyer, the sonar-equipment room was a beehive of activity. Several specialized Navy technicians and officers gathered around Nate Daschle, the chief sonar technician, as he searched the sonar monitors.

Commander Joe Vallario's concern was obvious as he asked, "Nate, what's the status of the tracking target? Has anything changed?"

"The *Scorpion* is still bearing northeast at nineteen knots, sir. It's being followed by the Delta 3! The Soviet sub is closing fast on the *Scorpion*, sir!"

Commander Vallario knew full well that the Delta 3 Soviet sub was a first-rate attack-class

3

submarine. The Delta 3's new state-of-the-art torpedoes were capable of destroying the *Scorpion* with the push of a button. Vallario wasted no time in picking up the communication mic. He gave a direct order to the CON room, "Battle stations! Battle stations! All hands on deck! Engage anti-submarine systems and arm the depth-charge pods! I repeat, battle stations! This is not a drill!"

Commander Vallario turned to his ensign officer, Brent Coors, and both men stared at each other. Their faces reflected the sudden stressful turn of events, but these seasoned Navy veterans had experienced sudden bursts of drama before when engaging the Soviets, and they knew how to handle the situation.

"What do you think, Commander?" the ensign officer asked. "Do you think they're serious, or are they playing games with us?"

Vallario quirked his eyebrow and smirked as he turned to Coors. "It's all a game, Chief. We're always playing the game of Who's Going to Blink First."

Suddenly they were interrupted by a shout from Daschle. "Commander! I think the Delta 3 is opening its torpedo doors! I hear faint sounds—I think they're from its torpedo door actuator."

After hearing that, all officers and crew nearby focused intently on Daschle. Vallario grabbed the mic again to give another command, but Daschle yelled out, "Wait! I hear something else—another sound that I'm having trouble identifying."

The room was silent as Daschle pressed his earphones tightly to his ears, struggling to comprehend the sounds coming from the sophisticated underwater sound-detection systems and sonar screens.

Suddenly Daschle shot up from his chair, ripping off his earphones and yelling at the commander, "Oh my God. I can't frigging believe it. Holy shit! It blew up! It blew up." Daschle's face was one of pure shock. He covered his eyes, shaking his head back and forth.

Vallario rushed toward Daschle and gripped his shoulders forcefully, shouting right into his face, "What blew up, Officer? Tell me!"

"I think it's the *Scorpion*! I think the *Scorpion* blew up, sir!"

Sonar Tech Daschle's training kicked in, and he quickly returned to his seat. He put his headphones back on and studied his sonar screens again for a few seconds. "We have a confirmation. Sonar indicates only one underwater target, Commander. She's gone, sir. The *Scorpion*. She's gone."

"Officer Daschle," Vallario commanded firmly, "Mark the time and position of this incident immediately."

"Yes, sir."

Commander Vallario stared down at Daschle. "Was there a torpedo launch from the Delta 3?"

"No, sir. I heard no launch, and I saw nothing on sonar to indicate a torpedo launch, sir."

"Are you sure of that, Officer?"

"Yes, absolutely, sir."

"Continue to track the Delta 3 and keep me posted as to its every move. Do you understand, Officer?"

"Yes, sir, Commander!"

Vallario turned back toward Daschle from the doorway. "Daschle, do you have any thoughts about what might have made those sounds you picked up near the *Scorpion*?"

Daschle shook his head. "I have no idea, Commander. I've never heard anything like that before. It just sounded like something else was there."

Vallario held Daschle's gaze for a little longer,

5

clearly puzzled. His glance shifted from Nate's face to the sonar screen, and then to his ensign officer, who followed him from the room. The commander was visibly shaken as he grappled with the bitter realization that just a few miles away, hundreds of feet below the surface of the water, one of the US Navy's most modern and elite submarines had somehow blown up in the middle of the night. He knew that none of the proud sailors on board the sub could possibly have survived—and he knew some of them personally.

If there was no torpedo, how the hell could it just blow up?

Vallario headed for the control room to report this news to High Command and to consult with his senior officers.

***

Six thousand feet below the ocean surface, a multitude of jagged remnants drifted down slowly through the pitch-black ocean water. Forty seconds later, two twisted hunks of steel and metal floated down farther and farther into the dark depths. An unearthly metallic sound announced the presence of the wreckage to the hidden creatures in that deep ocean realm. It took a full twenty-three minutes for the *Scorpion*, and the lost souls who went down with it, to reach their permanent grave, fourteen thousand feet deep on the ocean bottom.

[2]

Exploring the Blue Hole

June 4, 2032
Time: 14:37

In a blackness devoid of sound or movement, deep in an underwater cave system, seventeen miles from the Caribbean island of Abaco, a faint, distant light appeared. Several lights gradually approached, illuminating the movements of two scuba divers who drew near. The divers swam through the narrow passageways of an intricate and jagged underwater cave system. James Sebring led the way.

"Alex, I think we better turn around at this point. I checked my dive computer. We still have about forty-five minutes of air left in our main tanks. We have to leave a margin of safety for us to get back to the blue hole opening."

"Yeah, okay. I'm ready to head back now. It's been a great dive so far. I'm really enjoying it!"

"Okay, stop there," said James. "I'm going to pass by you to lead the way back. Be careful when I maneuver by you. Make sure to hold on to the safety line; it's our only way to find our way back to the surface." He began to turn back toward Alex Westwood, who was not only his diving buddy but his girlfriend.

Alex did as he asked, making room for James to pass by. James reversed his direction, securely holding the bright neon-green safety line. He moved carefully, taking great care not to disturb Alex's scuba equipment, especially her face mask. Losing a face mask could be catastrophic and potentially life-threatening in such a narrow underwater cave, hundreds of feet from an opening to the surface.

Alex Westwood called to him through her sophisticated underwater radio-communication system. "Wow, this cave is amazing. It's so huge and complex. Thank goodness we have the safety line to guide us back. We'd never find our way back without it!"

"Yeah, isn't this great? And make sure you always keep your hand on the line." He slowed down, looked back at Alex, and signaled for her to approach him carefully. "Come here and take a look!"

"What is it?"

Alex followed James upward. This part of the cave was larger. Unusual rocks protruded from the upper-right wall of the cave. James pointed to indicate the area of interest to Alex.

"This little shelf area was once an owl's nest. Probably about twelve thousand years ago, when this entire cave system was above water. Then the glaciers melted, and the sea level rose, flooding the cave."

"That's incredible. I can't believe that this was once all above sea level at one time," said Alex.

"Yeah, and look here." James reached into a small eroded, rocky shelf notched into the upper-right side of the cave wall. He grabbed what looked like a small bunch of sticks, holding them out for Alex to see. "These are the bones of an extinct owl that once lived here. Isn't it amazing?"

Alex moved her head closer to examine the bones. "Wow! Are there any other animal remains down here?"

"Oh, yeah, scientists from various universities have combed through these caves. They've found bats, small mammals, and even turtles."

James put the owl bones back exactly where he had found them and signaled Alex to follow him. As he headed down, his headlamp lit up a crevice in the cave wall a distance below them. He glimpsed something orange—a color that seemed out of place in the cave. Interested to find out what it was, he headed toward the orange object, but as he approached, he stopped short. Alex also halted immediately, noticing the change in his demeanor. "What is it, James? What do you see?"

Looking deep into the crevice, James warned, "Stay back, Alex! Don't look!"

Alex screamed, and James knew his warning had come too late. He had hoped to prevent Alex from seeing what it was—the remains of a diver who had obviously died long ago, still covered by his decaying scuba gear.

"Oh my God! What do you think happened to this guy?" she said, quickly backing away and moving in place nervously.

Alex realized that giving in to panic would interfere with the clear thinking needed to dive safely. She took a deep breath and reined in her emotions while James analyzed the discovery.

"It's actually very common that when cave divers run out of air, they freak out, panic, and find the nearest crack or crevice to try to get out of the cave," answered James. "There are a lot of these incidents where divers don't know what they're doing, don't use a safety line, and end up dead when they run out of air."

"How long do you think he's been here?"

"His fins, mask, and tank look old—probably from the seventies. Back then these blue holes were riddled with divers looking to find excitement and maybe treasure. Some didn't make it out alive, obviously," said James, looking at his dive computer. "We'd better get moving. We only have thirty minutes of air left in our primary air tanks."

"Yeah, okay, let's go. I'd really like to get to the surface."

James could hear the worry in his girlfriend's voice. Seeing the dead diver was a potent reminder that he wanted to get Alex out of the cave safely. He swam back down toward the safety line, which was only a few feet away. Alex followed closely as he glanced back at her to make sure she was all right. When Alex reached the safety line, she grabbed it tightly and trailed James as they both followed it back toward the entrance of the blue hole.

Alex was still unnerved by the sight of the deceased diver. She thought about her own mortality, the risks of being down hundreds of feet deep, in a dangerous underwater cave system, just one accident away from death. She wanted to get out of that cave as fast as possible but focusing on the technical details necessary to proceed safely helped keep her mind off the dangers around them.

After a few minutes of maneuvering through

the intricate passages, they moved upward, following the safety line into the narrowest section of the cave. James knew that once they got past that quirky section safely, they were home free—it was only fifty feet from the entrance of the blue hole. Then they would be able to relax.

As he entered the tight passage, he looked back to check on Alex and hit the side of the cave. The collision released a tremendous amount of silt and sediment into the water around them. They could see nothing at all through the murky water, and they lost sight of each other. When Alex realized she couldn't see James or even her own hands, she screamed again, terrified. She had never experienced a silt-out. The fear of drowning in that tight passageway was overwhelming.

"Alex! Alex!" James called out. "Don't panic! Keep your hands on the line and don't let go! Just relax and hold on to the line!"

"James, I can't do this. I can't," cried Alex.

"Just relax and breathe slowly. Concentrate on your breathing, and think about your hands on the line. The silt in the water will clear out in about a minute or so, and everything will be okay. Just hold the line and stay still, breathe slowly, and the silt will clear."

James knew that he and Alex were now in a very precarious situation. If Alex panicked and rammed into him, they could both die. He listened carefully and held on to the safety line tightly, listening to Alex breathing from her regulator. Alex's terror reminded him of some of his past cave-dive mishaps. He recalled the fear he had experienced being in an underwater cave, just inches from death. They waited silently, breathing, until they began to make out blurry shapes as the silt settled. Being able to see lifted

Alex's spirits tremendously. She realized they were going to survive and called out to him.

"James! James, I'm so happy we're still here. Oh my God. For a few seconds I thought we weren't going to make it!"

"Thank God you did the right thing and didn't panic." James grinned, giving her a thumbs-up. "You are one smart girl. I love you, Alex!"

Alex shook her head, acknowledging James's gesture. They shared a smile and began to move forward, as the water had almost completely cleared. They moved slowly and carefully, making sure not to disturb the sides of the cave. Finally, they exited the narrow passageways and swam the remaining short stretch toward the entrance of the blue hole.

As they neared the surface, James stopped in the water to let Alex pass him so she could exit to the surface first. Alex quickly and safely pulled herself to the surface. She ripped off her scuba mask and breathing regulator, took a deep gulp of fresh air, and let out a sigh of relief. James soon followed.

Elated, knowing they had both made it out alive, they grinned at each other, and Alex shouted, "Wow, what an experience that was! It was incredible, though that silt-out episode really shook me up."

"Yeah, it was a great dive. You really handled yourself well. I remember my first silt-out. They scare the hell out of you."

"The training really helped me. Without that I probably would have panicked. I guess that's what happened to that poor diver down there?"

"That guy probably didn't use a safety line, got lost, and ran out of air. We're gonna have to report that to the local police."

"Good idea. Maybe they already know who it was."

13

"Maybe they do, but I'm glad you handled yourself well and enjoyed the dive."

They started helping each other remove their equipment.

"Well, even with the challenges, I really had a great time," said Alex. "We'll have to do another dive next time I come down to the Bahamas, but let's do a cave that's not so dangerous."

James was relieved to notice the twinkle in her eye and smiled at the cute and sexy look she gave him. He was thrilled she had enjoyed the adventure. "There are hundreds of caves and blue holes around here. I know a few that would be perfect for us next time."

As Alex removed her wet suit, James was struck by the beauty of her body. She was vivacious and lovely. He loved her slim figure and found her enticing and sexy. He couldn't resist and moved toward her.

"Very cool... I'd love to do it again," said Alex.

James half heard these last words as he gazed at Alex. They were alone in a hidden cove, and she was standing on a sandy coral stretch of beach in her purple bikini. Her beautiful voice always turned him on. He reached out to hug her. She returned his embrace, and they moved into a kiss. A few moments later they headed away from the cave entrance toward their beach blanket.

The beach was sunny, the sand warm and soft, and not a soul was in sight. With adrenaline still surging from their adventure, they held each other closely. Before long, passion took over. As their bathing suits were tossed aside, physical desires took over, and it all became a blur of intimate and loving moments that seemed to last forever. Eventually, they redressed and shifted into quiet conversation about their dive, their careers, and their future. They shared their dreams of a time when they could be together every day.

As the sun started to move toward the horizon, James reluctantly packed their gear so he could get Alex to the airport in time for her flight. They packed their equipment and supplies into the cabin of James's twenty-eight-foot Sport Cruiser, which was anchored nearby, and headed toward Marsh Harbor.

[3]

Cruising to the Airport

Marsh Harbor was located in the center of Great Abaco Island, a little over an hour away by boat. About one mile out at sea from their secluded location, James hit the throttle. The full 660 horsepower from the two rear-mounted outboard engines roared to life, lifting the bow high into the waves and propelling the boat to a fast speed. Alex was forced backward due to the sudden acceleration but held on tightly to the seat.

"Alex, sit here next to me and relax. I'll get you to Abaco with time to spare. Enjoy the ride, sweetie," James shouted over the roar of the engines.

"Okay," Alex shouted back. "I don't see Abaco Island yet, but I know you must know where you're going."

"I know these islands very well. I still have to

be careful because there are a lot of hidden coral reefs and small sandbars around here that we could crash into."

"Whoa! We definitely would not want to run into a coral reef at this speed!"

"Absolutely not, but have no fear. I've gone diving all around these small cay islands. I know the waters here very well."

"I can tell. Hey, where is your company head-quarters located?"

"Over there—on the southeast side of the island." James pointed in the direction of his main manufacturing facility.

"You really are quite an entrepreneur."

Just thirty-seven, James had built up one of the largest ocean engineering firms in the world.

James smiled. "I'm just very lucky with how things have worked out. Couldn't have done it without my loyal friends and workers."

"Everyone I've met at your company is very nice, and you have a lot of really smart people working for you. Quite a team there. You must be proud."

James flashed a quick glance at Alex, then he returned his focus to piloting the boat. "I totally am, and I love what I'm doing! We both have a lot to be happy about. Things have gone so well for us!"

James's smile sent a little shiver of happiness down Alex's spine.

She held tightly to the bar in front of her seat as James quickly changed the direction of his sleek, modern watercraft. She let herself relax into the warmth of the sun on her face, the beauty of the aqua-colored, windswept Caribbean Sea, and the memories of their exciting excursion.

***

With the boat docked at Marsh Harbor, and Alex and all of her belongings packed into James's car, they traveled the short distance to Abaco International Airport. The small isolated airport was surrounded by a lush Bahamian jungle. Only one aircraft was out on the tarmac ready for takeoff. Several other airplanes and business jets were parked on the side of the large concrete runway.

James drove toward the airport security checkpoint and stopped at the guard booth to chat with the two security guards. Their welcoming greetings and gestures indicated they were on friendly terms with James. After chatting a bit, they signaled for him to proceed through the checkpoint, toward the middle of the runway, where a large white private jet was parked. Its sleek aerodynamic design, combined with a narrow blue stripe, gave off an expensive vibe. James pulled up and parked his car not far from the jet and accompanied Alex to the stairs while an attendant headed toward James's SUV to fetch Alex's baggage. The pilot approached to greet them politely but briefly, then continued to walk around the aircraft to complete his preflight safety check.

James turned to Alex and pulled her close. He looked deeply into her blue eyes and murmured, "I really wish you didn't have to go, Alex."

"I know. I wish we could be together all the time—but I just don't have a choice right now."

"Why don't you consider working for me? We can always use another good engineer in my company. You would love it here, and we can be together as much as we want."

Alex sighed. "I only have another six months left on my contract with the ITUS Project on La

18

Palma Island. Maybe I'll come work for your company then."

"Really? That's fantastic!"

The jet's steward approached and addressed James in a polished British accent. "I am sorry to disturb you and the lady, sir, but it's time for us to depart."

James had a hard time letting Alex out of his arms, and she gave him a last lingering kiss. Their hug tightened briefly, then they released each other and Alex boarded the plane.

James watched the stairway recede into the jet as the engines revved loudly. He walked toward the front of the craft, signaled with a thumbs-up to the pilots, and walked to his car. He waited to watch it take off. It would take six hours for his plane to reach La Palma Island in the Canary Islands, and he hoped the flight would be trouble-free and enjoyable.

[4]

Ocean Engineering Corporation International (OECI)

James zipped into his reserved spot in the management parking area in the front of the main building of the sprawling complex. The name over the entrance read Ocean Engineering Corporation International in big blue lettering over a virgin-white background. An abstract orange chevron design above the lettering added distinctive and colorful visual appeal. The receptionist in the main lobby immediately recognized him and greeted him cheerfully.

Before he could enter his office, Nicki, his administrative assistant, greeted him warmly, eager to speak with him. "James, so glad you're back. Did you and Alex have a good time together?"

Nicki Hammond was a young, tall, attractive, African-Bahamian woman. She was capable, very intelligent, and had excellent communication skills. She was well-respected and well-liked by James and his senior corporate officers, and everyone enjoyed her lilting accent and warm style of communication.

"Hi, Nicki. Yeah, we had a fantastic time. I only wish Alex had more time to stay, but she had to get back to her project."

"I hope you didn't take her cave diving with you. Please tell me you didn't do that."

James grinned. "Relax, Nicki. Yes, I did, in fact. Took her cave diving off of Abaco at the Crystal Hole. And before you say anything else—Alex loved it."

"Hmm. So did you two run into any problems during your dive? I can't imagine her going deep into that dangerous cave with you—that poor girl."

"Well, uh, yeah, there were a couple of issues, but Alex kept her calm and performed like a real trouper."

"Okay, good," said Nicki. "I'm just glad that you both made it out all right, and that you both had a nice time together."

"We had a fantastic weekend together. It was so nice being with her out on the open water, and she just loves it."

"Lovely, James. You'll have to tell me all about your trip, but you have a lot going on right now, so let me fill you in on what's on the agenda since you were away."

Nicki followed James into his office. The walls displayed pictures of many of his company's ocean engineering projects, including large ships, various submarines, and specialized marine-drilling rigs that were manufactured by James's firm. James sat down at his desk and turned on his computer, glanced at Nicki, who stood in front of his desk, and turned back to his computer.

"Ahem," said Nicki. "James, I have a lot to go over with you, so please pay attention."

James stopped his typing and looked up at Nicki. "Okay, what do we have?"

21

"First up, we have our research and development team heading out on the *Argonaut* today. They're ready to test out their latest underwater research sub. They want you to be there to go along during the test dive."

"Great. What time are they heading out?"

"Probably quite soon. I'll check with them when we're done here and let you know. Next up, we have a mystery visitor coming today from one of our contractors to discuss some business issues with you, but I'm not sure what company it is."

James nodded his head. "Okay, I'll meet with our mystery guest when they show up. What else is on the agenda?"

Nicki took a few seconds to search her memory, then raised her finger and exclaimed, "Oh! Tom wants to see you right away about something very important. I think it has something to do with your automated underwater drone exploration program. He was very insistent on reminding me to let you know as soon as you came in."

James's face lit up. "Okay, I'll check with Tom on that. I think I have an idea what that's all about."

"Okay, the last thing I have on your agenda is a call from Professor Aldridge in England. He said he has something important to discuss with you."

"Professor Aldridge! It's been a while. It'll be good to chat with him again. If he calls back today, make sure you track me down. I definitely want to speak with him."

"Sure. He seems to have become very special to you over the years," said Nicki.

James smiled. "I don't know if I ever told you this, but if it hadn't been for Professor Aldridge, I probably would not have this company today. I first met him when I was a student at Stony Brook University on Long Island some years back. I was in grad school, and he was a visiting professor in the Engineering and Ocean Science Departments. He happened to take a liking to me because he saw my interest in naval engineering and designing underwater robotic devices. He was very smart and innovative, and our shared mutual interests led us to a unique friendship.

"After I graduated, he encouraged me to start up my own company—even gave me financial support. Things took off quickly from there, and as the years went by, and the contracts came flowing in from private and government sources, my business boomed—and here we are today."

"Wow, what a story. I had no idea. No wonder he is so important to you."

There was a tap on the door as James's chief engineering assistant, Tom Walker, eagerly entered the room. "Hey, James. So glad you're back. The *Argonaut* is heading out in about thirty minutes to test dive our new research sub. You and I have to be on it, so let's get going, buddy. They need you there."

"Okay. Nicki, I'm heading out. If Professor Aldridge calls again, please tell him that I'll get back to him soon."

"Okay, I'll let him know, James. You guys be careful out there," Nicki said, heading back to her desk.

James grabbed his cell phone from his desk and followed Tom out at a brisk pace, their eagerness to get on board the *Argonaut* and test dive their new experimental submarine evident. As they headed down the hallway, Tom started to chat about some business projects. Then he stopped and grabbed James's arm. "I forgot. The data we downloaded from the Electric Fish program. Come with me. I know we're in a hurry, but this will just take a minute."

Tom pulled James into his office and headed to his computer, saying, "You have to hear this recording. This was captured by one of our deep-sea drones at a depth of about eleven thousand feet in the Atlantic."

"What was the location of the AUV?" James asked, intrigued.

"About a hundred and ten miles off the west coast of Africa, near Senegal. We've recorded this a few times before, but this time the audio resolution is much improved," Tom said, beginning the recording.

At first, the men heard only the normal sounds of soft aquatic motion. Then the sound drastically changed as a series of strange, elongated, near-disturbing sounds emanated from large wall-mounted speakers filling the room. Bewilderment played across James's face as he listened to the bizarre sounds. The effect of the stretched-out, bloop-like sounds interlaced with odd sound textures was eerie and rather startling. Both men stood there and stared at each other as the recording ended.

Tom raised an eyebrow. "So? What do you think?"

James shook his head. "I've never heard anything like it, but it sounds like a very large marine mammal. Or maybe even several creatures of some kind? It's definitely frigging weird!"

Tom nodded in agreement. "Yeah, I thought so, too. It sounds like a living organism, doesn't it?"

"Has anyone else listened to this?"

"Well, of course we're keeping this confidential, but I did have our staff marine biologists listen to it. No one has any idea of what it is, but they all agree that these sounds came from some kind of living aquatic animal, and that it definitely is not a whale or any other known marine creature."

James checked his watch. "We better head out to the *Argonaut*. They're probably waiting for us, and I definitely want to be there for our new sub test dive."

"Yeah, it's always fun heading on out with the *Argonaut* to test a new piece of equipment."

Both men left the room, still perplexed by the strange recording but excited to get to the research ship and get out to sea. As they left the building and headed toward the pier where the *Argonaut* was docked, they noticed one of their employees walking toward them.

"Good morning, Mr. Sebring. Hey, Tom! I just came from the *Argonaut*, and they're waiting for you guys."

"Hey, Chet. We're heading there right now. We're looking forward to seeing our new baby sub!"

"She's all ready for you guys to test her out. I just wish I could go with you guys."

"Why not, Chet? We can always use another deckhand to help out. Come along," James said with a smile.

"Oh, that'd be great. Thanks! Oh, Mr. Sebring, there's a well-dressed lady by the dock looking for you, sir. I told her that you'd be coming down soon."

Sure enough, a slim woman in a black skirt and white shirt approached along the paved pathway. She sported black heels and carried an expensive briefcase. A red bow adorned her lapel.

"Wow, she's a hot-looking lady," said Tom.

James answered, "Yes, she certainly is."

When she was near enough, the woman called out, "Hello! I'm looking for a Mr. James Sebring?"

James smiled. "Hello. I'm James Sebring."

"Oh, Mr. Sebring, it's so nice to finally meet you in person. We've spoken several times. I'm Diane Saveroff. I work for the Zepheron Corporation." Diane shook her head slightly as she spoke. Her smile was beguiling, and as James made eye contact with the attractive woman he noticed a soft breeze moving through her lovely auburn hair.

James looked confused for a moment. "Oh, you're Dr. Diane Saveroff?" he said, holding out his hand.

Diane laughed. "Yes, that's me. We've spoken several times about the Electric Fish contract. That's what I'm here about."

Still holding her hand, James exclaimed, "Please, call me James, Dr. Saveroff!"

Tom and Chet shared a quick smirk. It was obvious that the other two were quite taken with each other.

"Well, Dr. Saveroff," said James, as he released Diane's hand and began to walk toward the pier with the others, "I wish I had time to chat with you about our contract with Zepheron, but we're just heading out to sea to test one of our new subs."

Saveroff followed the men, saying, "That's okay. Perhaps when you get back you can find time for us to go over some of our proposals?"

"Yes, certainly, Dr. Saveroff. I can meet you in my office in a few hours. I'll be glad to look over your proposals then."

"Okay, that sounds great," said Diane. "Wow! That's a large ship. You must love going out on her to do your research."

"Yeah, she's a great ship—one of my favorites. One of the reasons I love my work so much is that I get to go out on the sea doing what I love."

Tom and Chet boarded the ship, which was ready to depart. Several members of the crew stood looking down as James and Dr. Saveroff continued to chat in a friendly manner. They couldn't help but notice how lovely she appeared in her stylish business clothes and how professionally she seemed to conduct herself in her discussion with James. It was a refreshing contrast to their usual work days.

Looking a bit disheartened, Dr. Saveroff said, "Okay, Mr. Sebring, I'll wait here in your lobby until you get back."

James gazed up to the ship, then out toward the sea, and then back at Dr. Saveroff. "If you want, you're welcome to join me on board the *Argonaut* for our test dive."

Excitement evident, Diane said, "I'd love to join you if that's all right with you."

"It will be my pleasure to have you on as a guest, but just be aware that I'll be rather busy, so I may not be able to talk with you much. There will be a lot of activity on board, so you'll have to be careful and try to stay out of the way, but it should be more fun than waiting in the lobby."

"Of course, Mr. Sebring. I understand. I'll stay off to the side and just observe the show."

James headed up to the ship and then stopped to look back at Dr. Saveroff. "Please call me James, if you don't mind. You make me feel a little old by calling me Mr. Sebring."

"Very well, James."

James led Dr. Saveroff up the incline onto the mighty *Argonaut*.

[5]

The Submarine Launch

The horn soon sounded to announce the ship's departure from the dock. The *Argonaut* slowly moved away from the dock, causing all on deck to become momentarily unsteady as they adjusted to the movement.

James escorted Dr. Saveroff to an area in the back of the ship that was isolated from the rear rigging, where the submarine was tightly strapped down and positioned. She had a clear view of the action, but she would be safe and comfortable there. While unloading the sub, workers would be moving around a great deal of equipment, and cables and hooks could become dangerous projectiles to those nearby.

The ship picked up speed and traveled effortlessly through the half-mile channel that connected the OECI headquarters to the open ocean. Dr. Saveroff stood in the isolated stern area, enjoying the sights and sounds along the waterway. She noticed that the sides of the channel were composed of layers of large boulders that were both gray and tan, stacked up high, rising twelve feet above the water's surface, which protected the channel from the wave and tidal erosion. She also enjoyed the many exotic birds that flew above the channel, circling in the air, creating a beautiful and dynamic scene against the backdrop of the blue and white cloudy sky. She didn't expect she would be getting such a beautiful boat ride when she visited the OECI campus and was happy to be part of this unexpected adventure.

The ship changed direction and increased speed as it left the channel and moved swiftly into the mighty blue ocean with its rough open waves. Dr. Saveroff held on tightly to a bolted-down seat, taking in all the nautical loveliness. She peered around the corner toward the bow of the ship and reflected on the mystery of the distant open sea before them. She viewed a near infinity out there, which filled her with a sense of isolation and wonder being in the midst of the majestic Caribbean Sea. She also pondered what it would be like to be in the submarine that was about to be launched. It seemed so dangerous and scary and couldn't imagine how anyone could be brave enough to get in that thing and travel down into the depths of the ocean.

The *Argonaut* was an older but proud ocean-eering vessel. She had served the sailors of OECI for more than a decade, delivering cargo and launching marine craft throughout the world. She was a beauty, three hundred and twenty feet long and sixty-eight feet wide, with a fresh coat of a royal-blue paint and a white topped deck. The five deck levels that rose above the surface deck were also bright white. Near the center of the boat, the front masthead light and the towering anchor light rose eighty feet high above the deck. The ship was always bustling, but the rear stern area was the stage of the ship where most of the launching and hauling was accomplished. Three massive crane hoists were located there that were capable of lifting large craft and gear weighing up to several tons.

Twenty-two miles southwest of the harbor, far from any land, they neared their destination in an isolated part of the Caribbean Sea. Dr. Saveroff had moved up to the first deck area, where she had a good view looking down at all the activity taking place at the stern. The boat was now slowing down, and crew members had gathered near the submarine, preparing to launch the craft.

As Dr. Saveroff continued to view the stern area, James walked down the stern stairwell accompanied by two men. They stopped to speak with other OECI workers who were involved with the preparation of the sub launch. She was impressed with the professionalism displayed by all the marine workers—they seemed to be highly trained and skilled at their specialized tasks. They were dressed in sharp-looking navy-blue jumpsuits emblazoned with the bold OECI lettering on their backs, and their bright orange safety helmets contrasted neatly with the blue of their jumpsuits.

A sudden gust of wind ruffled her clothes and reminded her of their location in the middle of a vast, choppy sea. She redirected her thoughts toward the activity taking place on the stern deck, excited at the prospect of watching the submarine launch take place.

James stood twenty feet away from the *Hydra 3* submarine. He watched as it was lifted into the air by the massive hydraulically powered robotic lift arm attached to the *Argonaut*. Even though the sub weighed nearly three tons, it reminded James of a large toy being picked up and moved above the Caribbean Sea to its new position.

The crew chief of the *Argonaut* approached. "Sir, the *Hydra 3* is ready to be placed into the ocean for her testing."

James smiled. "Good work, Carlos. Just make sure that all the telemetry links are tested properly before you get her into the water. We don't want to find out that we have some bad sensors while she's heading down to her test depth." Carlos had a reputation for being a stickler when it came to quality assurance. His crewmates thought he was compulsive and not always easy to get along with. But James loved his dedication and hard-driving attitude.

"We'll definitely run all the interface tests to *Will do.* make sure everything is all right with the links. It should take a few minutes, but we'll get it done."

The submarine test pilots were scheduled to take the craft down to a dangerous depth of sixteen thousand feet. At this depth the sub would be used by marine engineers and scientists around the world to explore new deep-sea environments.

"She's ready," Carlos said.

"Great," said James.

"Oh, by the way, our sub test pilots wanted to know if you want to go down with them aboard the *Hydra 3* during the systems test. They have an extra seat available for you if you're interested."

James twisted and looked up toward the first deck's overlook. Dr. Saveroff was watching him. She waved at him happily and yelled something, but he was unable to make out her words.

"Tell them maybe next time, Carlos. I have to

entertain a special guest on board, so I'll skip this one."

"Okay, I'll let them know." Carlos glanced back at James with a knowing smile. "I see that your *special* guest is waiting for you. You'd better go give her a tour of our ship."

As he walked away, James shook his head. Carlos knew him too well. "I'll do that!" He headed up to the first deck to join Dr. Saveroff.

She saw James approaching and turned to greet him. "Hi, James. You have quite a ship here."

"Thanks," he said. "As you can tell from up here, we have a lot going on here with the launch."

She looked down at the sleek gray-and-orange submarine suspended in the air. "She's beautiful, James. What will she be used for after she's fully tested?"

"The *Hydra 3* is a scientific research submarine that's going to be used by oceanographic research institutes around the world. I believe this model will be used by the Woods Hole Institution in Massachusetts."

"Oh, wow. I've been to Woods Hole several times for my job. Quite an interesting place."

"Yeah, we do business with all of the oceanographic institutes around the world—mostly dealing with their research submarines and other underwater sensing and exploration equipment."

"So you're a main supplier of submarines and automated underwater vehicles to these firms?"

"Yeah, we produce all of those. We also produce a line of remotely operated underwater vehicles that we supply to research institutes and various private industries, too."

"Sounds like it keeps you busy," she said, smiling.

James noticed the hydraulic arm was beginning to lower the *Hydra 3* into the ocean off the stern, so he half watched while continuing his conversation with Dr. Saveroff. "We're also very busy with the subs and remote underwater vehicles we sell to the petroleum industry. That part of our business has really increased. It's now our largest revenue source."

"Yes, I saw some of your equipment in use when I was in the North Sea area about six months ago," said Dr. Saveroff.

James nodded. "Actually, we have a big job going on right now in the North Sea—on the *Global One* offshore oil rig. It's just north of Scotland."

"I know about that job. That's one huge offshore rig."

"It really is. It's one of the largest rigs in the North Sea. I'm actually heading up there in a few days in one of my new ships to help out with its construction and deliver some equipment."

Dr. Saveroff gazed at the sea, then looked back at James, squinting against the wind. "You've got an exciting life, James!"

James smiled broadly. "Well, when you run a large global company like this one, there's always something going on somewhere in the world. Hey, let me show you around our ship a little, and maybe get a cup of coffee?"

She nodded and he walked toward the entrance to the ship, signaling for Dr. Saveroff to follow him inside. They headed toward the bow through a brightly lit hallway. After passing two OECI workers who greeted them, they walked past several rooms with closed doors. Continuing on, they passed what appeared to be a navigation plotting and chart reference room, which was occupied by a team of well-dressed seamen involved in technical planning.

James turned back to Dr. Saveroff. "I'm going to show you our dive control room, over here, coming up on the left." James led her into a large dimly lit room. Dr. Saveroff looked impressed by an array of large LED monitor screens hanging all along the wall, radiating colorful lights. The room was also equipped with microphones and other communication devices. Several desk stations were being utilized by technical personnel who were discussing the test dive.

Lowering his voice, James pointed at some technical staff nearby. "Those are the dive supervision officers who will be in contact with the two pilots aboard the *Hydra 3*. They'll be in constant contact with the pilots, as well as monitoring all of the telemetry measurements that will be transmitted by the submarine during the dive."

Dr. Saveroff peered around the room, looking at the brilliantly lit electronic equipment and monitors. She turned to James. "I'm impressed. This is a very well-planned, very professional operation. I'm assuming your personnel are experienced with these dives?"

"Oh, yes, my staff absolutely knows what they're doing. They have to be ready to handle any technical issue that may arise during a test dive."

"Do you get many problems when you do one of these?" She glanced back at the monitors.

"Well, over the years we have had problems. Things never go quite the way you expect. We've avoided any major events, but we have had some serious issues arise now and then—circumstances where we had to respond quickly when people's lives were at risk."

Tearing her eyes away from the *Argonaut*'s dive control center, Dr. Saveroff looked at James. "I have to tell you, I've been working for Zepheron for a number of years, and since we contract with other oceaneering companies, I've seen other dive-support ships. Your company operates at a higher level of proficiency than others I've dealt with."

James laughed. "Thank you for that compliment, and I only hope that it was genuine— and not because we're working a business deal together."

Dr. Saveroff flashed James a flirtatious gaze. "Of course, I'm serious. Everyone in the oceaneering business knows that OECI is the best in the business. You are always a step above the rest when it comes to innovation and quality. That's why Zepheron wants to continue our relationship with your company. And you." She completed her pitch with a wink, which James found quite charming.

"Let's go grab that cup of coffee in the galley and let these guys get the launch underway," said James.

"Good idea. I could use a cup of coffee, and maybe something to munch on."

They made their way one level down into the ship's galley, where they gathered coffee and pastries from the food-service counter, grabbed a couple of chairs at one of several tables, and sat down. Dr. Saveroff noticed that the galley was mostly empty except for a few other tables, which were occupied by ship workers enjoying a break. She took some sips of her coffee and a bite of her pastry.

"Good coffee, too."

"We serve the best food on our ships. I always want to keep my crew happy when they're working on board."

"I'm very impressed with both your ship and your new submarine."

"Thanks. The *Hydra 3* features the latest technology for performing deep underwater research."

"How deep can the *Hydra 3* dive?"

Dr. Saveroff appeared genuinely interested, and James knew that she had a great deal of expertise and knowledge in the field of underwater oceaneering technology. He also recalled she possessed an engineering degree, a PhD in physics, and had worked for another military contractor prior to her employment with Zepheron. Enjoying a sip of coffee, he took time to answer her question. "The *Hydra 3* is a highly advanced deep-sea exploration sub that we developed and can dive up to twenty-five thousand feet deep."

"Really? Twenty-five thousand feet? That's amazing, James. Not many subs can go that deep."

James quickly clarified, "Yes, it *can* dive to that depth, but we only certify it to dive down to twenty-four thousand feet at this time."

"That's still amazing. Tell me, if you don't mind—how much does the *Hydra 3* go for? As far as cost to the customer?"

James laughed. "I can see you're a real businesswoman, and yet you know that I *can't* readily give out that information due to our business relationship with the client who is receiving this sub."

"Yes, I understand that, but can you give me a *clue* as to what these deep-dive research subs go for in general?"

"In general, deep-dive research subs can go for up to twelve million dollars."

"Incredible! No wonder your company is doing so well."

"Well, as you know, Dr. Saveroff, they are very highly engineered and complicated."

"Yes, of course, I do know how difficult they are to build." Dr. Saveroff looked around the room and then back at James, sensing an opportunity to bring up their business relationship. She focused her eyes on James, continuing, "I'd really like to discuss our business contract with you if you don't mind. I know that you're busy with this test launch right now, but maybe we could chat a bit about our contract renewal?"

James checked his watch, thought to himself for a second, and answered, "I have a little time right now. What you would like to discuss?" He smiled gently, because he knew that Zepheron Corporation was desperate to renew their contract with his company.

"Well, James, Zepheron is very interested in renewing our contract with OECI concerning the Electric Fish program. We're ready to offer a new enhanced deal to your company if you will agree to a continuation of our partnership."

James nodded slowly. Electric Fish was their underwater surveillance drone program, which was used by the US Navy in surveillance of the world's oceans. The Electric Fish drones were capable of traveling down to incredible depths and could operate for missions of many months. "I see. I've been thinking about our arrangement for the past few months, and to be honest, I'm not totally happy about how it has been working out."

Clearly disappointed, Dr. Saveroff tensed up a bit. "Really? I'm sorry to hear that."

James took a sip of his coffee. He hated delivering awkward news. "I'm considering bypassing this whole subcontracting arrangement and taking my Electric Fish contract directly to the US Navy."

Dr. Saveroff leaned forward, her forehead creased with concern. "James, please hear me

37

out. We're ready to make a substantially higher monetary offer to continue our relationship. We are willing to—"

A loud pulsating siren blared from the ship's speaker system, interrupting Dr. Saveroff, who looked both shocked and confused. James jumped up and scanned the room as he and the rest of the crew members rose from their seats and quickly headed toward the exit doors.

"What is it, James?" Dr. Saveroff called out.

The look on James's face was ominous as he called back, "Something bad must have happened."

He was interrupted by Carlos, who ran into the galley, looking around for him.

"What is it, Carlos?" said James. "What's going on?"

"There's a problem with the *Hydra 3*! Come quickly!" Carlos replied anxiously.

"Okay, take Dr. Saveroff down to the rec room. And make sure she stays there. I'll meet you in the dive control center."

Carlos turned to her. "Okay. Dr. Saveroff, please follow me."

Apprehensive, Dr. Saveroff spared a fleeting look at James before quickly following Carlos in the opposite direction.

Wasting no time, James rushed back through the galley and out the door. Stress was etched across his face as he entered the dive control center. The dive-support operators were desperately calling out into their handheld microphones.

"What's the problem?" James shouted over the alarm.

"We've got a bad situation, sir," said Johnny, the dive supervisor. "We've lost contact with the *Hydra 3*, and telemetry readings are showing the pilots have lost dynamic control of the sub."

"What? How did this happen?"

"We're not sure, sir. Everything was fine till they reached nine thousand feet. Then we noted that some of the status-function sensors aboard the sub started to go out, and then we lost contact with the pilots."

"Have you tried the backup communications link?"

"Yes, we have, but we're unable to activate that link at this time, sir."

"Are you receiving any telemetry data from the sub at all?"

The dive supervisor looked down and then toward James and said, "None, sir."

James rubbed his chin, looking around the room, concern plain on his face, while all six dive control room operators stared at him, searching for answers as to what course of action they could take to alleviate the desperate situation.

"Okay. Johnny, keep trying to establish contact with them, and review the data link to see if you can figure out just what happened. Also, contact the bridge and get them to get a sonar fix on them to see where the hell they are now. We need to know if they're static or if they're sinking."

"Yes, sir."

The dive officers reacted immediately to their orders. James started to leave the room but then stopped. He turned to the dive officers and said, "I'm going up to the bridge to check the data on the sonar location of the sub—if they can find it. Notify me immediately if you find anything."

Johnny nodded in agreement. "Yes, sir. We'll notify you immediately if we obtain any more information."

∗∗∗

39

Several hours later, Dr. Saveroff sat by herself in the ship's recreation room, checking over some files on her laptop. She was starting to get annoyed by the combined sounds of the ship's engines radiating a low-pitched noise throughout the room, and the television mounted up high on the wall playing a local Bahamian TV news channel wasn't helping either. She was bored and confused and wondering what was happening with the sub test. She was also tired of being stuck in a confined room.

She stood up and started to move toward the doorway when one of the ship's crewmen entered and greeted her. "Hello, Dr. Saveroff. Mr. Sebring would like to see you, ma'am."

Closing her laptop, Dr. Saveroff replied, "Okay, let me get my things together."

"Of course, ma'am."

The crewman waited for Dr. Saveroff and then led her out of the room and up two flights of stairs, toward the rear deck of the ship. They made their way out through a rear door and proceeded to walk across the large open-air deck. James and a fellow crewmate were standing at the stern, near the railing. Even at a distance, she could tell they were having a serious conversation. Though she could not make out their words, Dr. Saveroff knew by the look of the men that all was not well on board.

She approached James and his crewmate slowly as the men continued their conversation. When James looked toward her, she saw a troubled, disheartened look in his eyes. She hesitated, unsure what to say, but James spoke first.

"Dr. Saveroff, I'm afraid we've had a serious problem with the submarine test."

Dr. Saveroff clapped her hand to her mouth, then moved it away. "Oh no! What happened?"

"We lost contact with the submarine, and we

don't know what's happening with it. It appears that the sub has lost all power."

"Will the crew be okay?"

James paused, unsure how to answer that question, but his assistant answered for him. "We're working on that problem right now. We have a whole team of skilled technicians and scientists searching for a solution."

James looked into Dr. Saveroff's eyes. She, too, was shocked and saddened at the implication—they simply didn't know if the crew was okay.

"Dr. Saveroff, I'm going to have to stay on board the *Argonaut* for a while, and I don't want you to be stuck here. I've arranged for one of my helicopters to come and pick you up. It should be here in a few minutes. When you arrive at my headquarters, my personal assistant, Nicki, will arrange for you to stay overnight in one of my onsite cottages. Nicki will take care of everything you need, so you don't have to worry about anything. When I get back to headquarters, I'll meet with you, and we'll try to go over the business issues then." James turned away, peering at the sea over the rail. Then he turned back and said solemnly, "Right now, I have to be with my ship and my crew."

Dr. Saveroff moved toward James and put her hand on his arm. "I totally understand, James. I hope everything goes well." A ship worker approached to escort her toward the landing pad as the sound of the approaching helicopter was heard.

James and his crew arranged for three other ships to come to their aid in the search for the missing submarine. They spent fifteen hours scanning the communication frequencies and searching the sea bottom using high-resolution sonar for any evidence of the missing *Hydra 3*.

Unfortunately, that extensive search found no trace of the missing experimental submarine and her seemingly doomed crew.

[6]

An Unusual Request

Two days later, at the OECI headquarters, James summoned his dive control officers and his engineering quality-assurance team into the conference room for a meeting to determine the cause of the loss of the *Hydra 3*. The quality-assurance team was ready to present their preliminary findings.

From his chair in the middle of the long oval table, James listened intently to their review of the data from the fatal submarine tragedy. But after listening for an hour, he was beyond impatient. He just wanted to get to the bottom of the tragedy that had taken both the submarine and the lives of the two pilots.

Kent grew anxious as well, knowing that James wanted answers, and finally he interrupted the endless droning. "Look, we all know that the data readings during the dive initially appeared normal. But exactly seventy-three minutes into the dive, something happened, and the submarine inexplicably lost all power and went into static freefall. Find the answers and tell us what the hell happened at that point in time! What caused that power outage and the loss of buoyancy control?" Kent banged on the table twice, releasing some of his pent-up frustration.

Bobby Saxon, one of the QA team members, spoke up. "If I may, I'd like to interject something..."

James stared at Bobby, unamused, and said, "Please do, Bobby. Somebody tell me *something* I can use."

"I was going through the data broadcast from the line feed from the *Hydra 3*, and I noted that the pilots had activated the hydrophone prior to the mishap. I believe that there is something on the audio of the hydrophone that could maybe give us something to go on."

Kent leaned forward. "What do you have, Bobby?"

"Well, when I went over the audio file and filtered out the background noise using audio software, at exactly eleven seconds prior to the onset of the accident, I could hear something from the submarine that was... unusual."

Kent looked at him, exasperated. "Well? What was it?"

Bobby continued, stammering. "I-I'm not exactly sure what it was, but there was a weird sound that seemed to be coming from the inside the sub just prior to the accident."

Kent tossed his pen onto the table. "That's exactly what you just said."

"Bobby," James said, his voice taut, "Can you determine what the sound is?"

"I-I can't tell exactly what it is right now, but I'm going to go over it again and see if I can make out where it's coming from. It's possible it's a sound coming from the actuator control of the ballast tanks. But I can't be certain."

Taking a deep breath, Kent said, "At least we have something to go on. Go over that audio file from the hydrophone and see what you can find."

Kent made eye contact with each of the other members of the review committee. "And I want each person on this team to go over everything you can—all the data from the dive, the blueprints of the submarine, and even the video from the ship. We need to find out exactly what happened!"

With the meeting essentially over, James stood to address the committee members.

"I just want to say that we're all a little worn out after these past couple of days. I know that everyone here knew our test pilots, Ted and Ray, and their families well, so whatever we do here to find out what caused this tragedy, we're doing it for them. Go get some rest, and then get back to work. We have a lot going on for the next couple of weeks, but I want everyone here to go over the findings from this meeting with a fine-tooth comb. Let's figure out just what happened to that submarine. Thanks for your help, everyone."

All of the OECI workers filed out of the room, except for Kent, who stayed to have a few words with James. As Kent was leaving, James called him back with a new thought "Kent, I want you to go over all the construction notes and blueprints for the *Hydra 3*. See if you can uncover anything that would indicate any issues during the construction of the craft."

Kent nodded his head. "I was already planning to do just that."

"Oh, and another thing, I want you to make me a list of all of the personnel who were involved in the construction of the sub. I want you and your team to interview all of them to see if they have any ideas on what could have happened during the dive."

"Okay. I'll get right on it."

"Good man," said James, giving Kent a friendly smack on his shoulder. Kent left, and James was about to follow when he saw Nicki standing in the doorway, holding her notepad and grinning at him.

James smiled at Nicki. "Please tell me you've got some good news for once."

"Yes, I do, James. I have Professor Aldridge on the phone right now on hold. He wants to speak with you."

"Oh, great. Uh, send it to my office line. I'll take it there."

"Sure."

James quickly headed to his office, just down the hall from the conference room. His phone started to ring just as he walked into the office. He sat down in his chair, took a moment to catch his breath, and picked up the phone to greet his friend. "Hello, Professor Aldridge!"

"Hello, James!" replied a familiar, friendly voice. Professor Aldridge was an elderly gentleman, soft-spoken with a British accent.

James relaxed back into his office chair, smiling broadly. "It's so nice to hear from you. It's been a long time."

"Yes, it has, James. You know, I have been thinking of you lately, and I wanted to give you a call."

"I'm glad you did, Professor. We'll have to get together sometime in the near future."

"Yes, indeed, James. I'm looking forward to catching up with you about everything going on. I, myself, have been very busy lately, and I'm back to lecture at Cambridge again."

"Good, Professor. I'm very glad to hear that. All the students at Stony Brook always enjoyed your lectures."

"Yes, that was a while ago, wasn't it?"

"It certainly was, Professor. Hey, it just so happens that I'm going to be heading up to the British Isles in one of my new ships in the next couple of days."

"Really? Why is that?"

"I'm bringing the *Aquatarus* up to a job that we're working on in the North Sea—just above Scotland. It's a big oil-rig job, and we're being subcontracted to help out with the construction."

"Great, then maybe you'll have time to stop in and visit me in England."

"Of course. I look forward to it. I'll have Nicki arrange it with your secretary."

"Oh, James, before I forget, I have something very important to talk to you about."

"What's that, Professor?"

"I have come across a piece of information that may be of interest to you and your company."

James sat up straight, his interest piqued. "What is it?"

"First of all, I have to tell you that I cannot divulge the source of the information due to my relationships with my many contacts and the nature of my work."

"Of course."

"I have to also tell you that I could have easily disregarded this information, but since the source of it is so reliable and trustworthy, I felt compelled to share it with you."

"Okay."

After a few moments of silence, Professor Aldridge began to speak. At first he spoke in his normal soft-spoken way, but then he became more strident as he explained the strange information he had come across.

"I was told that at a certain location in the middle of the Atlantic Ocean, west of Africa, at thirty-one degrees latitude, there is something of interest on the bottom of the ocean that is highly significant."

James was silent for a moment. "I see. Is there anything else that you can tell me about the location?"

"Unfortunately, that's all that I can tell you at this time, but due to the nature of my contact, I'm sure there is something very important there."

"Well, you certainly have piqued my interest. I'm very tempted to stop there on my way up to the British Isles and survey that area. This may mean I'll need to give you a rain check on that visit."

"I totally understand, James. You know, of course, that the depth is very great there, so any exploration will involve advanced technology."

"I understand that, but we happen to have our best deep-sea exploration equipment on that ship, so I'm rather confident that if there is anything down there to be discovered, that we can find it."

"Good then, James. I thought that you would be intrigued. Just allow me to give you one piece of advice, though."

"What's that?"

"I strongly advise you not to share this information with anyone else—not even the ones closest to you."

"Okay, Professor, you have my assurance on that."

"Right, then, James, I'm going to go now, but we'll speak again soon, and I do hope we'll find time to meet up on your trip up north. If you do take on this little side trip, I certainly will be interested in the results of your exploration."

"Of course. I'm looking forward to seeing you again as well, and thanks for the information. I'm certainly intrigued."

"Okay, then. I'm going to email you the exact coordinates. I'll send it via my protected server, so look for it, and again, please keep it confidential."

"You have my assurance, Professor."

"Have a jolly good time on your trip, and see you soon. Goodbye, James."

"Goodbye, Professor."

James hung up the phone and sat in his chair thinking about Professor Aldridge's unusual request. He tried to think if there was anything in that general area of the Atlantic and turned to his computer to search for information. After surfing the internet for several minutes, he came upon a webpage that displayed an atlas of the Atlantic Ocean. The latitude markings on the map included many small islands that populated the Atlantic Ocean. He stared at the screen, pondering the vastness of the area at thirty-one degrees latitude, to the west of the coast of Africa, and wondered what could lie below the surface of the sea there.

***

Three hours later, James headed to the break room to get a cup of coffee. He found Nicki and Kent having a vociferous conversation in the hallway outside the break room. They both appeared somewhat disconcerted.

James called out to them. "Hey guys, what's going on?"

Nicki immediately held out a piece of paper. "James, we've got trouble."

48

Kent moved to James's side. "Wait till you see this."

James pulled his head back for a moment, confused. "What is it?"

Nicki raised her eyebrows. "Well, one of our marine scientists here in Research was surfing the net and found this article on one of the science news websites. It mentions our company by name in the article."

James looked perplexed. "So what's the big deal with that? It's not uncommon for us to be mentioned in scientific articles. We're probably mentioned in a lot of scientific articles."

Kent grabbed the piece of paper out of Nicki's hands. "I'm going to read this to you, and I think you'll see the problem right away." Kent took a second to focus on the paper. "This is the headline: Famous Oceaneering Company Discovers Ancient Deep-Sea Marine Monsters."

"What—"

"Let me continue," said Kent. "In what may be a stunning development, it has been reported by insiders at the engineering company Ocean Engineering Corporation International that a new large unidentified marine animal has been discovered. The discovery of the new sea creature came about when marine scientists at OECI were studying data from their Electric Fish underwater surveillance drone program."

Kent went on. "It has been reported that OECI conducted a multiyear study of the deep sea using hundreds of automated underwater drones. Professor Egan Suffield from the University of Hawaii commented, 'As strange as this sounds, it was highly probable that one day there would be a discovery of a new class of large underwater marine organisms.'"

"Are you sure this news is legit?" James asked after a brief pause.

"Yes, Nicki and I checked it out before showing you to make sure it was from a trustworthy source. It was also posted on a news video."

"Okay, then let's think about this for a moment before we jump to any conclusions on what to do."

They settled into the break room. James quickly scanned the article again, shook his head several times, and tossed the printout onto the table.

"I think that the best way to handle this is to issue a press release stating that OECI would like to clarify the previous news issued concerning Electric Fish," said James.

Nicki grabbed her notepad and started to take notes. Kent sat silently.

James continued. "You can include something like this: OECI has developed the Electric Fish underwater surveillance program in conjunction with other prominent scientific research organizations. Its purpose is to map the ocean's depths, since most of the underwater regions of the world remain virtually unexplored."

"The Electric Fish program has extensively surveyed the deep oceans, making many impressive discoveries over the past several years. Unfortunately, there have been some misrepresentations about some of our recent findings. Please rest assured that OECI will issue a full report on the progress and findings of the program in the near future. If you have any further questions concerning our program or OECI in general, please contact our PR Department. Okay, I think that's good enough."

Nicki continued to jot down some notes, then put her pen down. "Fantastic. I'll get that typed up and distributed."

Kent nodded, noticeably relieved. "Nice work."

James just smiled. "I've learned something over the years in dealing with the press. Always use the news services to your advantage, because there is no such thing as bad publicity if you word things right."

Kent and Nicki both smiled. James always had an interesting way to size up situations.

"Oh, James," said Nicki, "Dr. Saveroff is anxious to meet with you to discuss her contract proposal."

"Oh, that's right!" he said, slapping his forehead. "I forgot about her! Is she still staying at the visitor cottages?"

"Yes, she is. We've taken good care of her, but she's insistent on meeting with you."

"Okay, set something up. I'll talk with her. Kent, is everything ready for our launch of the *Aquatarus* tomorrow?"

"Yes. We've got everything loaded on the ship, and she's ready to leave. Captain Hayes and her crew are all ready to depart at four p.m. tomorrow."

"Good, good. Oh, there's one other thing that I forgot to mention to you, Nicki."

"Yes?"

"For being such a good employee, I'm sending you on an all-expense-paid vacation."

"Wow! I don't really know what to say. Where to?"

"The North Sea!"

"The Nor— James, that's not funny."

James and Kent both laughed. Kent was so amused that he doubled over with laughter and smacked his hand on the table while Nicki glared at them both.

James finally stopped laughing, looked sincerely into Nicki's eyes, and said, "Sorry. Seriously, though, I need you to come with us. It's just for a few weeks. We have so many important things going on, and I'm going to need your assistance. What do you say?"

After a few moments of thought, Nicki threw up her hands. "All right, I'll come! It sounds like it'll be an interesting adventure. I'll ask my mom to help out watching my kids while I'm gone."

"Great, Nicki. You'll have a great time."

"You'll love the *Aquatarus*," said Kent. "It's a really big, comfortable ship. There's even a workout room."

Nicki still didn't look completely convinced. "How's the food?"

"We have a professional chef on board," said James, "And the cafeteria is almost as big as a cruise ship's. You'll even have your own spacious suite."

Nicki sighed. "Okay, then, I better get going and start making preparations." She left the table muttering, "Can't believe I'm going to the North Sea. My mom's going to go crazy."

"Kent," said James, "Find out exactly how that leak got into the hands of that site."

Kent nodded. "I'll get our IT guys to check out our computers to find out if anyone on the inside sent out any information."

"Good. Now let's get going. We have a lot to do before we leave tomorrow."

Kent sighed. "We sure do."

Later in the afternoon, James headed out of the main building and walked on the paved pathway toward the guest cottages, which were located on the company grounds, near the shoreline, west of the channel harbor. The sun was already sinking, and the light on the shoreline was shimmering softly off the small waves of the bay. James stopped for a moment and took in all the beauty of the scenery around him, contemplating how lucky and proud he was to have built such a magnificent company. He fully appreciated being able to do what he enjoyed so much and never took for granted the wonder of a profession that explored the oceans of the world.

James reached the guest cottage where Dr. Saveroff was staying and knocked on the door. She peeked out the window, her face brightening once she saw that James was at the door. She opened it excitedly and greeted him with a smile.

"James, so glad to see you. I've been waiting to meet with you for the past several days, but I know that you had a lot going on."

Dr. Saveroff appeared to be ready to go for a jog. She was wearing black leggings and an aqua halter top. He was momentarily flustered by the wave of attraction that swept over him.

"Hi, Dr. Saveroff, yeah, uh, I'm sorry I couldn't meet with you sooner, but I'm..."

"No need to worry. I totally understand. I hope that the submarine accident is being resolved."

"It's being investigated as we speak," James answered soberly.

"I know their families must be taking it hard," she said.

James remained quiet for a few seconds before she broke the silence. "Would you mind taking a walk with me? I was just about to go just before you came."

"Sure. And we can chat a little."

"Great." Dr. Saveroff closed the door to the cottage, and they headed down the paved pathway that led toward the shoreline.

"It's so beautiful here. I've been trying to focus on my work, but I just love this area and walking on all of these lovely paths."

"Yeah, I love to walk here, too. I find it good for thinking about things, especially when work gets hectic."

Dr. Saveroff smiled. "What do you like to think about?" They continued their stroll, gazing at the shoreline scenery.

"Oh, I like to think about some of my projects, and some of the more interesting work trips that we've had out at sea. ~~And lots of other things, too~~. It's just very relaxing being out here, searching at the bay, feeling the wind, and taking in the views."

"It certainly is a perfect combination of relaxing and stimulating here." She paused for a few moments. "Do you think we could take some time to discuss my company's business with you? We have a lot to go over. I have our proposals back at the cottage, if that's okay."

James glanced at his guest briefly but kept walking, clearly enjoying the moment. "That's why I came out here. Unfortunately, I'm leaving tomorrow on the *Aquatarus* on a scheduled trip, so I won't have time to go over your proposals."

Dr. Saveroff clearly was disheartened by James's words. "Oh no. I was looking forward to working out a contract extension. I really think that we can work out an amicable deal that benefits both our companies."

James stopped walking, looked directly at Dr. Saveroff, and saw how disappointed she was. "Well, how about this: If you want, you can come aboard the *Aquatarus* with us, and during the trip I'll definitely find time to meet with you and go over things. I could even drop you off in the Canary Islands, or if you prefer, England, during the voyage. Would that work for you?"

Dr. Saveroff paused for a moment, thinking through her upcoming commitments as she looked out over the bay. Then she laughed. "You know what, it sounds crazy, but that would be fantastic. Thanks for the invitation, and for finding time for me. I really appreciate it."

"Just remember that I can't guarantee any-thing. As of right now, I'm reluctant to make a deal. But I'll be open-minded and consider

54

everything you have to say."

"That's fine. I only ask that you consider what we're willing to offer."

They both stopped walking and stood in a somewhat awkward silence, but James was pleased by Dr. Saveroff's broad smile and her evident excitement at their upcoming sea voyage. He also couldn't help but appreciate how attractive she was in the light of the afternoon sun.

James averted his eyes and peered in the direction of the channel harbor, where his company ships were docked. He pointed toward the harbor in the distance and said, "If you look over in that direction, near that large orange crane hoist, you can see the *Aquatarus*."

"Wow, what a beautiful ship. She's huge."

James nodded his head as he looked out over the harbor. "There is no better experience than being out on the sea."

While still observing the *Aquatarus*, Dr. Saveroff reflected on James's words. She took in all the coastal scents and sounds and breathed with an air of calm contentment as she stood there taking in that beautiful scenic location.

After a short while, they resumed their stroll, enjoying the enchanting natural environment along the beautiful bay shoreline of the Bahamian island. They were both excited and anxious about the upcoming journey, which would take them out into the mighty Atlantic Ocean aboard the magnificent *Aquatarus*.

[7]

Aboard the Aquatarus

It was thirty-three minutes past eight o'clock in the evening aboard the *Aquatarus*. The sun was setting in a magnificent kaleidoscopic show of orange, red, blue, and white in the western sky of the Caribbean Sea. The *Aquatarus* had been at sea for the past four hours, heading northeast at twenty-three knots toward the archipelago island nation of the Azores.

James looked one last time at his laptop screen, studying the area of the Atlantic Ocean southwest of the Azores before he turned it off and closed it down. He was struck by how isolated that group of islands was, out in the middle of the Atlantic Ocean. It was about eight hundred miles west of Spain. He grabbed his jacket, left his cabin, and walked a short distance to the cabin adjacent to his own and knocked on the door. The door opened, revealing Kent standing there.

"Hi. I'll be ready in a minute."

"Sure. Take your time," said James as he entered the room.

Kent ripped off his shirt and quickly put on a crisp white officer's shirt and a well-ironed navy-blue tie. He briefly finished his grooming rituals in the bathroom, then walked toward James, asking, "How do I look?"

James laughed. "You look like you're going on a hot date. C'mon, let's go."

They headed out the cabin door and down the hall, talking as they descended two flights of stairs. After a long walk through the ship's large cafeteria, they entered the executive dining room suite. They were immediately greeted by the top executive staff, ~~who were~~ looking very dapper dressed in their jackets and ties. *rose*

Captain Hayes ~~had also~~ promptly ~~risen~~ to his feet as they entered. He waited for James and Kent to be seated, then addressed the gathering. "I would like to welcome our company president, James Sebring, and his executive officer, Kent Walker, aboard the *Aquatarus*. As ~~the~~ captain of this ship, it is my honor and privilege to toast our special guests. So please raise your glasses and join me in giving both James and Kent a special toast on this voyage."

It was clear that Captain Hayes was an experienced veteran of the sea. He knew just how to perform an official seaman's welcoming ceremony, making special guests feel at home on his beloved ship. Captain Hayes spoke slowly and clearly, even though he had already indulged in a few glasses of the fine champagne. "To James Sebring, Kent Walker, and all the other employees of OECI who are aboard this ship tonight. We, the crew of the *Aquatarus*, wish you a great and special voyage. We hope that your stay on board ~~this ship~~ will be one that you will enjoy and always remember."

Everyone seated at the large dinner table smiled cheerfully and drank to the toast. Their glasses were quickly refilled by the attentive dinner assistants.

Kent took his seat at James's side, but James remained standing, compelled to say a few words.

"Thank you, Captain Hayes, for that wonderful greeting. I have known Captain Hayes for quite some time, and every time I come aboard this ship, he always provides the warmest of welcomes. Some of you are on this ship for the first time, and I just want you all to know that we are in good hands. There is no finer captain on the sea than Captain Hayes."

Captain Hayes smiled in his seat and nodded his head, acknowledging James's compliment.

James continued to speak, radiating charm and intelligence. "This ship, the *Aquatarus*, is the most modern dive-support ship in the world. She is the flagship and pride and joy of our great company. I would not trust any captain other than Captain Hayes to operate this vessel."

Captain Hayes ducked his head and grinned as the staff broke into appreciative applause. James paused, surveying his senior staff. "We have a very important mission ahead of us over the next few weeks. I know you are all focused on accomplishing that mission and getting the job done. Feel free to learn about and to experience this great ship—and hopefully to have some fun, too. Thank you all for joining us on this voyage. Let's get the job completed and have a wonderful time doing it!"

As James took his seat, all those gathered gave him polite applause and settled back into their seats. The servers sprang into action, and the finest of foods obtained from around the world were served in a plethora of culinary

splendor. They enjoyed their dinner to the enter-
tainment of a musician located in the background playing Debussy on a grand Steinway
piano. *was*

After dinner had been served, *and* while the guests
were involved in fruitful discussions, James
slipped away, entering the galley through a side
door.

As he walked to the beverage station to get
himself a bottle of his favorite brew and chat
with other crew members, he noticed Nicki and
Dr. Saveroff seated together at one of the galley
tables enjoying their dinner with the general
staff. They both spotted James.

"James! We're over here!" Nicki used her hand
to get James's attention and waved him over.

James smiled and proceeded to walk over to
them. Both women seemed to be enjoying themselves. They were each holding a glass of wine
and were smiling brightly.

Dr. Saveroff peered up at James while holding
her wine aloft. "My, my, James, you look very
handsome tonight."

"Thank you! I can see you ladies are enjoying
yourselves."

"Yes, we are," said Nicki. "Dr. Saveroff and I
had a wonderful dinner. We're both amazed at
how good the food is here, as well as how impressive and spacious the ship is."

James pulled out a chair and sat down. "Well,
this ship does have the best chefs aboard any of
our ships—but our entire fleet has excellent
chefs from all around the world."

Dr. Saveroff laughed. "Yes, the food is of first-
rate quality. It's actually better than the food on
most of the cruise ships I've been on."

James nodded his head and then asked, "So
tell me, how are your accommodations?"

Nicki put down her wineglass. "The rooms are

really nice, and very comfortable." She pouted slightly. "I'm a bit sad you've never invited me before. We took a look around, and we're just astounded at how huge this ship is."

"Yes, how big is the *Aquatarus*?" asked Dr. Saveroff.

"The *Aquatarus* is the largest ship in our fleet—five hundred and fifty feet long and ninety-two feet wide."

"Wow!" said Dr. Saveroff. Then she whispered to Nicki, "I have no idea what that means." They both snickered.

"Oh. James, listen," said Nicki after settling down. "I was going over your schedule, and it looks like you're going to have a scheduling conflict coming up in the near future."

"Really? What's up?"

"You may have forgotten, but remember you were invited to speak at the Ocean Science Technology Symposium at Stony Brook University on the twenty-eighth?"

James banged both his hands on the table in surprise. "Oh, that's right. Okay, I'll have to think about that. We'll figure something out in the next few days. It's a pretty important event. There'll be a lot of press coverage, and some big shots there, and OECI should be represented."

"Okay. Keep me posted on that, and I'll send them a message that someone will be attending."

"Yes, good. I'll have to change our plans a little, but we'll work it out somehow."

Nicki gazed up from her tablet toward James and continued, "Oh, I also got a text message from Alex a few hours ago. She said that she's going to call you tomorrow about something very important."

"Okay, make sure you find me when Alex calls wherever I am. I definitely want to take that call."

"Who's Alex?" Dr. Saveroff asked.

"Oh," said Nicki, "Alex is James's girlfriend."

Dr. Saveroff smiled at James and said, "I hope I get to meet her. She must be something special."

Nicki laughed. "Alex works on the ITUS Project on the Canary Islands."

"The ITUS Project? I know about that. That's one of the largest engineering projects in the world, isn't it?"

"Yes, it is," said James. "Alex has been working on ITUS for the past three years. She's looking to move on in the next year or so, and I'd like her to come work with me here at OECI—but we'll see." He shrugged.

At that moment, Captain Hayes approached the table, greeting James's guests politely. "Well, hello, ladies. I hope you're enjoying yourselves on our ship tonight. How is your trip going so far?"

Dr. Saveroff stood up and held out her hand to the captain, who grasped it warmly. "I'm having a fantastic time on board," she said, "And I'm sure Nicki is, too. You have a wonderful ship here, Captain, and you must be very proud of it."

"Why, thank you, ma'am. Yes, we're very proud and lucky to be on this magnificent ship, and we do our best here to make our guests happy and to get our jobs done." He tipped his hat to the ladies. "Would you mind if I have a word with James outside?"

"Of course not."

James stood up and excused himself, saying, "Enjoy the rest of your evening, ladies! I'll be seeing you tomorrow. Dr. Saveroff, I should be able to meet with you sometime tomorrow to go over your business proposals. Nicki will arrange a time."

Dr. Saveroff nodded. "Thank you, James!"

James walked off with Captain Hayes. Dr. Saveroff watched as he followed the captain out of the galley. She turned to Nicki and said, "He's such a charming man. How do you like working with him?"

"James? Oh, I love working with him. He's very easy to work with, and there's always something interesting going on at OECI."

Just then, Nicki's cell phone rang and she excused herself. Dr. Saveroff relaxed in her chair, took a sip of wine, and observed her pleasant surroundings. Music was playing and she was having a very enjoyable evening, relaxing on a boat away from the rest of the hectic world. But she also knew in the back of her mind why she was really there. And what she had to accomplish.

***

James followed Hayes to the promenade, where they could see the ocean from high above water. "It's a beautiful evening tonight," said the captain.

Peering out into the murky sea before him, James heard the waves and saw the ocean swells until visibility ended in the mysterious realm of darkness that surrounded them. "Indeed it is, Kipp. A very beautiful evening."

"I've asked you up here because I'm interested in the location we're traveling to. I told the bridge crew that we're heading there to do some undersea research, but I know you're up to something."

James laughed. "That's a good story. I'm glad that you kept it a secret. I want to keep this closely guarded. I don't even want any of the officers to know anything about where we're going."

Hayes appeared puzzled. "So why *are* we going there, James?"

"Well, there's apparently something very important on the bottom of the ocean there—and we're going to find out just what it is."

"What could possibly be there?"

James met the captain's gaze and held it. "I don't know, but whatever it is, it must be very important. All I can tell you is that I got the information from a very reliable source."

Hayes shook his head. "Okay, guess I'll just tell myself we're in for a little adventure. We should arrive at that specified location in about forty-eight hours."

"Good work. We're meeting tomorrow morning about our upcoming dive there, right?"

Hayes nodded. "Con room at zero nine hundred. I'll try to be there. I'm going to head back up to the bridge now."

"Very well, Kipp. See you tomorrow."

James watched Hayes go, then leaned against the railing and continued looking out into the captivating darkness of the ocean.

***

could eliminate

Restless and a little excited about the voyage, Dr. Saveroff quietly left her room and ventured out onto the deck of the ship. As she made her way toward the promenade, she turned the corner and found James staring out into the sea all by himself. She stood still and continued to watch James, wondering what he was thinking and realizing he was probably just taking the time to enjoy the beauty and majesty of the sea before him. She decided to let him be in his quiescent thoughts and went back to her room to get some rest.

[8]

Located on Radar

Atlantic Ocean
West of Africa
31 degrees latitude

James was having a pleasant morning. After enjoying a breakfast of waffles, home fries, and bacon with some of his staff, he proceeded to the ship's dive command center to attend the dive-preparation meeting. This important meeting would review the details of the deep-sea dive scheduled the next day, and James wanted to be as prepared as possible to prevent any potential problems.

He headed belowdeck to the con room, which was located deep within the ship. The room was dark, lit only by the LED monitors on the walls. He was welcomed by the dive commander, Scott Voss. Kent stood next to him and nodded at James in greeting.

"Morning."

"Hey, guys. Hope I'm not interrupting?" asked James.

Scott clapped his hand on James's shoulder and escorted him to the table. "Not at all. Kent and I were just reviewing some of the Electric Fish data, and we'd like to show you something."

"Okay."

Scott grabbed his laptop and sat down. "Give me a second. I'll get my data up on the big monitor there."

A few seconds later the large central wall monitor lit up, displaying a large map of the oceans of the world. James leaned back in his chair and rubbed his chin while peering at the map.

"What I've got here," said Scott, "Are the near-time actual locations of all of our underwater surveillance drones."

James shook his head, impressed. "Didn't realize we had so many. How many drones are actively exploring right now?"

Scott looked toward Kent, squinting. "What do we have, Kent? About two hundred and twenty or so?"

"The last count that was confirmed by telemetry was, I believe, two hundred and twenty-three active," said Kent. "We did have seven drones go missing. No idea what happened to them. There were also twelve that sunk to the bottom, and we're still getting signals from them."

"Interesting. How many do we have running in the Atlantic? I've lost track."

"We have forty-seven AUVs operating in the Atlantic. There are also sixty-four operating in the Pacific. The rest are scattered about in the other oceans."

AUVs were their autonomous underwater vehicles. OECI used them to explore the vast depths of the world's oceans. They were capable of recording sounds, pictures, and sonar images and could operate for months before needing servicing.

"How are they holding up to the deep-sea environments?" asked James.

"Well, they're generally working well, despite the limited lifespan."

The AUVs were launched from OECI's science research ships and were programmed to glide down on an angle to a specified depth. They then used passive buoyancy lifts to glide back up *toward* the surface, all while recording data. The cycle was repeated many times till the battery life was exhausted. Their early-generation drones had notoriously short lifespans.

"So, what are their lifespans now?"

"Our second-generation drones, which use silver-zinc batteries, last about six to eight months, depending on conditions like current and pressure."

"That's certainly an improvement. Well, let's go over the data. What have we found? What the hell is down there? And how the hell did this get out to the press?"

"First of all, I have no frigging idea how the hell the press caught wind of our undersea anomaly finding. All I can say is it had to be someone familiar with our AUV program. Luckily, they don't know half of what we've found."

"Good, just make sure that everyone involved keeps their mouths shut going forward."

"Don't worry. I've already taken significant measures to prevent any future data breaches."

"Good, so tell me what the hell we're dealing with."

Scott leaned forward, his demeanor intensifying. "Well, it all started about four months ago when we were receiving the telemetry data from the AUVs in the South Atlantic. We recorded some unusual sound patterns. We record all kinds of sounds routinely, but there's a lot more living marine organisms down there than we thought."

"Go on," said James.

"We've developed special sound software to filter and identify any new species that we find. So we're able to use this to identify the location of the sound and of the organism that produces it. About four months ago at a depth of eleven thousand feet, four hundred miles west of the coast of central Africa, we detected and recorded a series of new sounds. What was astonishing was that we found these same sounds in other locations, which meant these organisms were actually moving around at incredible depths."

"That's remarkable."

"Yes, and whatever these organisms are, they're moving quite fast, so they must be very large creatures."

At that moment, several of the dive personnel started to arrive and take seats at the table. Scott lowered his voice. "I'll fill you in on more details later."

James nodded in agreement. With the leak, they had to watch what they said in front of general personnel.

When everyone had arrived and taken their seats, the meeting started. Scott and Kent took command and started to review all of the equipment and procedures that would be employed the next day. James sat back in his chair and listened to them go over operations for the remotely operated vehicles and the undersea sonar scanning drones. The ROVs and drones would be used for locating objects on the sea bottom.

It was all fairly routine until one of the crewmen asked Scott, "Sir, do you mind if I ask what we will be searching for on the bottom? And why all the secrecy?"

Scott and Kent looked at each other and then at James. "James, would you mind answering that?"

The room was dead silent and all of the personnel seated at the table had their eyes fixed on James. He knew they sensed something unusual about the upcoming dive.

"All right. Fair enough. I'll answer that question. I know that you've already been told that we are heading to a special location in the Atlantic with the purpose of conducting a scientific research dive. Well, this dive tomorrow will be a bit more involved than that. I don't want to reveal the specifics of what we know about the location, but I want you all to handle this dive with all the skill and precision that we hired you for. I don't know exactly what we're going to find tomorrow, if anything, but anything we do find or discuss during this dive is to remain confidential. We've already had an unauthorized leak. This is very unfortunate, and I don't want anything like that to happen again."

James took a breath and again looked around the room at his crew. Their faces tightened with signs of stress and anxiety as he continued, "I realize that you are the most skilled and the best in the dive-support business, and that's why you work for OECI. I just want you all to know that we appreciate all that you do. Thank you!"

Scott got the attention of the crew and immediately continued their prep discussion.

James relaxed and sat back in his chair again, mentally zoning out a bit, knowing that Scott and Kent would handle the rest of the meeting. His thoughts drifted toward Alex. He wondered how her work was going. He hadn't heard from her for a few days and was looking forward to her next visit. As the meeting progressed, he started to daydream. His conscious thoughts blended with his imagination, projecting a weird movie onto the screen of his mind's eye. He saw himself descending into the rough blue Atlantic in one of his special submarines. He gazed out of the view window of the sub and saw something swimming toward him. Suddenly, a voice brought him back to reality.

"James. James! Captain Hayes wants to see you immediately on the bridge. It seems important."

James shook off his daydream and stood up, looking at the crew member who had been sent to fetch him. "Okay, thanks for getting me."

They made their way up toward the bridge and were immediately greeted by Captain Hayes.

"Thanks for coming up, James. Sorry to pull you out of your meeting. We've got something going on, and I wanted to let you know."

"What is it?"

"Follow me."

The captain led James over to the ship's radar control area and pointed to one of the monitors. "We're apparently being followed by an unidentified ship. It's twelve miles due southwest of our location."

"Are you sure?"

"Yes, very sure. Two hours ago we started to notice an unknown target following our course, so we started tracking it. It's a surface vessel."

"Do you have any idea what it could be?'

"Unfortunately, no, but whatever it is, it's a fairly large ship. Somewhere around twenty-seven thousand tons. We tried to communicate with them, but we got no response."

James was puzzled. Who would want to follow them? He placed his fingers on his chin, deep in thought.

"Why the hell would a large ship want to follow us?"

Captain Hayes raised his eyebrows. "I'd assume they're interested in finding out where we're going."

A chill ran through James as Professor Aldridge's words came back to him. *I strongly advise you not to share this information with anyone else—not even the ones closest to you.*

"Have they figured out where we're headed?"

Hayes shrugged. "No way to tell for sure. Guess we'll going to find out tomorrow morning when we get there."

James shook his head, then relaxed a bit. "Keep tracking our mystery ship and keep me posted. I'll let some of my staff know. Maybe we can send the helidrone out for a flight to check it out. I'll hold off for a while until we know more."

Captain Hayes nodded his head in agreement.

"We're pretty much ready for launching the ROV and the AUVs tomorrow, just as long as the weather cooperates," James said. "I'll check back with you later tonight so we can coordinate tomorrow's dive."

∗∗∗

Later that day, when James had returned to his private cabin, he noticed a message from Nicki on his desk. He smiled as he read it.

James, I spoke to Alex earlier today. She wants to speak to you. She left me this message:

James, call me as soon as you can. It looks like I'm going to have a few weeks off from work soon, so maybe we can get together. Love, Alex

James grinned, filled with warm, calm feelings as he thought about the possibility of seeing Alex again. Maybe she could join him on the *Aquatarus*? Some private time together with all of his scheduled work would be difficult, but it wasn't impossible. His romantic planning was quickly extinguished, however, when he heard a knock on his cabin door. James walked to the door and saw Kent.

"Hey, I'm heading to the cafeteria. Want to join me for dinner?"

James stared at Kent for a beat. "Uh, yeah, sure. Can I meet you there, though? I have to call Alex right now. After I talk to her, I'll come on down and join you and the guys." James glanced at his watch. "I shouldn't be longer than ten minutes."

"Great, see you then."

James closed the door and reached for his cell phone. He dialed Alex's number and waited. After three rings, Alex answered.

"Hey, James, it's so nice to hear from you. We haven't spoken in a while."

"I know, Alex, I'm sorry, but we've been very busy here."

"That's okay. I understand. Are you on the boat now?"

"Yeah, we're taking the *Aquatarus* out for a special research dive tomorrow." He paused. "So what's going on with work?"

"Oh, I have some good news. I'm going to have a few weeks off from work here on La Palma."

"Wow! That's great. Would you like to join up with me, maybe? How did you arrange to get that much time off? I thought you guys were swamped."

"I don't know, really. It's the strangest thing. For some reason management is shutting down the project for a few weeks and almost all of the employees are getting an unscheduled vacation." She lowered her voice slightly. "Word is there's something going on here, but hey, might as well make the most of it, right?"

James chuckled. "Yeah, let me get Nicki to look at my schedule for the next week, and I'll see if we can hook up somehow."

"Fantastic! I haven't seen you in a week and I miss you already."

"I miss you too, Alex. Maybe once I get you on board I can figure out how to finally steal you away from ITUS for good."

Alex laughed. "We'll see. You know I want to complete my contract. There's plenty of time to join your company."

James sighed with exaggeration. "You're so hard to get. Anyway, I gotta head to dinner. Nicki will give you a call."

"Okay. Should I text you or her the days that I'll have off?"

"Just text us both so that I can see too."

"Perfect, just give me a bit and I'll get that to you. I'll let you go now."

"Great. I can't wait for you to see the boat."

"It'll be fun for sure. I love you!"

"I love you too, Alex. Bye. See you soon."

[9]

Launch

It was a beautiful morning on the *Aquatarus*, with plenty of sunshine and calm seas. The magnificent ship had reached its secret destination in the central Atlantic Ocean earlier, and Kent was searching for James to notify him that the AUV launch was ready to commence. He had checked the control center, but James wasn't there. He headed into the ship's cafeteria and was looking around the large spacious galley when he spotted James seated at a table, having coffee with Dr. Saveroff. As he approached, he caught snippets of their conversation. Both were smiling and chatting while they ate their breakfast. James turned as Kent approached.

"Morning, Kent!" James called.

Kent nodded his head. "Good morning, James. Morning, Dr. Saveroff. I see you're both enjoying your breakfast."

The pair were sitting at a table near a large

73

glass window with a brilliant view of the serene ocean and the blue sky sprinkled with white dreamy clouds. Dr. Saveroff looked away from Kent and out at the sea. "It's just so beautiful here on this amazing ship. It's hard to believe that we're in the middle of the Atlantic Ocean having breakfast hundreds of miles away from dry land."

Kent laughed. "Trust me, after you've been on the boat for a few weeks, you start to get used to it." He directed his attention toward James. "James, we've reached our destination and we're ready to launch the AUVs."

James's coffee mug clanged lightly against the table as he put it down. "All right, I'll be down there in a few minutes. You guys can get everything ready."

"Will do," said Kent. He nodded at Dr. Saveroff again before heading out of the cafeteria.

***

James leaned back toward Dr. Saveroff. "I'm sorry to interrupt our business discussion, but I have to get to the stern. I lost track of time."

Sitting in the sunlight, Dr. Saveroff squinted her eyes as she looked at James. She was clearly interested in what they were doing, but professional courtesy forbade her to ask outright. "That's too bad. I was hoping that we could wrap up our negotiations and come to an agreement."

"I have to get out there, but I promise I'll have more time for you in the next few days."

James rose and started to walk toward the cafeteria exit. Dr. Saveroff also got up and followed right behind him. As they walked, she asked, "Do you mind if I ask you just what you're launching today?"

James glanced at her. "We're just testing out

some of the equipment that we developed. It's no big deal... just a routine test."

Closely trailing James onto the promenade, Dr. Saveroff again inquired, "Does your test have anything to do with the Electric Fish program? I'd love to see what they look like!"

"Well, no, the equipment that we're testing today really doesn't have anything to do with Electric Fish equipment. Maybe later I can show you a few of the EF robots in our test lab—if you're interested."

It was clear that Dr. Saveroff was fishing for information. She obviously wanted to know more than whether it had to do with Electric Fish. James continued to walk down the promenade, heading for the ship's stern as Dr. Saveroff continued to follow him. A grand view of the ocean opened up to their right with not another ship in sight in the vast, calm sea. James opened a doorway to a stairwell leading down to the deck, where he was greeted by Carlos, who had just come up the stairs.

"Hi, James. We've got everything out on the deck and we're ready to launch."

"Thanks, Carlos. I'm heading there now. Say, do you have some time to do me a favor?"

Carlos took a quick look at Dr. Saveroff, noting her black jogging tights and turquoise sweater before looking back at James, a little uncertain. "Sure, what do you want me to do?"

James placed his hand on Carlos's shoulder. "I'd like to introduce you to my lovely guest, Dr. Diane Saveroff, who is representing the Zepheron Corporation. Please escort her to the helicopter pad and have the helidrone pilot take her for a little ride around the ship. I'd like her to get the full experience of taking a voyage on our ship, and I know she'll appreciate the fantastic ocean view."

Carlos smiled knowingly, and James felt assured that he understood that James wanted him to get Dr. Saveroff out of his way, at least for a little while. The distraction worked.

"What exactly is a helidrone?" asked Dr. Saveroff. "I've never seen one before."

James laughed. "It's just like a helicopter but a little different. You'll love it, and I know you'll love the view. I'll catch up with you later. Enjoy your flight around the ship!"

Dr. Saveroff started to leave with Carlos but then looked back at James uncertainly as he rushed down the stairs. James waved and smiled, encouraging her to go. Carlos's voice faded as he led her away. "You'll love the helidrone. Come on, let's go."

Relieved, James quickly headed down the stairs, anxious to get out to the work platform. He wanted to be there when they lowered the AUVs. After racing down three flights of stairs, he arrived at the stern. Crew stood working in the distance, and he saw the AUVs nearby. He made his way toward them, overwhelmed with pride as he watched the launching crew work, all properly dressed in their orange jumpsuits and

safety helmets. His company's emblem was emblazoned on the helmets, and the jumpsuits were
embroidered with OECI in large blue lettering.

"Hey, Scott. How's everything?"

"Hey, James. You got here just in time."

"Looks like a great day to launch. What do you
think?"

Scott smiled. "Yeah, we lucked out—the weather report looks nice and clear, and so far the
currents are light. It looks like we'll be able to
launch the two bottom-scanning AUVs without
any difficulty."

"Great."

Scott made some final checks and gave the go-
ahead for launch. James looked up at one of the
two AUVs being lifted up by an enormous white
hydraulic crane. They watched as the AUV was
slowly lowered into the ocean. The operator
deftly performed a series of delicate maneuvers,
and the large torpedo-shaped neon-green drone
entered the ocean and floated on the surface six
yards away from the ship. The crane arm immediately withdrew upward, and the drone floated
free.

"Keep it away from the ship!" called Scott.

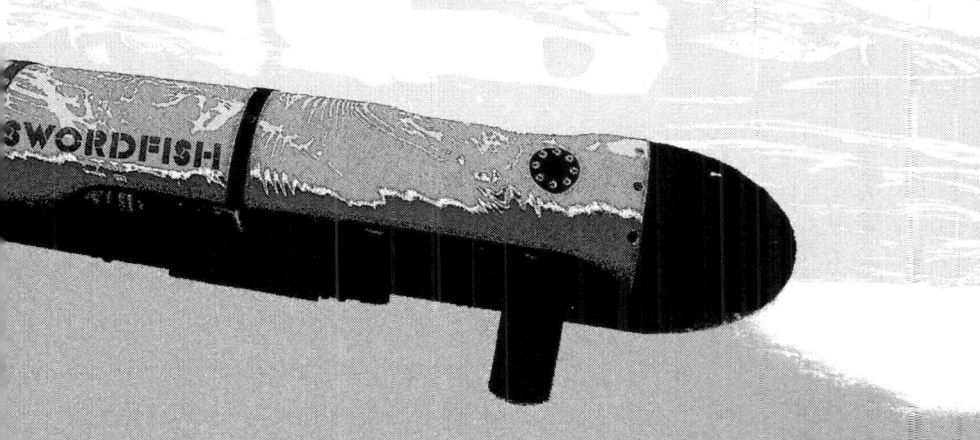

A small orange, floating seacraft was already in place to assist with the drone launch and quickly powered up, speeding to the floating object. Crewmen aboard the small craft used a specialized pole with a cushioned hook to corral the drone and keep it from bumping into the ship. A single small collision with the ship could damage the drone, cost thousands of dollars in repairs, and delay the launch.

Scott and James peered down over the side, watching them work. "One down, one to go."

While still looking down at the drone bobbing in the sea, James smiled. "Good work, Scott. Which drones are we using today?"

"Our two best Deep Search Class AUVs: *Dolphin* and *Swordfish.*"

James nodded approvingly. OECI sold a lot of those drones to some of the best navies around the world. The Deep Search Class was among the most advanced models. They had OECI's newly developed Aqua-Search, the most advanced underwater search technology in the world.

"I'm somewhat reluctant to sell this new tech to some of our customers," said James. "Especially those dipshits at Zepheron."

Scott burst out laughing. "I hate dealing with those dimwits, too. Heard you got one of their reps on board. Wanted to taunt her a bit?"

James smirked good-naturedly. "We gotta pay the bills, so I have to deal with sleazy clients sometimes. And we do make a lot of money from them, at least indirectly."

"Thought you said you were trying to get around that Electric Fish subcontract from Zepheron. Deal with the Navy directly?"

"I am, but it's complicated. They have powerful political friends in high places, so it's not easy. We'll see what happens."

As James looked overboard to check the

status of the AUV in the ocean, he noticed it starting to slowly sink below the surface. Happy with a smooth launch, he relaxed and turned to Scott. "I'm going to head on down to Control to watch the descent."

"All right. We'll have the other AUV in the water in a few minutes. They'll both be running their programmed descent to the bottom. I'll join you in a few minutes; I just want to make sure the second is launched correctly." He looked out over the water. "We're starting to get some ocean swells, and I don't want them running into each other."

James nodded. "See you later."

***

An hour later, Scott arrived in Control and joined James, Kent, and the rest of the dive control team. Both of the AUVs had successfully made their programmed descent to the bottom, and they were now cruising in a sweeping pattern, scanning for any anomalies.

As time passed, Scott and another team member were carefully scrutinizing several of the monitors displaying both the real-time under-water sonar scan results and the visual imaginary of the ocean bottom. James was chatting with Kent when he heard Scott call out to him in an excited tone.

"James! We found something on the bottom!"

James quickly made his way to where they were standing. "What is it?"

"Look here," Scott said, pointing at a monitor. "We're detecting some debris. It appears to be wreckage of some sort."

"Wreckage?" James leaned closer, studying the high-resolution images, which were constantly changing due to the scanning movement of the

AUV. To anyone else, it would be too much to process, but James and his crew had years of experience and were experts in deciphering such patterns.

The view panned over an area, and James sucked in a breath. "Oh yeah! I see it! Wow, it looks like it's spread out all over the place. What do you think it is?"

"Can't tell just yet, but whatever it is, it must have been large to leave such a huge debris field."

James could barely contain his excitement as he stared at the many monitors in amazement. How privileged was he to know what so few marine scientists ever got to experience? He marveled at how far the industry had come, giving him the chance to view the deep bottom of the Atlantic Ocean in such amazing high-resolution detail.

"How deep are the AUVs now?" he asked.

Scott stood behind James. "Right now, the *Dolphin* and *Swordfish* are hovering about three hundred and fifty feet above the bottom. It's about fourteen thousand and a hundred feet deep there."

James whistled. The Atlantic Ocean in the area ranged from nine thousand to seventeen thousand feet deep. Fourteen thousand was deeper then James thought it would be at this particular location in the Atlantic.

"How are the AUVs holding up?"

"Well," said Scott, indicating the screen with a wave of his hand, "All the telemetry indicators are looking really good, and the batteries are at about eighty-five percent charge."

"So, we'll most definitely get to find out what's here?"

Scott grinned. "Oh yeah."

One of the crew walked up behind James and tapped him gently on his shoulder. "Sir, you have a call on the ship's intercom system. You can take it in the back of the room, sir."

James looked up at the crewman and nodded his head. "Okay, thanks."

He walked to the back corner of the room where the intercom was located and picked up the wall-mounted phone. "This is James."

Chester Verona, the pilot of the ship's helidrone and helicopter, was on the other end of the video call line. He was on the top deck of the ship, near the heliport landing pad. James could clearly see Dr. Saveroff in the background checking out the helidrone holding her flight helmet,

"Hi, Mr. Sebring. I understand you want me to take your friend, Dr. Saveroff, for a little flight around the ship? Is that correct?"

James laughed a little. "Hey, Chester. Yeah, if you don't mind, take her for a little trip around the ship for thirty minutes or so. She represents a customer, and she's getting in our way here. I don't want her to learn too much about what we're doing right now, so keep her occupied and entertained."

"Understood. We'll keep her busy for a few hours."

"Good. Tell her that I'll meet up with her later."

"Will do."

James walked back to the monitors. Just as he reached them, several members of the team cried out in excitement.

Scott shouted, "James, come take a look at this!"

"What is it?"

Scott turned around. "We found the center of the debris field, and we can see numerous fragments of a metal structure of some kind."

"Wow! I see it."

"Looks like it was broken into many pieces and crushed by the pressure."

James noticed something unique about a large section of the metal structure he was observing. "Stop it there! Take a look at that section!" James pulled out a pen from his shirt pocket and pointed to a portion of the screen.

Everyone leaned in to look at the metal section that James pointed at, silent for several seconds as they all tried to make sense of what they were looking at.

James turned toward them. "What does that look like to you guys?"

Kent looked at Scott and then at James, shock all over his face. "That looks like a conning tower on a submarine!"

James nodded his head in agreement. "Exactly! We're looking at the wreck of a submarine here, guys."

Scott focused on the image. "Yeah, this is definitely the wreck of a submarine. Look over here." Scott used his finger to indicate another area of the monitor. "This is the aft section of the sub, and you can even see its propeller here."

"What do you think happened to it, and what country was it from?" asked Kent.

James peered at both Kent and Scott. "I don't know, but I want you to continue scanning the wreckage area, and have the team research what submarines could have sunk in this area of the Atlantic." James quickly checked the digital clock on the wall near the monitors. "I'm going to head to the upper deck to check with Nicki on some items. I'll meet up with you guys later."

"Okay," said Scott. He turned back to his crew with a determined look. "You heard the man. Continue with the bottom search. Let's find out what the hell this thing is."

James started to walk toward the doorway and then stopped and called back to the crew, "Oh, and send the AUVs out on an outer scan of the wreck periphery, just in case there's more to this wreck than we think. That sub could even have collided with a ship, which could still be down there somewhere, too."

"Good idea," said Scott, nodding.

James left the room, his mind buzzing. *Just what the hell have we gotten into, and how the hell did Professor Aldridge know about this wreck?*

[10]

The Mysterious Discovery

Chester secured Dr. Saveroff in the flight compartment of the helidrone and slammed shut the hatch on her side of the craft. He got into his compartment, closed his hatch, and prepared the craft for takeoff. Before he started the engine, he turned back to look at his passenger. "Dr. Saveroff, are you comfortable and ready to go?"

"I have to tell you, I'm a bit nervous, but I'm ready and kind of excited."

Occupying the bubble-glass compartment directly behind Chester, Dr. Saveroff took a deep breath as he gave her a thumbs-up and started up the gas turbine engines. Instantly, the six independent turbine blades sprang to life and spun effortlessly, generating a unique high-pitched whine. The sixteen-foot-long craft lifted high into the air and rose quickly above the large octagonal pad.

Dr. Saveroff turned her head and looked out

at the helicopter pad painted with bright yellow lines. It shrank as the craft moved higher and higher into the air, until she could see the entire *Aquatarus* ship. She was amazed by the power and speed of the helidrone and how swiftly it flew through the air. With adrenaline pumping, she called out to the pilot, "Woo! This thing is amazing! How the hell can it move so fast and turn so quickly?"

Chester turned his head to look at her and returned her huge smile. He spoke to her through his helmet microphone. "Awesome, right? This craft has six computer-controlled external turbine blades which swivel independently and steer the craft instantaneously in any direction. Kind of like a dragonfly!"

"It's unreal! I love it!"

Chester hit the throttle located on the steering pod system, and the craft accelerated swiftly as they flew west toward the open ocean. Dr. Saveroff immediately felt the intense g-force as they flew. She looked back and saw the *Aquatarus* becoming smaller and smaller until it was a little speck way off in the distance.

A thrill of excitement rushed through her. Both the amazing view and the velocity she was experiencing was more than she could have imagined coming out here. As they sped faster and faster westward, high above the water, she shouted to Chester again through her helmet mic, "How far are we going to go? Don't we have to save some gas to get back to the ship?"

He laughed heartily. "Don't worry, Dr. Saveroff. We still have plenty of gas to get back to the ship, and this craft has inflatable pontoons if we have to make an emergency landing." He hesitated for a few additional seconds and then continued, "But we wouldn't want to do that because that would be very risky."

She couldn't have agreed more. "No, we wouldn't want to do that."

Dr. Saveroff shuddered as she pictured landing on the rough ocean waves below and decided that she'd much rather stay in the helidrone. She took a breath, relaxed, and scanned the vast ocean vista before her, taking advantage of her once-in-a-lifetime opportunity.

As she searched, she noticed a small speck floating on top of the ocean in the distance. Interested what it was, she squinted at the mysterious object as they sped along. Then she realized it was larger than she thought. It looked like some type of floating vessel. She called out to the pilot. "Hey, Chester, do you see that object off in the distance?"

"Yeah, I just noticed it! I wonder what it's doing out here near our ship?"

Chester piloted the helidrone downward, heading directly toward the vessel. It took them two minutes of flight time to reach the mysterious-looking military craft. It was heading northeast, directly toward the *Aquatarus*. As they flew by the ship, they saw no one on deck. Dr. Saveroff stared at the vessel and felt a shiver of apprehension at the sight of the shadowy, unattended craft.

"Chester, what is this ship doing here? Do you have any idea?"

"Sorry, Dr. Saveroff, I have no idea, but it almost seems like it's following the *Aquatarus*."

"Wait a minute... I can see some letters on the side of the ship, near the bow. Can you get us a little closer?"

"Sure." Chester piloted the helidrone into a holding pattern and drifted closer and closer toward the starboard bow. It took several seconds for Dr. Saveroff to decipher the words on the side of the ship.

"It says OSOSCELOS," she shouted. "That's the name of the ship!"

"That's a weird name for a ship," he said. "I wonder what kind of vessel this is?"

Chester steered the helidrone closer to the ship so that they were now only a hundred yards above the bow, near the navigation tower. The ship was moving, but they couldn't see anyone on board anywhere. It almost seemed like a ghost ship.

Chester seemed just as uneasy as she felt. "I can't even see through the windows of the tower. They're tinted gray. Very strange."

Suddenly, an earsplitting, pulsing siren sounded, and a dozen sailors bolted out of a side door. The sailors, dressed in dark-gray uniforms and carrying military-style rifles, gathered on the side of the ship and pointed their weapons directly at the helidrone. Chester hit the throttle and the helidrone jolted upward and away, high and fast out above the sea.

"Holy shit!" he shouted. "Did you see that? We've got to get the hell out of here and back to the *Aquatarus*."

Although Chester wasn't looking at her, Dr. Saveroff was so rattled that she simply nodded her head, her face beet red. Her upper lip twitched and she was sweating, her heart pounding in her ears. "What the hell was that? Have you ever seen a ship like that before?"

Chester shook his head. "No, ma'am. I've never seen any vessel like that. It looked military, but it had no clear military identification on it."

Chester kept the helidrone speeding away on full throttle for a few minutes, until they could barely see the mysterious dark-gray craft in the distance. Dr. Saveroff allowed herself to breathe a sigh of relief, and they both relaxed when they caught sight of the scarlet-red *Aquatarus* with Neptune's Trident clearly emblazoned near the bow. As they approached from above, Chester slowed the helidrone down and began to circle the ship.

Dr. Saveroff studied the vessel as they hovered high above the stern. She decided to see if she could take advantage of their little scare. "Chester, what are all those white cranes on the back deck of the ship for?"

"Those are hydraulically powered lifting devices we use for transferring large oceaneering materials on and off of the ship. This ship is often used in offshore oil-well construction and other oceaneering projects. It's also used to launch large watercraft into the sea—such as submarines, ROVs, or automated underwater vehicles."

"I see. They're huge!"

"Yeah, they can move many tons of equipment when they have to."

"How many crew members are on the ship?"

"Well, that depends on the job, but typically about a hundred twenty to a hundred and eighty crew members are on the ship at any given time."

Chester skillfully piloted the helidrone down onto the ship's large landing pad. Dr. Saveroff admired the view as they flew lower and lower until finally they landed with a slight bump. Chester turned off the fan turbines and turned to her. "I know we had a bit of a scare, but I hope you enjoyed your flight with me today."

She smiled. "I had an excellent flight. This helidrone is an amazing craft."

Chester smiled back. "Yes, she is amazing. I love piloting this thing!"

He exited the helidrone, assisted Dr. Saveroff out of the vehicle, and then escorted her off of the landing pad and into the ship. She knew

Chester would report the incident with the ship to James, but she couldn't help but wish she could tell him the story herself.

* * *

Two hours later, James met up with Nicki in the central command suite near the bridge. James knew that he had some future commitments on his schedule that could pose a problem, and he wanted to straighten them out.

Nicki had already arranged James's upcoming engagements on the table. As soon as he walked up to the table, she got right to it. "James, as I mentioned before, we have an issue here next week. The *Aquatarus* is scheduled to deliver some equipment to the North Sea Project, but you're also booked for Stony Brook then."

"The symposium is definitely my priority. Any ideas about how can we work this out?"

"I think we can get our corporate ship to meet up with us en route, and we can transfer over the equipment that needs to go to the North Sea job. It shouldn't be a problem, because she already has a full crew."

"Where's the *Pemaquid* now?"

"Luckily, she's docked in Lisbon. She's available to meet up with us in a few days if needed."

"Great, let's do that. We're still going to be here for a few more days, so have the *Pemaquid* start to head this way for a rendezvous. Hopefully we'll have some calm seas in a few days so we can transfer the equipment over to them."

"All right, I'll make the arrangements. And I'll confirm your attendance with Stony Brook."

"Thanks, Nicki. It'll be fun speaking at my old school. You'll join me as my guest, right? I can show you the school and the area. You'll have a great time."

"Thank you. I'd love to." She smiled sincerely. "And, James, I'm so glad I joined you on this voyage. I'm really enjoying it."

"I'm glad you came. I don't know what I'd do without you. I only wish Alex were here with us."

"Oh, don't worry. I already made arrangements for her to fly to Long Island. She'll be meeting up with us when we arrive in Port Jefferson."

He spread his arms out. "See? You're amazing. We'll all have a good time."

"Oh, before I forget, I got an email from the engineering team on Abaco. They have something to report about the *Hydra 3* accident. When you have some free time, give them a call."

Some of his happiness dimmed at the reminder of the accident, but that quickly bloomed into determination. "Okay, I'll do that. We're going to find out what happened to the crew."

The phone rang, interrupting their discussion. She picked it up and listened to the caller, looking at James. Her eyebrows lifted in response to whatever she heard on the line. After listening for a few moments, she removed the phone from her ear and said to James, "It's the dive command center. They found something."

***

Several members of the crew were huddled around the live feed from the *Swordfish*. Scott glanced over his shoulder and called him over. Everyone was keyed up with excitement. "We've identified the vessel."

"Well, what is it?"

Scott gestured toward the conference table. "Rebecca, will you show Mr. Sebring our findings?"

His chief science officer, Rebecca Ciani, indicated some documents she had set out for him to examine. A highly respected member of James's crew, she had been employed with OECI for more than ten years. She held a master's degree in marine biology and additional training in the field of marine archaeology. The crew regularly relied on her for her extensive knowledge and insightful advice on oceaneering science matters.

"What do you have for me?"

"I cross-referenced the computer library for known vessels that went missing in this part of the Atlantic south of the Azores, and I came across several candidates for this undersea wreck. After studying the visual data that the *Swordfish* provided, I confirmed that this debris field is the remnants of a US Navy submarine, the USS *Scorpion*."

James's eyes opened wide in astonishment. He glanced back at the live feed briefly, then turned back to Rebecca with a confused expression on his face. Scott and Kent joined them.

"Look here," said Rebecca, pointing at an old photograph. "In this picture, you can clearly see the masts of the conning tower, the one you first spotted. This picture is from when the *Scorpion* was first launched in New London, Connecticut in 1959. Do you see the four conning towers and how one of the masts is higher than the other three?"

James studied the picture intensely. "Yes, I see it. It's very distinctive. One of the masts is the periscope and the other three are the antennae and the sensing hoists."

"Correct. Now look at this photo from the *Swordfish*'s feed. It's a photo of the broken and partially crushed mast that we found in the debris field."

James compared the two pictures and then understood what she was getting at. "They're exact. Wow, good work, Rebecca!"

Rebecca continued. "The *Scorpion* sunk in May of 1968 under suspicious circumstances while following a Soviet ship convoy. To this day, the US Navy has no idea how it sunk."

James nodded. "I remember reading about it. The Navy thought that it may have been carrying a torpedo that accidentally self-detonated but when they took pictures of the crushed hull they found no evidence of that."

"Exactly," said Rebecca. "I found out through contacts that the Navy still periodically uses AUVs here to conduct testing for the release of materials from the nuclear reactor and weapons that the *Scorpion* carried."

"That means there could be several nuclear weapons still sitting right there in that crushed hull!" James stood up, refocused, and looked around the room at his team. He was alarmed but proud they had successfully located the mysterious item that Professor Aldridge had sent him to find.

"Good work, everyone! Remember, all of this must be kept completely confidential." Approaching the video image of the *Scorpion's* wreckage, he added, "I want precise pictures taken of every inch of this site. Let's see if we can determine what happened to this submarine. Maybe we can help the Navy figure out why it sank." He sighed, realizing they had to take additional steps. "Do not disturb the wreck in any way. This is a memorial site. Ninety-nine of the Navy's finest submariners lost their lives here."

Rebecca and Scott glanced at each other. "What? Is there something else you want to tell me?"

"We found another debris field separate from

the wreck of the *Scorpion*," Scott said. "That's actually the reason I called you down here."

Shocked, James shook his head in disbelief. "What? Where is it?"

"At your suggestion, we sent the *Dolphin* out on a wide sweep in case there was any other debris from the *Scorpion*. We found an entirely isolated debris field three miles away, northeast of the *Scorpion* wreck. At first, we thought it was another section of the *Scorpion* that had drifted while sinking, but when we got the high-resolution photos back from the *Dolphin*, we were amazed to find that this wreck had nothing at all to do with the *Scorpion*."

Rebecca placed some enlarged photos onto the conference table. She pointed at something in the photo. "This is a picture of the elevated view of the ocean floor below us. This debris field over in this lower-left corner is the wreck of the *Scorpion*, and over here, in the upper-right corner of the photo, this is the newly discovered, unidentified wreck site."

Rebecca placed another large photo on the table. "This is a photo captured by the *Dolphin*. It was taken approximately fifty feet above the unidentified wreck." Lifting her gaze, she looked at James and the crew before continuing. "Notice how different and unusual this wreck is compared to the *Scorpion*?"

James eagerly pulled the photograph closer and studied the enlarged images. Still peering down at the mysterious images, he said, "It's obvious why. This looks like an ancient wreck."

"Exactly," said Rebecca. "If you look at this image, right here you can see the faint details of a large wooden structure. These seem to be the three masts lying on their sides, broken off from the boat. Also, these things scattered about the bottom, on both sides of the hull, appear to be the contents of the unidentified craft." Rebecca looked up at James. "This appears to be some kind of ancient marine craft, buried deep in the ocean bottom."

"How ancient do you think it is?"

She shook her head. "I don't know. I've never seen anything like this before. It could even be pre-Colombian, for all we know. But it's in fairly good condition, considering that it is buried in silt, more than ten thousand feet below the surface."

Still somewhat perplexed, James shook his head and looked at his crew. "All right, you guys know what to do. Prepare the ROV and send it down to do a survey. Let's find out what the hell this thing is. Try to obtain a few samples from the wreckage, and then take them to the lab for examination. We don't have much time. We have to rendezvous with the *Pemaquid* in a few days for a materials transfer, and then we're heading to Port Jefferson for the conference."

Scott nodded. "We'll get the ROV ready and launch her in a few hours using the moon pool. That way we won't attract too much attention. We'll be up well into the night, but I'll let you know what we find down there."

James laughed softly. "I can't believe we found two separate wrecks!"

Just then, Kent walked over to James and spoke softly to him. "I have to talk to you about a few things. Got a moment?"

The look on Kent's face let James know that whatever he had to say was important. He nodded toward an office over to the side of the larger room. "Yeah, let me grab a cup of coffee first."

Both men walked into the small kitchen area. James grabbed two cups from the cabinet and poured the coffee. As he finished adding sugar and cream to their cups, Kent began to speak. "I just got a call from Abaco. They told me that they got a recent sound identification hit from one of our Electric Fish drones!"

"Really? What kind of hit?"

"One of those same unidentified creature sounds that we've been recording."

"How far down is it, and where did you locate it?"

"This is the part you won't believe—it's about twelve thousand feet deep, and it's only about twenty-one nautical miles from our current position, where the ocean gets deeper."

That's some coincidence. "So, what now?"

"Well, we've been tracking these unidentified creatures, and some of our past hits have been in this area."

"This area? Can you show me on the monitors?"

"Yeah, I will, but I have to tell you about something else, too."

"What else you got?"

"I spoke to the captain a little while ago, and he told me that ship that was following us is still there—and it's even gotten a little closer."

"Have they identified it?"

"Well, Chester flew past it when he took Dr. Saveroff for a ride, and they were able to read the ship's name. It is called the *Ososcelos*."

James grinned. "I heard that they didn't get a pleasant reception from that ship."

"No, they certainly did not. Anyway, the captain researched the name and found out that the US Navy does not have a ship named the *Ososcelos* in its fleet. More importantly, even with extensive research, he was unable to find a country of origin for the *Ososcelos*."

"Hmm. Any thoughts as to whose ship it could be?"

Kent shrugged. "Maybe the CIA, KGB, JSOC?

You know that there still are several nuclear torpedoes in that sub—just laying there on the ocean bottom."

"Yeah, but I don't think that our military or the Russians would follow us in this way."

James raised his eyebrows. "You think that ship has something to do with the other unidentified wreck?"

"That didn't occur to me, but it's possible. Maybe there's something in that wreckage that's important."

James nodded. "Maybe. If so, we're going to find out just what it is."

[11]

Nighttime Alert

Hours after James left Control, he settled into his room for the night for some much-needed rest. The excitement and mysteries of the day had exhausted him. He lay in bed trying to put the pieces together. What had occurred at this strange location deep on the ocean bottom? How was Professor Aldridge involved in all of this? His mind drifted as he thought about the sea and the waves that surrounded him each day on his glorious vessel.

In his mind's eye, he could see below the depths of the water near his ship, and he peered down deeper and deeper into the vast dark waters of the abyss. He traveled through the deep sea toward a distant glow. As he traveled, he felt the cool current around him. Swimming along, he startled as he became aware of a nearby presence that suddenly sped past him. He stopped in the water and looked about, trying

97

to get a better view of the long black shadowy object that had passed by. He saw nothing as he scanned the cold darkness.

Worried, he peered down again toward the mysterious glow he had been moving toward. He was relieved to see that it was still there, and he continued to swim down toward that intriguing luminescence. Strange sounds moved about him, and an intense fear gripped him as the shadow reemerged in the pitch-black darkness. He felt more than saw the flutter of the dark mass as it moved out of sight once more.

He searched farther down into the abyss toward the radiant glow. It was still there, but it was now dimmer, and it seemed to be moving away from him ever so slowly. He jerked back as he felt another, much larger object move by in the cold blackness. A sense of shock overcame him as something called out to him and touched his body.

"James! Wake up! We've got an emergency! There's an intruder on board, and we're trying to apprehend him. Get up!"

James immediately sat up in bed, rubbed his eyes, and tried to focus. Kent stood before him. After such a deep sleep, it took a moment for James to orient himself. He waved a hand to redirect the flashlight shining directly into his eyes. "What was it you said? Someone's on board the ship?"

Kent switched on the room lights, and James squeezed his eyes shut. "Yes. An intruder was discovered on the ship trying to sneak into the lower decks."

"Shit." James dressed frantically and quickly followed Kent to the promenade deck.

As they ran toward the stern, the ship's general quarters alarm sounded. They quickly turned and headed down the stairs, bursting through the doorway onto the deck. Though the lighting was dim, they were just able to make out someone chasing two men. A full-blown fist fight broke out, and they raced toward the fracas.

When they caught up to the confrontation, James lunged at one of the two individuals dressed in tight black clothing and knocked him to the ground. The other intruder pulled out a weapon and pointed it at James. Kent grabbed the armed man, and they struggled for control of the weapon. The first assailant managed to rise and charged at James. The two men battled, exchanging punches and kicks for several seconds. James fought frantically, hoping backup was coming soon. The man was very skilled in martial arts.

Kent's attacker got the upper hand and knocked him violently back toward the ship's railing, briefly incapacitating him. The assailant rushed to his partner's aid and delivered a brutal kick to James, catching him in the ribs. James fell forcefully onto the deck of the ship, scraping his face, and he could only watch as the two black-clad intruders ran toward the stern and jumped overboard.

Struggling for breath, James managed to get to his feet. Everything hurt as he stumbled around. He gazed at the place where the men had vanished from view.

What the hell is going on? Who were those thugs?

As James approached Kent to help him to his feet, armed crew members ran toward them.

"Are you all right?" James asked.

Kent groaned from the pain and wobbled for a few seconds before peering up at James. "Depends if getting my ass kicked qualifies as all right. Holy shit, I'm sore."

"Are you guys okay?" one of the crew asked. "Anybody hurt?"

James sighed, steeling himself against the pain. "I think we're all right, just a bit beaten and shaken up."

He turned his attention toward the stern railing, where crew members were using high-powered searchlights, scanning the water where the intruders had jumped overboard.

"Do you see any of them in the water?" James asked. "Anything there? A boat, raft, anything?"

"Nothing. Nothing's there. They escaped somehow."

James grunted in frustration. "How could they just disappear? We didn't hear any motors."

Still shaken, James and Kent walked to the railing. All eyes peered intensely into the dark waters below the ship. After searching for ten minutes, they stopped to speculate.

"There's nothing here. Those bastards must have come in a mini-sub and disappeared under the sea," said Kent, obviously infuriated by the intrusion as well as the physical assault.

James rubbed his forehead, still in pain. He found the ship's security officer, a tall, stern blond man with a muscular frame. "Gary, I want you to get all of the security staff and search this ship from top to bottom. See if those goddamned intruders took or disturbed anything. I want to know what they were doing on this ship and what they were after. Got it?"

"Yes, sir!"

"Good. Report to me directly by zero eight hundred hours."

"Yes, sir!"

"And from now on I want armed security officers patrolling the ship night and day."

Gary nodded sharply. "Yes, sir. I'll see to that."

"Good."

As James was about to open the doorway to the stairs heading up to the general quarters, he noticed several people, including Dr. Saveroff, looking down at them from the upper balcony, apparently awakened by the commotion. Not in the mood to explain, he didn't stop.

***

Minutes later, back in his suite, he was just about to enter his bathroom when he heard a knock at the door.

His first impulse was to ignore it, but he reconsidered. It might be information about the intruders. He opened the door and was surprised to see Dr. Saveroff's frowning face.

"Are you all right, James? You look hurt!"

"I'm okay."

"What happened out there? The alarm woke me up. When I checked the hall, everyone was racing out of their rooms to find out what was going on."

James's partly bruised and swollen face told the story of what he'd been through. He moved to the side to invite her in. "I don't know what happened. We had some intruders on the ship. Kent and I caught up with them on deck, and then we fought them."

Dr. Saveroff searched James's face and placed her hand on his cheek. "You've got a cut on your face. Here let me clean that off and get you a bandage."

James tried to push her hand away, but the doctor resisted. She walked into the bathroom and came back with a wet hand towel to clean James's wound. The action stung, and James winced and instinctively grabbed her hand. As he held it, he looked up at her, noting her sincere worried gaze. This close, he couldn't help but notice her big blue eyes, her lips. Her soft feminine touch made his body warm in reaction to her. A few seconds went by as they stared at each other, the silence deafening.

Then James gently removed his hand from Dr. Saveroff's and let her complete her first-aid assistance.

As Dr. Saveroff finished, she said, "There. That looks better now. Let's get you some ice. That should help with the soreness tomorrow."

James looked thoughtfully at her. "Thanks for your assistance, and I know it all seems a little crazy. Here we are at four in the morning. You must regret—"

Dr. Saveroff lifted her hand to stop him. She shook her head. "Don't worry. I don't understand everything that's going on here, but I can see that it's important for your company, and I know it's none of my business. I just want you to feel better. Maybe I can get off at the next port, and we can work on our business interests when you get back." She raised an eyebrow and smiled. "Of course, when you are feeling better."

James smiled broadly. "All right. I promise you, we'll work on our shared interests together soon. I'm going to get some sleep now, and you should too. Hopefully we won't have any more disturbances tonight."

"I certainly hope not! I'll see you tomorrow. Nicki and I are going to breakfast together in the morning. You can join us if you like."

"Okay, maybe I will," he said, sitting on his bed with a groan. "Keep in mind that we're going to have armed security guards monitoring the ship from now on, so you'll probably see them around."

"Okay. Good night, James."

Dr. Saveroff closed the door behind her. James lay back in bed, trying to relax. It felt strange to realize the vessel that he had been so proud of earlier was now tainted with vulnerability.

***

Nicki made her way down a flight of stairs from the executive office suites and entered the second-level deck. As she walked along the railing, she peered out toward the gorgeous seascape that Mother Nature had provided. She approached James's cabin and knocked on his door. After knocking vigorously with no response, she became worried and decided to enter his room. As James's personal assistant and his unofficial boss-arounder, her access and authority were not to be questioned.

As she entered the dimly lit room, she saw him crashed on his bed like a tuckered-out panda cub. She immediately went to the windows and slid open his drapes, calling out loudly, "James! Get up, get up! What the hell did you do last night?"

Nicki's efforts were successful, and James crawled out of bed, slowly rubbing his arm. He looked around the room and muttered to himself. Finally, he noticed Nicki. "Oh God, Nicki! What time is it?"

"It's seven thirty, and you need to get up."

James moved carefully and swung his legs out onto the floor, gazing up at her. "What a night. I got to bed very late. Did you hear what happened?"

"Yes. I can't believe you and Kent got into a fight with those thugs! What were you thinking? You both could have been killed."

James took a deep breath, exhaled slowly, and slowly rose to his feet. He walked into the bathroom, splashed some water on his face, and looked in the mirror. Nicki watched from the bathroom doorway as James examined his face. He had four facial abrasions, including two on his left cheek and two near his mouth.

She shook her head. "I'm going to have the ship's doctor examine you and Kent today. I'm also going to tell him to check your mental faculties."

James laughed and threw the towel onto the bathroom vanity and went to his dresser. He grabbed a pair of pants and a shirt and put them on. Catching Nicki's eye, he said, "I'll let the doctor look us over later, but I think we'll be all right. Have you heard anything about those bastards that got on the boat?"

Nicki frowned. "No, I didn't. I actually came here to tell you something else very important."

James stopped what he was doing and gave Nicki his full attention. "What is it?"

"Scott and the dive control team found something very unusual last night at the site of that unidentified wreck."

"Really? What did they find?"

"I don't know, but they managed to bring some items up from the wreck. Scott said that the finds were amazing, and they want you to come see them right now."

James eyes bulged with astonishment. "Where are they now?" he asked, rushing to finish dressing.

"They're at the moon pool."

"Okay, I'm heading there right now. Where's Dr. Saveroff?"

"We're going to breakfast right after I leave here."

"All right, just make sure you don't tell her anything about what's going on with the findings."

"Don't worry. I have her completely focused on our business relationship and contract negotiations."

"Good girl! Definitely keep her out of the way and out of the picture. I may join you at breakfast after I go down to the moon pool. If not, I'll catch up with you later."

Anxious and excited, James hurried from the room. He couldn't wait to see what his dive team had found.

"Okay," called Nicki. "And don't forget to see the doctor. I'll know if you didn't."

[12]

From the Bottom

James couldn't get to the moon pool fast enough. It was located far from his quarters, at the very bottom of the ship, below the stern. He entered the spacious rectangular indoor complex that housed the moon pool. The Aqua-Search ROV was being lifted out of the water by a cable hoist, and James watched as the crew gently set it down on the side staging area.

James walked toward the ROV, where Scott and several other dive control personnel had gathered.

"Heard what happened to you and Kent last night," Scott said as James approached. "You all right?"

"Yeah, we're all right, but something very strange is going on."

"Indeed. Well, come here and take a look at what we found."

James followed Scott to a pile of debris that

had been brought up from the dive and placed on a raised platform. Scott used a pencil to point at the items. James bent over slightly to observe them closely. He had no idea what to make of it.

"What is this stuff?" he asked. "Do you have any idea?"

"It's hard to tell because everything is encased in sediment," said Scott.

"It's like a concretion—almost like a clay cement."

"Yeah, but if you look closely you can make out certain artifacts that were either part of the ship or its cargo."

James squatted down and picked a few items up and studied the minute intricacies. "It looks like there are metallic items and some wood pieces."

"Yeah. Rebecca said that in order for these items to form this kind of solid concretion, the wreck has to be very ancient—possibly thousands of years old."

"That old?" said James.

Scott nodded. "There's still a lot more detritus like this to be recovered, too."

"Fantastic! What does Rebecca recommend we do with this?" said James, indicating the load they'd been examining.

"She recommends we deliver it to an underwater archaeological specialist who has experience in separating and identifying this type of undersea discovery."

"All right. I think I know one who I can work with. I'll look into it. What else did you guys find down there?" James tore his eyes away from the intriguing mass and looked up at Scott.

"The ancient wreck site is somewhat scattered, so we're not sure how large it actually is. It looks like when the vessel hit the bottom all those years ago, some of the contents got blown out of the ship and scattered. If we had time for another dive we could map it out better. We're using GPS to mark the exact positions of everything, so the next time we come back, we can resume our mapping of the area without wasting time."

James cursed inwardly. Who knew what else was down there that they couldn't reach. But they had to get moving to meet up with the *Pemaquid* tomorrow. He stood up. "All right, good work. Pack this stuff up for shipping. I have someone in mind in England who I'm sure will be able to tell us more."

"Sure, we'll get it ready for transport."

"Good. We're going to get underway in the next few hours, so get all the submersible equipment secured, and make sure the crew knows that everything that we found on the bottom is highly confidential. We cannot allow another leak."

"Don't worry. I've already taken extreme measures to keep this discovery a secret."

James nodded. "Just keep an eye on everything and everyone. For all we know, those intruders were here to steal this stuff. I've got security patrolling the ship night and day."

"I'll tell the crew. We're all taking everything very seriously—especially with what happened last night."

James lowered his voice. "And I want a detailed report on what we found out about the *Scorpion.* I want pictures of it from top to bottom, as well as any dive notes you and your team took during the excursion."

"Okay, I'll have Rebecca work on that immediately."

James glanced at his watch and clapped Scott on his arm. "I'm heading up to the bridge to talk to Hayes. I'll check with you later."

***

On the bridge, James approached Captain Hayes, who was at the bow window, peering through binoculars toward the vast open sea.

"Hey, Kipp. Beautiful day today out there."

"Hey. I'm glad you're up here. I was looking for you earlier."

"What's going on?"

"Well, for one thing, that ship that was following us for the last few days disappeared sometime late last night—apparently shortly after your encounter with those two intruders."

"So they took off after they got their thugs back on board. What do you think they were after?"

Hayes put his binoculars down and checked out the cuts on James's face. "Looks like you got clocked pretty damn good last night."

"Don't worry about it. I'll be all right."

"Anyway, I don't know," said the captain, shaking his head. "I can't imagine why a ship like that would send agents onto our ship to snoop around. The only thing that makes sense is that it has something to do with the wreckage."

He'd been unable to shake the same thoughts ever since the fight. "So, it has to do with either the *Scorpion* or that unidentified shipwreck that we found nearby."

Hayes looked at him gravely. "As I understand it, there are several nuclear weapons still on board the *Scorpion*. Maybe it has something to with that?"

James didn't want to admit it, but the thought terrified him. Ancient artifacts were one thing. Nuclear arms were something completely different. "It's possible, but it wouldn't be easy to get at those nukes, *if* there are any, they could have corroded into an oxidized pile of uranium by now."

"True," said Hayes, fiddling with his binoculars. "Although maybe they already knew about this other wreck that we've discovered here, and they're trying to chase us away from it, thinking that we haven't discovered it yet."

"Good point. I hadn't thought of that."

"I also finally managed to find out something about the *Ososcelos*."

"What did you find out?"

"I researched every source I could. It's registered in South Africa, and it's a privately operated ship owned by a billionaire named Callum Namesbury."

James shifted his focus and rubbed his chin, searching his memory for a few seconds. "That name sounds familiar, but I can't remember where I've heard it before."

"I'll contact my friends in the US Navy to see if they know anything more about the *Ososcelos* and Namesbury. We'll see what the hell they're doing here, out in the middle of the Atlantic, spying on us."

"All right. I want us to set sail at fourteen hundred hours to meet up with the *Pemaquid*." He was looking forward to Port Jefferson. New York was always great to visit.

"Affirmative. I've already got the coordinates."

James turned to leave, then remembered something. "Oh, one other thing before we leave. I want to have the officers and some of our available senior staff on the stern in an hour. I was thinking we could have a memorial for the crew of the *Scorpion*."

"That's a great idea. I know the crew will be honored to participate."

James looked out at the horizon pensively. "We'll pay our respects, and then we're going to

make damn sure we find out why that submarine sunk in the first place."

Kipp nodded his head slowly, his thoughts no
doubt turning to the sailors who had perished
on the *Scorpion* so long ago. "I'll be there as
well."

The two men stood there in silence for a bit. "I
wonder how many sailors died on that wooden
shipwreck not far from the *Scorpion*," said Hayes.

"I don't know. It must have gone down in a
terrible storm."

"I do know one thing," said the captain.

"What's that?" asked James.

"They were scared as hell."

***

Over the past several days, Nicki and Dr. Saveroff
had fallen into a pattern of having lunch and then
enjoying a pleasurable stroll around the upper
promenade. Both women shared a sense of
adventure and were enjoying themselves despite
the recent intruder incident. And although Nicki
was still keeping Dr. Saveroff occupied and out of
James's way, the two women were developing a
sort of friendship.

Nicki and Dr. Saveroff walked briskly toward
the back of the ship. High above the ship's flat
work area, they could see the crew beginning to
gather at the stern. Intrigued, they stopped
walking and observed the assembly.

"I wonder what they're doing out there?"
asked Dr. Saveroff.

"I don't know, but it looks like they're performing some type of nautical ceremony," said
Nicki.

Some of the crew were dressed in their official
uniforms.

Nicki frowned, confused herself as to what

was taking place. Then she realized what must be happening. She had to play along so as not to tip off Dr. Saveroff. "Must be for a special occasion. Captain Hayes likes to do these sometimes," she said casually.

It was a hard sell, though. James, Captain Hayes, and several of the senior officers and crew stood solemnly silent and proud, just a few feet away from the magnificent open sea. The ocean wind blew, and two large folded flags were placed before them on the deck. Nicki watched, not wanting to say more, hoping that Dr. Saveroff would lose interest.

***

As per tradition, Captain Hayes held a small ship's bell in his hands that he intended to ring at the appropriate time.

James slowly looked over his crew with pride. He then directed his gaze toward the flags at his feet and spoke solemnly, "As we stand here today, in this lonely spot in the Atlantic Ocean, we take the time to remember the many men who lost their lives tragically so long ago. As we listen to the bell toll, we should grieve, but we should not forget to celebrate their lives. As we hear the bell, we remember these lost sailors, and we hear their voices."

The crew stood tall, silent, and still for several seconds. Then Captain Hayes rang the ship's bell seven times to commemorate the Navy sailors whose lives had been taken by the sea. After some moments, two officers dressed in official ship uniforms lifted the flags and slowly lowered them into the water. The crew watched as the flags slowly drifted away from the boat and into the endless ocean. Captain Hayes led the assembly in one last final farewell salute to the lost souls. Some of the crew members wiped tears from their eyes.

The ceremony had just ended when one of the officers from the bridge approached rapidly. Noticing that his officer was carrying a pair of binoculars and looked anxious, Hayes called out to him. "What is it, Hank? What's going on?"

"Sir, we've got a large plane approaching from the northeast!" He pointed at the sky and attempted to hand the binoculars to Hayes.

Hayes looked at his officer in confusion, then grabbed the binoculars and searched the northeast. After a few moments, he spotted the approaching aircraft.

Sensing something serious, James and several of the crew members stood silently, waiting while the captain focused on the approaching craft. Finally, a bit unnerved, James asked, "What is it, Kipp?"

Still observing the speck in the sky through the binoculars, Kipp exclaimed, "Well, I'll be damned!"

He lowered the binoculars and turned to James. "It's a US Navy plane. Coming in fast and low."

"What? What kind of plane?"

Hayes again observed the approaching airplane through the binoculars. "It appears to be an MC-12 Liberty. It's a reconnaissance plane."

"Oh God. It looks like they found us above their submarine," said James.

By this point, a low-toned hum could be heard, and the plane was close enough to be seen with the naked eye.

Captain Hayes lowered the binoculars, looked up toward the airplane, and then at James. "The better question is how they found out that we're here."

James shook his head. "No way to tell. But

they have satellites, drone buoys, and the capabilities of using acoustical monitors to sense ships. God only knows what else. They have to be here for the *Scorpion*."

The airplane was approaching fast and loud. James stood with his crew by his side as the large grayish multipropellered plane advanced. Just as the airplane was about to fly overhead, James called out, "Okay, everyone! Let's give our visitors a nice welcome!" He waved at the plane, and the crew and captain joined him. The airplane flew on past them, and James said to Hayes, "I suppose they were taking pictures of us as they flew by?"

"Oh yeah. That plane has some of the best cameras and sensing equipment in the Navy."

Even though the spy plane was nearly out of sight and could hardly be heard, James took one last look up in the sky. Whatever was going on, they still had work to do. He turned and shouted to his crew, "All right, everyone, let's get going. We have to get this ship prepped for our rendezvous with the *Pemaquid* tomorrow, so get your asses in gear! We depart at eighteen hundred hours."

Captain Hayes ran a tight ship, and everyone proceeded quickly to their assigned duties. Hayes headed back to the bridge. He had several tasks involving navigation and engineering to complete before the rendezvous and equipment transfer the next day.

James stayed behind for a moment of solitude and thought. He walked back toward the stern and peered out onto the open ocean. Fog was approaching in the distance. He recalled a memory from his childhood, remembering how frightened he had been as a kid on his father's fishing boat, off the coast of Maine. They had been sailing far from the coast when they were quickly engulfed by a thick fog. He remembered how his father had settled him down and taught him to use the onboard instruments to navigate back to the coast and to safety. James smiled as he relived the pleasant memory and that spirit of adventure.

He only allowed himself a few moments of re-flection. It was time to check back with Nicki. Time was short, and there was much to be done. Before leaving, he turned back toward the sea and searched for the memorial flags they had set adrift. He was unable to find them.

Lost to the sea forever, just like those sailors.

As he left the stern, the fog had nearly over-taken the ship.

[13]

Rendezvous with the Pemaquid

It was just past noon, and the *Aquatarus* was moving swiftly north at twenty knots, heading for the open ocean rendezvous with their sister ship, the *Pemaquid*. They had traveled through a thick fog all night and were still in it, but luckily it was starting to lift and they could now see the ocean for at least a mile or two.

Captain Hayes peered through the mist nervously. The *Pemaquid* was nearing their location, and the fog was making their rendezvous a more difficult and dangerous endeavor. Fearful of a possible collision, Captain Hayes called out to the radar technician, "Stefan, give me a position fix on the *Pemaquid*. I know she's out there, but I can't see her yet."

"I've got her on my radar, sir, she's heading in our direction at approximately seventeen knots." Stefan turned toward Hayes and added, "Captain, they're roughly seven miles from us bearing

116

south at ninety-seven degrees, sir. We should be able to see them any moment now."

"Very good, Stefan, keep your eyes on them and let me know as we near their position."

"Yes, sir."

Then Hayes yelled a command to the helms-man, "Reduce speed to seven knots!"

The helmsman responded. "Aye, aye, Captain, ship's speed reduced to seven knots."

Captain Hayes grabbed his binoculars and called out to the other officers who were on watch on the bridge. "All right, crew, all eyes on the north horizon. Let's get the *Pemaquid* in view and get this rendezvous underway."

Within a minute, the bright blue and white colors of the *Pemaquid* were spotted by the crew through the light fog, and the final approach was initiated. The two ships slowly and cautiously approached each other until they were just twenty yards apart. A loud signal alarm was sounded both inside and outside of the ship, alerting the crew of the arrival and possible danger of an approaching large sea vessel.

Captain Hayes intently viewed the slow approach of the *Pemaquid* and voiced yet another command to his bridge officers. "Approach the *Pemaquid* on the port side and use the automated-positioning tractor drive once we're aligned for the transfer of the equipment."

"Yes, sir, Captain!"

"It's a little rough out there today, and I don't want an unexpected collision with our guests."

"Don't worry, sir, we'll be operating in automated-positioning mode once aligned. We're on it, sir!"

"Good. I'm heading down to the stern to oversee the equipment transfer. Stay in contact during the transfer and notify me immediately of any contingencies during the process."

"You got it, Captain!" shouted the first bridge officer standing watch.

Captain Hayes grabbed his hat and radio and left the bridge, heading for the stairwell to get down to the rear stern area. As he made his way down the stairs to the large flat aft deck, he immediately noticed that several large piles of equipment and boxes had already been assembled, awaiting transfer to the *Pemaquid*. As he approached the huge white crane off to the port side, he saw James and Kent standing near the crane control booth, already sharing a conversation with the operator.

"How everything going with the transfer?" Hayes asked.

"So far so good, Kipp. We think that we have everything out on deck that needs to be transferred to the North Sea, but we're still checking."

The *Pemaquid* had slowly and carefully positioned itself alongside the *Aquatarus* and was now making final adjustments to its position so that the transfer could commence.

Hayes peered at the large assemblage of equipment on deck. "Lot of stuff going out. I want to get this transfer going as soon as possible. Sea's starting to get rough. Wind speed is increasing, and the weather is going to get bad in the next several hours."

"Don't worry, Kipp," said James, "We'll get this stuff moved onto the *Pemaquid* quickly. We were going to deliver it ourselves and help out with the compressor construction but we got sidetracked with the *Scorpion* dive."

Just then there was an announcement heard coming from the captain's radio that the *Pemaquid* was now properly positioned and ready to receive the equipment. James looked toward the crane operator holding the stick controls and gave him a thumbs-up and a smile.

The operator maneuvered the huge crane lift over toward the equipment sprawled out on the deck.

James and Kent left the crane booth and headed toward the pile of equipment lying on the aft deck, careful not to get in the way.

James looked at Kent and yelled over the whirring of the crane, "Where's our special package for the British archaeologists?"

Kent smiled. "Oh, you mean the package containing the mysterious sunken ship fragments?"

"Yes, that package. We definitely want to make sure that doesn't get damaged in the transfer."

"Don't worry. Come here and take a look at how I labeled it." Kent pointed toward the large wooden crate that contained the ancient shipwreck materials.

The large box was covered in easy-to-read bright-red lettering:

DANGER!

HIGH EXPLOSIVES

HANDLE WITH CARE

James laughed out loud and looked at Kent. "Brilliant! I love it. What made you think of it?"

Kent snickered. "Well, you told me to make sure this package gets to Cambridge safely and undisturbed. So, I figured that anyone who sees this package will be very careful when handling it. By the way, why did you decide to send it to them?"

"I contacted Professor Aldridge, and he recommended that I send it to Cambridge. He knows them personally and thought they would be the best at identifying what we found."

"What do you think they are? Don't you think it's strange that the *Scorpion* and that other ancient shipwreck were both found in the same general area?"

James shrugged. "I don't know what to make

of it. But we're going to find out what happened."

Both men heard the loud gearing sound of the crane and noticed the crane maneuvering toward them. James grabbed Kent's arm and pulled him away. "Let's get out of here."

They headed up the port side of the ship, a safe distance away from the hazard and noise of the crane. They peered overboard at the magnificent ship that was the *Pemaquid*, which was floating parallel with the *Aquatarus* as the crane moved the items.

"I'm heading up to my office to touch base with Nicki," James said. "I also want to go over those photos of the *Scorpion* that we took with the ROV. There's something that I saw in those photos that piqued my interest."

"What was it?"

"I'm not sure, but I want to take another look. But I want you to stay here and make damn sure that our special archaeological package gets on the *Pemaquid* safely."

"Don't worry, James. I'll tell the captain about our highly explosive package." He grinned.

James laughed. "Good. I'll talk to you later."

***

It was two days later, and the *Aquatarus* continued on its journey, heading northwest toward the Long Island Sound. They were now four hundred and fifty nautical miles from Port Jefferson Harbor.

James sat in his cabin looking over the underwater photographs of the unidentified shipwreck. He had arranged the photographs in two rows on his office table and was precisely examining each photograph, at times using a magnifying glass. What was this unusual ancient vessel, and where it could have come from? It was thousands of miles from any known land formations. Just which ancient people could have built such a ship seaworthy enough to venture into the vastness of the Atlantic Ocean?

James set aside the ancient shipwreck photos and replaced them with the photos of the wreck of the *Scorpion*. The first photo was the sonar overview picture that showed the silhouetted locations of both the *Scorpion* wreck and the ancient wreck. The distance between the wrecks was a mere two miles. Then he examined the close-up pictures of the *Scorpion* fuselage. He was amazed at how intact parts of the sub-marine were while other sections were twisted and mangled hunks of metal.

Noticing something peculiar in a photo taken of the bow of the *Scorpion*, he carefully man-euvered his magnifying glass. There appeared to be an indentation or crease in the metal section. Intrigued, he leaned in, trying to make it out, but then Nicki tapped on James's office door, breaking his concentration.

"Hey, James. Just wanted you to know that I made arrangements for Alex to be picked up from Gabeski Airport on Tuesday morning. I had a chat with her, and she's all excited to meet up with you and attend your presentation."

"Thanks for making those arrangements and for reminding me about my presentation. I'm kind of losing track of time here on the ship."

"You're welcome. And I have a guest here who wants to see you about something. Do you have some time?"

"Is it Dr. Saveroff?"

"Yes."

"Oh, good. Please send her in."

Dr. Saveroff entered James's office and paused to look around the room.

"Very nice office you've got here."

"Take a seat, please," James said, gesturing to one of the seats in front of his desk. "I hope you're enjoying your visit, and I must apologize that I haven't spent more time with you discussing our contract."

Dr. Saveroff immediately turned on her ever-present charm now that she knew business would be discussed. James couldn't help but notice how nice she appeared sporting dress jeans and a stripped red and white shirt.

"I understand, but I must stress that my company is very eager to renew our Electric Fish contract."

James sighed. "I hate to break it to you, but unfortunately I'm leaning toward not renewing that contract with Zepheron. At least with what you presented to me the last time we discussed this. But I do need to discuss something else with you while you're here."

"What's that?"

"I've been notified by some of my crew that a day ago you were seen at night, wandering around the lower-deck levels looking around in some of our high-security areas. Namely, you were found in our operation control area, apparently checking out our equipment there with a camera on your possession. Please explain what you were doing there."

Dr. Saveroff appeared momentarily startled but recovered quickly. "James, I'm so sorry to have concerned you and your crew about my visitation down below. I have to say that it was late at night, and I went for a little walk because, frankly, I was bored. I'm just so fascinated by your marvelous ship, and I wanted to explore some of the areas that I hadn't seen before. And I figured that I'd take a few pictures of the more interesting areas so that I could show some of my friends because I know they're going to ask me all about my experience."

James peered inquisitively at Dr. Saveroff, listening as she went on. So far, her explanation seemed reasonable.

"Please do not think that I was trying to secure any unauthorized information from your ship or do anything hostile to it. I was just enjoying myself, taking a nighttime stroll to some of the more secluded areas that I hadn't seen before."

Dr. Saveroff seemed sincere, and when she finished, she waited for James's reaction.

James smiled gently and shook his head slowly. "Okay, Dr. Saveroff, fair enough. I imagine if I was on a big ship like this for several days, I probably would want to check out some of the hidden areas of the ship too. But just to give you a little warning: Our ship's security is on full alert now, especially after we had that little intrusion of uninvited guests a few days ago. So I'd strongly advise you not to wander into any of the lower decks of the ship without an escort. If you feel the need to visit any of the high-security areas of the ship, just talk to Nicki, and she will make arrangements with one of our security officers to escort you around. If that's permissible."

Dr. Saveroff smiled and nodded. "Thank you for that offer, and from now on I certainly will be more careful. You've been so generous, and I've had a wonderful time. I'm afraid, though, that I must press on about the contract. We're going to arrive in Port Jefferson Harbor in the next few days, and I really don't want to leave the ship without a business deal in hand. Perhaps you can tell me why you're leaning toward not renewing?"

James lifted his eyebrows and relaxed in his

chair. "Dr. Saveroff, I'm going to be blunt with you. You're a very nice young lady, and you're a very smart businesswoman too, but I don't really like the Zepheron Corporation, and I'd rather not deal with them. We've had this business deal for a few years. I design and build the drones for the US Navy, but I have to sell it to them as a sub-contractor through your company.

"Unless Zepheron improves the terms of our contract and the monetary value, I'm going to have to break away from their business deal and go on my own and see how things proceed. I'm very confident that I'll have no problem getting my own contracts with the US Navy and other government agencies around the world."

Dr. Saveroff's face fell slightly, and she looked around the room. She reached for the small photo. "Is this a picture of your girlfriend?"

"Yes, that's Alex. She's meeting up with me in a few days in Port Jefferson. We haven't seen each other in a few weeks, and we're looking forward to getting together."

"She's a very pretty lady."

She put down Alex's photo and looked at him with admiration. "You really have it made here, James. You've built up an amazing company, this ship is a true wonder with a state-of-the-art design, and your corporate headquarters in the Caribbean is the envy of the industry. Even I would love to work for you."

James laughed lightheartedly. "Well, if you want to change careers, Nicki can give you an employment application, and we'll see how things go. I could always use an experienced engineer and an attractive saleswoman who knows how to engage customers and get their attention."

They both smiled at each other. "Well, thanks for that offer, but... I have a commitment to my present employer, so I don't think that I'll be leaving my job anytime soon. But I'm going to contact my superiors at Zepheron as soon as I get off this ship and see if they're willing to enhance their business offer."

Dr. Saveroff stood up abruptly and held out her hand. James stood up alongside her and warmly shook her hand for several seconds. "Dr. Saveroff, it's been a pleasure, and I'll certainly consider any revised offer that you bring. I'm going to be in Port Jefferson for several days, so just give Nicki a call. It was so nice having you, and I'm sure we'll meet again."

Dr. Saveroff placed her hand on James's arm. "The pleasure is all mine, James."

They shared a few moments of extended smiles, then she quietly left the room. James sat for several seconds and wondered if he really would ever see her again.

[14]

Arrival at Port Jefferson Harbor

The *Aquatarus* proudly sailed into the mouth of the Port Jefferson Harbor and boldly sounded its ship's horn to announce its arrival. The large vessel slowed its speed and headed toward the bustling village of Port Jefferson, two miles south of the harbor entrance. The harbor was quite large and was surrounded on both sides by large sandy, earthen cliffs. Along its way, the ship passed by industrial sites that included a petroleum-tank storage farm, a gravel storage and shipping yard, boatyards, and various recreational marine businesses. There were also some exclusive house estates that adorned the shoreline with a great view of the blue-green waters of the harbor.

James and other members of the crew made their way out onto the starboard side of the ship to experience the amazing view that the harbor provided. They had been at sea for more than two weeks and were excited to finally get a chance to visit a nice seaside port and enjoy much-needed relaxation.

Since the *Aquatarus* was such a large ship, and the harbor had a constant stream of boats leaving and arriving every hour from the Port Jefferson docks, Captain Hayes moored the ship along the southeast side of the harbor, away from any boat traffic. A large tugboat supported and guided the *Aquatarus* into its approved mooring site. The village of Port Jefferson knew of the arrival of the *Aquatarus* and greeted her by sending a ship carrying the harbor master and several village dignitaries, including the mayor.

They circled the huge *Aquatarus* slowly and pulled up alongside, using their amplified PA system to announce their welcome to all aboard. James and his crew smiled brightly and waved vigorously, pleasantly surprised by the gracious hospitality. They were all anxious to get off the ship and enjoy the town, and James was eager to see Alex, who would be arriving the next morning.

The next day, James left the ship and traveled the short distance to the village docks by way of a small shuttle boat. As he walked off the dock, he saw his large escort vehicle waiting for him to arrive, with Alex anxiously waiting inside. As James approached the large blue SUV, Alex jumped out of the passenger door and ran into his waiting arms. They hugged and kissed and smiled at each other.

"It's so good to see you, Alex. I missed you so much. I'm so glad you're here."

"I missed you too. I'm so glad I was able to get time off from work."

"Me too." He put his arm around her. "We're going to have a great time here, but let's get going. You can tell me all about your trip here on the way to Stony Brook. The presentation's in just a few hours."

"Great, I can't wait to finally see you talk in public. This will be cool," she said, grinning.

James escorted Alex into the back seat of the SUV and then jumped in right behind her, closing the door. The SUV sped off onto the roadway in the direction of Stony Brook University, which was only a few miles west of the village.

***

A tall blond-haired individual standing on the sidewalk watched the vehicle leave until it disappeared up a large hill. He checked his watch and looked around, then pulled out his cell phone and made a call. "Hello. I'm in Port Jefferson now. I spotted our target."

"Good. You know what to do, so make arrangements and stay in touch. And whatever you do, *don't* lose him."

"Will do," he responded in a low voice. "I'll check back in later."

The man strolled away onto a street that led toward the village center. He quickly disappeared into the crowd of people walking the streets of the busy hamlet.

[15]

The Ocean Science Symposium

James and Alex arrived minutes later at the Stony Brook University main entrance. Large banners along the roadway advertised and promoted the Ocean Science Symposium taking place that day.

Their escort pulled up in front of a building to let them out. As James and Alex got out, they marveled at how large and modern the Staller Center for the Arts was. The Staller Center complex was situated in a huge mall-like setting, surrounded by towering red-and-brown brick buildings. Lines of people were moving toward the entrance doors to attend the symposium. There was an electric vibe about the crowd, eager and excited to attend this long-anticipated event.

James flashed his identification to the campus police attendants who were verifying the IDs and credentials. After moving through a security scanning device, both he and Alex were escorted to a special dignitary section up front and center to the performance stage.

Soon enough, the Ocean Science Symposium started, and James and Alex sat through and enjoyed a long list of speakers, all of whom delivered intriguing presentations. There were presentations on the health and physical state of the oceans and on many other scientific topics dealing with the ecology, chemistry, and geology of the world's oceans. Alex was particularly interested in the presentation dealing with the ITUS Project, which included her own work.

After several hours of presentations and a lunch buffet, it was finally time for James to start his presentation. It took a short while for the symposium technician to load up his visual material, and then he was formally introduced to the large crowd. James smiled in greeting and began speaking, loudly and clearly.

"I want to thank you for inviting me to give a talk at this fantastic symposium here today. It's been a while since I've been back to Stony Brook, where I did my undergraduate and graduate education, and I have to say that this university has really changed since I was last here some nineteen years ago. I can't believe all the construction and the new buildings that have been added here, and I am very glad to see that their ocean science and engineering departments have been expanded and enhanced."

James paused and took a quick moment to gauge his audience, a mix of university faculty, business professionals, and visiting university professors from around the world. He was very happy to see many young interested students were in attendance.

"When I found out that I was going to speak here, I wondered, *what* in the world am I going to talk about?" he said with mock incredulity. This got a chuckle from the audience. "Eventually, I decided to tell you how I got started in the ocean engineering business and how instrumental my education here at Stony Brook was to my success.

"During my time at Stony Brook, I happened to have a British professor here who got me interested in underwater robotic technology and design. When I left, I got a job working at a defense contractor designing underwater submersible surveillance systems. Did that for a few years. Then I decided to go on my own, since I... didn't like working for other people."

Another chuckle. "I formed a company and decided that the Caribbean was a nice place to base a company, so with the help of my professor, who eventually became a good friend of mine, I hired a small staff of engineers and technicians and started up what would eventually become Ocean Engineering Corporation International, or OECI."

A slideshow started up behind James, displaying a photo of the corporate headquarters of OECI.

"This is a picture of our corporate headquarters, located in the Bahamas on the island of Abaco. We're an integrated ocean engineering company and produce a wide variety of products for marine and defense industries throughout the world."

As James spoke, he went through several slides of OECI products. "Our products include underwater construction and service vehicles for the deep-sea petroleum industry. We also build deep-dive exploration submarines for ocean research institutes around the world and the petroleum exploration industry.

"One of our best-selling products: underwater

surveillance drones for both military and ocean science research. Our robotic drones include both shallow-sea and deep-sea exploration types. We also have a division that is involved in marine vehicle and ship construction. In recent years, we have been getting very involved in the underwater ocean-exploration business, since I believe that will be a growing field of the future.

"Why is that, you may ask? Because I think that the oceans will be of great importance in our future, both for resources and energy. Keep in mind that most of the oceans are totally unexplored. We know almost nothing about them. In fact, we know more about the moon than we do about our oceans, and the more we explore the deepness of the oceans, the more amazing discoveries we will find."

James took a pause and a sip of water. The attendees remained focused on him.

He continued on. "I'm going to give you a little history of underwater ocean-exploration. For thousands of years, men have attempted to make vessels that could travel underwater, but by the 1920s, none had been able to travel below four hundred feet. The first real attempt to find out what lies deep below the ocean's surface was by two virtual amateurs. Their names were William Beebe and Otis Barton.

"Beebe was a famous ornithologist and director of the Bronx Zoo. He teamed up with Barton, a young engineer who came up with a design that he believed could take them safely into the bathypelagic zone, which goes down to thirteen thousand feet, where there is no sunlight. Now, keep in mind that most biologists of the 1920s thought there was no life in the deep ocean and that it was too cold and the pressure was too high and that no life could survive those deep, dark depths.

"Well, Barton designed a four-and-a-half-foot hollow cast sphere, made of steel one inch thick, that he called the Bathysphere. It had a bolt-on hatch and several windows that they could look out through to see what was in the water as they went down. They first tested this five thousand-pound Bathysphere in 1930 off the coast of Bermuda, far out at sea, with no one in the craft. They used a strong steel cable to lower it into the water to a depth of a thousand, five hundred feet.

"When they brought it back up, they could see that there was water inside that had come in under pressure, and it was leaking out of the hatch. So Beebe knocked off the wingnut holding the hatch, and as the nut cleared the threads, the pressure inside shot the wingnut forty feet across the ship, nearly killing a worker who was on the deck.

"What that test showed them was what would happen to them if they were inside at that depth with water coming in at them. You see, the pressure below the ocean keeps increasing as you travel down, and it is very deadly if it enters your vessel."

James then showed a brief video of the large metal wingnut being blown out of the Bathysphere hatch and onto the ship's deck. The audience reacted skittishly to the wingnut. James pulled out a normal-sized empty Styrofoam coffee cup and placed it on a table in front of him for the audience to see. Then James pulled out another Styrofoam cup, but this one was one-third the size of the first. He placed it near the first one.

He smiled. "This smaller Styrofoam cup was once a normal-sized cup that was brought down just three thousand feet below the ocean's surface by one of our submarines, and look what the pressure did to it. All those little spaces inside the Styrofoam were compressed by the pressure at that depth, about one thousand pounds per square inch."

James looked at the audience. "Now, how many people here would like to go for a ride to that depth in one of my submarines? Any takers?"

Many in the audience shook their heads in amazement, with some laughing and others chatting among themselves about the thought of being subjected to the danger of that pressure in an underwater vessel.

James grinned. "I see we have a few volunteers here willing to put their lives on the line at that depth. Okay, well, anyway, after solving their leak problems and several successful test dives, on August 21, 1934, Beebe and Barton entered their Bathysphere off the coast of Bermuda for a manned test dive. They went down for several hours and passed their previous dive record of eight hundred and five feet, and they eventually went down to a depth of three thousand and twenty-eight feet."

"As they went down, the waters became darker and darker, until there was no sunlight. They had lights in the craft and reported seeing strange creatures that nobody had ever seen alive before. The Bathysphere had survived the dangerous dive, and when it was brought back up and the hatch was unbolted, Beebe and Barton emerged as international celebrities. Their achievement was front page news on newspapers across the world, and many scientists were jealous of their discoveries. For years, mainstream academia remained skeptical of their accounts of animal life in the deep.

"In the decades after that famous dive in the Bathysphere, underwater explorers were able to build high-technology submersibles that took them deeper and deeper into the depths of the oceans. Then, in January of 1960, two ambitious explorers named Piccard and Walsh journeyed down to the bottom of the deepest known part of the ocean, to a depth of thirty-six thousand feet. Their submersible was called a bathyscaphe, which used gasoline as a ballast, and they named their craft the *Trieste*."

"After they made it to the bottom safely, Walsh peered out through a thick Plexiglas window and saw a large flat fish on the bottom sediment. It was quite an amazing discovery because no scientist at the time had ever thought any marine creature could survive the intense pressure and cold below a depth of twenty thousand feet."

Visual images of the bathyscaphe being lowered into the sea and of its interior came on screen. James paused for a moment and looked at Alex. She smiled, silently mouthing some encouraging words. James smiled back and continued.

"Okay, who wants to see some of my company's newest ocean exploration submarines and drones?" Most of the students raised their hands. James clicked to the next slide. "This here is our Hydra-class deep-sea exploration submarine, which we sell to ocean research institutes and the petroleum industry. We have two different models, and they are capable of undersea depths of greater than twenty thousand feet and are fully autonomous and untethered. As of right now, there are no competitors to our deep-dive technology."

Several visual pictures of the submarines were displayed on the screen.

"Now here we have shown some of our newest underwater Remotely Operated Vehicles, or ROVs, which are used in the deep-sea petroleum and underwater marine-engineering industries. These ROVs are fully capable of underwater physical tasks such as turning valves, tightening nuts and bolts, underwater welding, and other assorted tasks that are too dangerous for underwater divers."

James waited for the audience to view the pictures of his underwater ROVs and then continued.

"And, finally, I'm going to show you our most advanced underwater exploration system, which we have developed over the years. These are our proprietary technology automated underwater vehicles, or AUVs, which we sell to the United States Navy and to a few ocean science institutes around the world. We call these our Electric Fish underwater surveillance drones.

"These underwater drones are launched by ship and are capable of performing extensive underwater surveillance and are programmed to record sensory data for whatever purpose. Now, as far as the military uses of the drones, I cannot tell you about that, since I'd have to kill you." Hearty laughter rang out. "But I *can* tell you that my company has an underwater exploration program of its own, and we have hundreds of these AUVs exploring the oceans right now. As we speak."

Several visual images of the Electric Fish drones appeared for the audience, displaying their long, sleek, narrow neon-green torpedo-sized shapes. Some of the pictures were taken of them speeding underwater, and others displayed oceanographers removing electronic parts from their structures for servicing.

"I guess you're wondering what we're finding down in the deep depths of the oceans, right?"

The audience murmured, and many people nodded.

"Well, we're finding amazing things deep in the oceans. We've seen many new species of fish and aquatic animals below twenty thousand feet, creatures that we had no idea about previously. Some of these organisms are quite large, and some of them are very strange-looking.

"For instance," James said, bringing up a slide, "This ghost jellyfish." Some in the audience gasped. "It's fifteen feet wide and seven feet long and looks like it came from outer space. We named it the ghost jellyfish because, well, it looks kind of ghostly, don't you think? And how about this new species of shark?"

He moved to the next slide. "This one we named the fanged shark because of the large protruding fangs from its mouth. Notice the lack of dorsal fins along the top of the shark, typical of normal sharks that inhabit surface waters. And here we see a few more pics of some of our new deep-sea discoveries, including the dragon fish, which looks somewhat like a large eel with a big mouth and a very long body. By the way, we found this fish at twenty-seven thousand feet.

"And this goblin fish, which also has a very large mouth and long, spiny teeth and very large eyes. Notice also that many of these deep-ocean species have large eyes or no eyes, very large mouths, and translucence or bioluminescence. These adaptations help these creatures cope with the high-pressure, low-oxygen conditions that exist in the sub-abyss realm."

James stopped for a few moments and noticed the event coordinator standing on the side, signaling that his speaking time was about up.

"And I think that about wraps things up, so I want to thank you all for listening to my presentation and for allowing me to speak here. It's a great university with fantastic facilities.

Have a wonderful time with the rest of the conference. I've really enjoyed myself here. Thank you all!"

James was about to leave, but the event coordinator walked over to James, shook his hand, and then announced on the microphone, "I just want to remind the audience that James is offering a tour of his magnificent ship, the *Aquatarus*, to anyone who has a VIP pass, at 5 p.m. at the Port Jefferson Harbor dock area.

"Now, I think we have a little time for some questions from the audience if James doesn't mind answering them?"

James smiled and nodded. "I'd love to entertain some questions."

The event coordinator searched the audience and asked, "Do we have any questions for Mr. Sebring?"

Several hands rose quickly from the audience, and James pointed to a young lady in the front row, who got up and asked, "I loved your presentation, and I can see that you have seen firsthand the condition of the oceans in traveling the seas. How would you rate the conditions of the oceans today?"

James grabbed the microphone, grinning. "Good question. I'd have to say that overall they're in relatively good condition, considering we have over seven billion people on the planet. But they're constantly threatened by pollution and overfishing. We have a very bad plastics problem, with tremendous amounts of plastics and other debris being dumped into the ocean and floating on the surface."

"We also have a problem with overfishing and with ghost fishing gear scattered throughout the oceans and bays of the world. For those who don't know, they are the lost or abandoned fishing nets and traps that remain in the oceans that entrap and kill sea creatures. My company is a member of Global Ghost Gear Initiative, which is working with the fishing industry, governments, academics, and charities trying to control this problem that is threatening the oceans."

The woman sat down, and the event coordinator looked about the audience and selected another question from the audience.

An older, distinguished gentleman stood up and asked his question in a slow, deliberate manner. "We all know that there is a serious energy problem in the world today. Gasoline is over five dollars a gallon, and everything is going up in price from it. I see that you do a lot of business in the petroleum industry, so you must know something about it. What are we going to do about the energy problem in the future, and is your company involved with a response to this issue?"

James stared at the gentleman and took a deep breath. "Wow! Another good question. You are bringing up one of the most important issues threatening the world and our lives today. You are right that we have a major problem. This is because the world is facing the problem of peak oil and of declining energy returns."

"For those who don't know what peak oil is, it is the idea that total oil production in the world has reached a top and is now going in decline. We're not going to run out of oil, it's just that oil production cannot grow anymore and will always be in decline. All of the world governments know about this. They've known about this for a long time, but they don't want to talk about this in public. Just look at where all the military action is today—in the Middle East and elsewhere, where the major oil-producing fields are in the world. Now, there will be responses to this, and one of them is war.

Another one is developing the poor-quality oil fields in the world, like the shale oil or tar sands that you see being developed throughout the world. Those cause a lot of pollution."

James paused for a moment, took a sip of water, and took a long look at the audience. They were dead silent and appeared to be pondering James's words of warning.

"Okay, what are we going to do about it, hmm? Well, I've been discussing this problem with my contacts in government, politics, and industry for years, and I've taken my own actions with my business investments because I see an opportunity here.

"We have partnered with a major energy company, and we're developing a fuel derived from ordinary seawater, using electricity generated from ocean energy to produce it. This fuel can be burned in typical automobiles with little modification and is completely renewable. And amazingly, this fuel does not produce carbon dioxide when burned. This fuel is called anhydrous ammonia and actually has been around for a long time, used in making fertilizer. We're going to invest millions in this alternative fuel because we're heading for a serious energy problem."

The event coordinator again looked for a question from the audience and pointed to a well-dressed woman in the middle rows. The woman stood up and asked, "I'm a news correspondent with *CBM News*, and I'd like James to respond to several reports over the past few months that his company's underwater drone-surveillance program has discovered a very large previously unknown underwater creature. These reports also indicate that James is working with a government agency to keep this new discovery quiet and out of the public view. Is there any truth to these news reports, Mr. Sebring?"

The symposium crowd immediately began chatting among themselves about this outlandish news report. The stunned event coordinator looked out into the audience and called out, "Quiet down, please, and let Mr. Sebring respond to this unusual report."

James smiled at the news reporter. "These reports about us discovering some kind of very large previously unknown underwater monster are not true. This is an exaggeration of some of our new underwater discoveries, which we've made while examining the data from our Electric Fish program. As I said before, our drones are searching below depths of twenty thousand feet in the oceans for the first time. No scientific study has ever been done there before. We have found many undiscovered creatures down there that we are studying and learning about. I can definitely tell you that we have *not* found a large 'monster' down there yet. If we do... we will announce it to the world. I hope that answers your question, miss."

The lady remained standing as the crowd became noisy and restless. James saw the opportunity and left the stage, walking over to the side area, where Alex joined him. They walked out onto the sloped aisle and headed up toward the exit doors, where they were met by several symposium attendees and reporters.

Just as James and Alex were about to leave, a young lady who stood by the door called out to James. "Mr. Sebring! Mr. Sebring! Can I get your autograph?"

James heard the unusual shout and stopped, his eyes landing on a studious-looking young woman, most likely a student. James moved toward her and asked, "Young lady, are you a Stony Brook student?"

"Yes, Mr. Sebring. I'm an engineering major just like you, and I've read all about you and your company. You're quite an amazing person."

James laughed. "A lot of people think I'm a little crazy, but I thank you for that compliment, young lady. What would you like me to sign?"

"Here, Mr. Sebring, please sign my marine science textbook if you don't mind."

James grabbed the textbook. "What's your name, miss?"

"Andrea. Andrea Fiorentino."

"Okay, Andrea. I'll sign it right on the inside cover, is that okay?"

"Sure. That will be cool."

James grabbed a pen from his front pocket, glanced at Andrea, and then wrote on the blank inside cover.

Dear Andrea, best of luck to you in your journey through life. I hope you find a career in the ocean science field, just as I did. All the best to you! James Sebring OECI

He handed the book back to Andrea. She opened the front cover and read what he wrote and said, "Thank you, Mr. Sebring."

The young lady held out her hand to James, and he noticed her bright eager smile as he shook her hand. "Oh, by the way, here's a couple of VIP passes for a tour of my ship later today. You're welcome to come aboard to see it if you'd like." He held them out to her.

Her face lit up with a smile as she gladly accepted the passes. "Thank you so much! I'd love to see the ship."

She turned to her friend standing next to her and held the passes out for her to see.

As James started to leave, he turned toward the young lady again. "Maybe you'll work for my company someday."

James grabbed Alex's hand and escorted her

through the busy entry lobby and out the main entrance doors, where they spotted his chauffeur waiting patiently for them outside.

He was quite pleased at how things had gone.

[16]

A Strange Call

Late in the afternoon that same day, James and Alex relaxed on the upper-deck promenade on the *Aquatarus*. They were watching Kent and Rebecca escort the VIP guests across the rear section of the ship, explaining the equipment and the various activities that took place on that deck during a typical mission. Alex turned to James. "Want to go down and meet to our guests?"

"I don't know... I'm a bit tired from the conference, and they seem to be enjoying the tour. Maybe we'll catch up with them later when they head to the galley for some refreshments."

"I think you should chat with them! It would be interesting to see what they think about the ship. A lot of them have never seen a state-of-the-art ship like this."

"All right, how about we join them in the galley when they take their first break?"

Just then, Nicki came up the nearby stairwell,

out of breath, and called to them. "Hey, guys! I've been looking for you all over the place. James, I have to talk to you right now."

"What's going on?" asked James, one eyebrow raised.

"Not sure, but we got a strange call a little while ago on your private business line from an individual who wants to speak to you about something very important. He seems to know a lot about you and said something about the *Aquatarus* being in the middle of the Atlantic Ocean last week."

"How?"

"I don't know, but he said that he'll call back and that he has something very important to tell you."

Nicki held out James's cell phone, and it started ringing as if on cue. She looked at the display screen. "It's him calling again now! What do you want to do?"

James grimaced with a puzzled look. "Give me the phone."

Nicki handed it over.

"Hello? Who is this?"

"Is this the famous James Sebring? The president and founder of OECI?"

"Yes, that's me. Who are you, and what do you want? How did you get this number?"

"Well, Mr. Sebring, it's not important that you know who I am right now, but what is important is what you were doing out in the middle of the Atlantic Ocean. You spent a lot of time and money out there searching for something, didn't you?"

"You know very well I'm not going to answer that."

The caller laughed mirthfully. "Don't worry, Mr. Sebring, I'm not here to cause you any trouble, but I suggest you meet me while I'm in town. I think it's very important for us to have a chat about your little adventure and about something much more important. What do you say, James?"

James flashed a tense grin at both Nicki and Alex and responded to the mystery caller. "Where are you right now?"

"I'm at the Chandlers Hotel here in Port Jefferson. It's right on the harbor. I can see your ship from where I'm sitting. I'll be at a table in the restaurant. I'd advise you to come alone, because what we're going to talk about is far too important for anyone else to know."

"All right, I'll be there in twenty minutes. I'll see you then."

"It will be good to finally meet you, and I know that you'll find our conversation very interesting."

James hung up and stared at Alex and Nicki. They'd both heard the strange conversation, and their faces reflected an unsure anxiety about who the mystery caller was.

"Do you know who this person is?" asked Alex.

"No, I didn't recognize his voice at all. But I have to meet him to find out what's going on. He seems to know something important. Remember that ship that intercepted us last week?"

Nicki pulled out her phone. "I'll get one of our ship security officers to follow you."

"No, that won't be necessary. I'm going to go alone, and I'll be all right."

Alex grabbed James's arm and looked at him with concern. "Please be careful."

"Don't worry, Alex. It's a public place, and I'll be careful." He smiled at her. "When I get back, you and I are going to have a wonderful dinner together somewhere in town. Now that you're with me, we're going to celebrate!"

James hugged her briefly and then left, heading for the strange meeting with the mystery caller.

***

James made his way into Port Jefferson Village and walked the short distance to the Chandlers Hotel, passing by many people enjoying the dusk hour and the many offerings of the busy village. He walked along the boardwalk, which led to the restaurant entrance. As he entered, he moved toward the bar area, searching the crowd. He was a bit uneasy and unsure what to expect and who to look for.

When he got to the bar, he looked about the tables in the dining area and peered around slowly. Then he noticed a middle-aged man sitting at a table by the window, waving his hand slowly in the air. James had found his mystery caller. As he approached, the man got up from his chair and held out his hand in greeting.

"Well, James, so glad to finally meet you, my friend."

James shook his hand. "Glad to meet you, too, but unfortunately I don't know your name yet."

The man chuckled. "Sorry about that. My name is David. David Simmons."

"Okay, David, nice to meet you."

At first glance, the tall man seemed sincere and nonthreatening, but James was still a bit unnerved about his real intentions.

"Sit down, James, relax. I know this hastily set up meeting between us is a bit unusual, but I think you will find the information I'm going to share with you very intriguing and potentially beneficial."

James sat down and made a quick visual check around the dining room, looking for any potential accomplices. Everything seemed normal. Just a small crowd at a lovely seaside inn enjoying the late day.

"Would you like a drink?"

James thought for a few seconds. "Sure, I'll have a drink."

David signaled to the nearby waitress, and she came over to the table.

"What are you drinking?"

"I'll have a Tanqueray and tonic."

David gazed up at the courteous waitress. "Tanqueray and tonic and a whiskey sour."

A few moments of silence then proceeded as James and David made eye contact and studied each other. James noted David's unusual grin, as if he and James had known each other somehow previously.

James broke the silence. "So tell me, David, why am I here? What do you want to tell me that's so important?"

David picked up a large white envelope off the table and tossed it across the table to James.

"Go ahead. Take a look inside."

"What is it?"

"You'll see. Go ahead and open it up."

James picked up the envelope and pulled out a small stack of photographs. He examined the first one, and suddenly his eyes lit up as he sighed. He looked at the second photo for a few seconds, then went to the third one, and on to the fourth and fifth. He cringed, shocked and startled. He lifted his head, dropped the photos, and peered directly at David. "How the hell did you get these photos? Who do you work for?"

It was obvious from the look on his face that David was pleased with James's reaction. David shifted his seated position and bent over the table slightly to get a little closer. In a lower tone of voice, he said, "James, what I'm about to tell you is very confidential and classified. I work for the CIA, and those photos were taken of your ship by one of our surveillance aircraft last week. We know why you were there, and I have to tell you that any items that you removed from that wreck site are the property of the US government."

James relaxed a bit. "I see what's going on here. Look, I understand that it is a sensitive issue for the military since it's a wreckage of a United States nuclear submarine. We had no intention of disturbing the site, and we also recognize that it's a memorial for the hundred or so sailors who lost their lives there. We respect that site."

"Good. I'm glad you understand the importance of the matter, but again, if you removed anything from that site, you must return it. The United States Navy takes these matters very seriously. And, ironically, since you're also a contractor for the Navy, your status as a contractor could be jeopardized."

"I understand, and I will check with my personnel, but I don't believe that we removed anything from that wreck. We just sent down robots to observe it and photograph it. Nothing else."

"Very good."

A brief silence took place as James handed back the envelope to David. He put aside the envelope and peered at James with a more serious grin. "Now, I have another matter to discuss with you, James. A very important matter."

James folded his arms. "What's going on? Why all this cloak-and-dagger stuff?"

"I'm going to discuss with you a matter that is of very high importance and security to the United States. And we are requesting your help and assistance."

"Go on."

David picked up a different envelope and pulled out a large color photograph and handed it to James. "Take a look at this photo. This is a recent photograph taken of Gough Island, located in the southern Atlantic Ocean, roughly a thousand, seven hundred miles west of Cape Town, South Africa."

James studied the photograph and continued listening.

"We have reason to believe that nefarious activities are taking place in the waters just south of Gough Island. Those activities may involve the testing of some type of nuclear weapon. About seven months ago, our GEOStar satellites detected some unusual electromagnetic radiation being emitted from the waters off the south coast. More recently, we detected belts of radioactive emissions near the island using one of our CIA recon ships, but we're not sure who or what is involved with these activities. Then about a month ago, one of our satellites recorded these pictures."

David handed two more photos over to James, who took the photos and examined them.

"Are these some type of unusual surface waves?"

"Exactly. Those are pictures of pressure waves that are normally formed from underwater ex-plosions."

David took the photos back and said firmly, "James, we're asking you to help us find out what is going on in that area. We would like to contract you and your ship to travel down to that island and do a deep-sea search of the area and report back to us on any information that you find. Your ship would be the perfect cover story so as not to alert any of the potential adversaries that are using the area to test their nuclear cap-abilities. We're willing to make you a very good offer for the use of your ship in this investiga-tion."

David handed a small envelope to James. James grabbed the envelope and opened it slowly and examined the small piece of paper inside.

"That's a very generous offer. But tell me, David, who do you suspect is using this area to test their nuclear weapons?"

"That's a very good question. Right now we suspect it could be one of several countries co-operating in testing their nuclear devices. We highly suspect the South African government or the Israeli government is involved, or maybe both of them jointly using that area for testing. It may turn out to be some unidentified adversary. We don't know, but that's where you come in. That area has undersea depths that reach fourteen thousand feet, so you'll have to use one of your more advanced subs. What do you say, James? Are you up for the challenge?"

"How do I know you're legit?"

"You saw our surveillance plane fly overhead when you were standing on the back of your ship next to Captain Hayes."

James was amazed by how much he knew. He grinned boldly. "Okay, I'm willing to work with your agency. I accept your financial terms. When do you want me to start?"

"Now, James, as soon as you can. You will find a one-third down payment made into your business account by tomorrow morning. Other payments will be made as you proceed to the island and complete your undersea investigation. Take these instructions; it includes exactly what we want you to look for. We'll be in contact with you as you proceed. Just one word of advice..."

"What's that?"

"Just look and act normal, just as if you were doing one of your usual dives. And keep a lookout for any contact with any boats or aircraft that approach you. They may want to know what the hell you're doing in their nuclear-testing area and may be hostile. We'll be watching, and will send you protection if necessary."

"All right. This will certainly be an interesting change for us."

"Yes, it will. But keep this mission a secret from most of your crew. Only tell your those who absolutely have to know."

"Understood. I'll use a cover story."

"Good. If you need to contact me, call me at the phone number listed in the envelope, or you can give me information by ship email. Obviously, I have your number, so I'll be contacting you as needed."

David stood up along with James and they shook hands. David smiled. "Good luck to you, and have a safe mission, my friend!"

James started to leave but stopped and looked around the restaurant, his eyes coming to rest on his ship all lit up in the Port Jefferson Harbor, looking very proud and stalwart. He thought about the possible dangers involved with the unknown, then turned to leave.

There was a lot to do before they could leave and not a lot of time to do it. And he still had to spend some time with Alex.

[17]

Enjoying the Night Out

A few hours later, James and Alex took the short boat ride from the *Aquatarus* to the Port Jefferson dock and arrived at the brightly lit-up town. They were all dressed up and eagerly strolled the streets, looking for a nice place to have a quiet dinner together. After checking out a few restaurants on the busy main road, they meandered on to the more mellow Bohemian east part of the village, where coffeehouses and jazz clubs offered up a mellower mood to visitors.

"Feel like Italian food tonight?" Alex asked. "Check this place out."

James looked at the sign. "Hmm... The Tasty Tomato. A great name for a restaurant. Let's take a look at the menu."

They gazed at the menu hanging in the restaurant window.

"Looks good, and they even have rigatoni with homemade Italian sausage. I could go for that," said James.

"Yeah, it looks comfortable, and I'm in the mood for Italian food. Let's go in."

James opened the door to the modest, homey restaurant, and they went inside. A waitress greeted them and escorted them to their seats in a quiet, comfortable area. "I'll bring you your menus. Would you care for a drink?"

"Sure, we'll have a bottle of a nice Pinot Grigio."

"I have a nice local Pinot Grigio from the East End Wineries."

"That will be good, thank you, miss," James said as he and Alex turned to look at their menus.

Soon enough, the wine was served, and James toasted the special occasion.

"To my gorgeous lovely lady and our bright future together, sailing the oceans and exploring the world."

Alex laughed and clinked her glass to James's and said with a sparkling smile, "Thank you, James. Only a few months to go on my contract, then I'm free to go."

The waitress arrived with their orders and set them on the placemats in front of them. "Here you go. Can I get you something else?"

James waved her off and they began eating. After several minutes, Alex grabbed her wine-glass, took a sip, and gazed at James. "James, if I do work for your company, what would you want me to do?"

"Oh, I don't know... You could work in under-water robotics R&D, or you could help me with the marine equipment design section."

"Most of my experience is in structural engin-eering, so this will be all new to me."

James laughed and reached for her hand. "You are one sexy lady when you talk work and science. I'll fill you in on the 'plans' I have for you when we get back to the ship."

Alex laughed merrily, nearly knocking over her

wineglass. She rubbed James's hand softly and looked into his eyes. "I can't wait to get my first company 'training session' tonight, James. I'm a *very* quick learner."

They both laughed and spent the remainder of their dinner chatting about their lives, their jobs, and their futures. The meal itself was wonderful, and they thanked their waitress and the other restaurant staff with kind comments for serving up such a pleasant evening. Alex and James left the restaurant in a happy mood and strolled the street, arm in arm, heading north toward the village pier.

They passed several other couples enjoying the cool starry-skied evening. As they made their way by the Port Jefferson library, suddenly they heard the frightening sound of tires screeching and screams from a nearby woman yelling, "Watch out!"

James quickly turned to see what was causing the commotion and saw a large passenger sedan veer off the street and onto the sidewalk, accelerating at high speed, directly toward him and Alex. Alex screamed in terror, and James, totally stunned by the sudden danger, reacted instantaneously by thrusting his body into Alex's, pushing them both into the side of the nearby building and out of the way of the runaway car.

The automobile violently crashed into the brick building directly in front of them, just inches away, part of it smashing inside the building. James slowly got up and helped Alex get to her feet. The driver's door of the vehicle swing open, allowing the rogue driver to get out of the badly damaged car. The driver ran down the street, attempting to escape from the scene, limping slightly. James yelled to Alex, "Stay here! I'll be right back."

"Where are you going?"

"That was no accident."

"*What?*"

"Stay here!"

James had nearly caught up to the driver when the driver pulled out a small handgun and pointed it at James. James ducked quickly and rolled to his left, onto a driveway. The man paused and nearly took a shot at James but decided to continue to run. Other people on the street were watching him.

James sprang to his feet and continued his pursuit but soon lost sight of him. He kept running, searching the alleys and roadways before giving up. On the walk back to Alex, James heard the sound of police sirens.

What the hell was that all about? Why would someone try to run them down? This had to have something to do with the Atlantic discovery. He shook his head and continued back to Alex, who was being comforted by other people. The earlier happiness he'd felt during dinner faded, replaced with fear and anxiety.

***

The next morning, James and Alex got together for a pleasant breakfast in the ship's reserved section of the dining room. They had shaken off the previous night's dangerous encounter and were able to relax with a great view of the harbor. Hans, the ship's dedicated chef, approached them with a magnificent platter of delectable food choices.

"Here you go, you two," Chef Hans said in a thick Austrian accent. "I prepare a few morning treats."

"Why thank you, Hans. That is so nice of you," said Alex, eyeballing the delicious-looking foods in front of her.

"This here is special Austrian sausage with freshly cut ham and some pineapple too. Please enjoy!"

"It looks great, Hans. Thank you so much," said James, his mouth watering.

James and Alex dug into the specially prepared food items. As they ate, they took in the view of the harbor and Port Jefferson Village through a large plate-glass window. Alex sighed. "You know, I could get real used to this kind of work. I'm starting to consider not going back to work on La Palma."

James laughed and took a sip of his morning Bloody Mary. "Well, it's hard work, but after a few trips like this, you get into it."

Alex laughed. "Seriously, though, after I complete my contract, I'm coming with you, James. I was thinking maybe I could work in the marine equipment design area?"

"That's perfect, Alex. You'd fit in perfectly, and every now and then we could do these special work cruises."

"I would love doing these work cruises. They're like an adventure, and this ship is so beautiful. By the way, where are we heading today after we leave Port Jefferson?"

James stared at Alex with a heightened gaze. "We're heading to an unexpected destination that's a bit of a mystery. Something strange happened when—"

Captain Hayes walked up to their table. "James, sorry to interrupt you and Alex, but we have a visitor that just arrived by private boat that wants to board our ship."

"Who is it?"

"It's Dr. Diane Saveroff."

"What does she want?"

"She wants to meet with you. She said she wants to talk to you about the contract negotiations."

James stood, a little aggravated. "Excuse me, Alex. I have to meet with this lady to see what she wants. I'll be right back, so relax and enjoy your breakfast, hun."

James put his hand on Captain Hayes's shoulder, lowering his voice. "After I come back, let's depart quickly and head for our special destination. Understood?"

"Understood."

"Did you come up with a cover story?"

Kipp nodded. "As far as they know, we're heading there to find a missing Electric Fish drone that sank to the bottom of the ocean."

"Excellent. That works perfectly."

James turned to Alex. "I'll be right back."

As James approached Dr. Saveroff on the arrival platform, she smiled at him and gave him a friendly wave of her hand. "Hi, James, I'm sure you're surprised to see me so soon."

James held out his hand in an act of politeness, which Dr. Saveroff received warmly, and said to her with a confused grin, "Yes, I am, Dr. Saveroff. How can I help you?"

"Well, you know how important our business relationship is and just after I left you a few days ago I had quite a few discussions with senior management at Zepheron."

She smiled. "They gave me permission to offer you a totally new incentive with our contract renewal, one that I think you will find very attractive. Do you have some time now to go over it?"

James scratched his head and looked around the platform uncomfortably. "Well, that's very kind of you to secure me a better incentive, but right now we're leaving Port Jefferson, so I'm afraid I can't do any negotiations right now."

Dr. Saveroff thought to herself for a few moments. "Well, where are you going?"

"We're heading into the South Atlantic Ocean on a special job."

"Well, how about I come along with you for a few days? We did it before. Then I can go over everything concerning the new contract and you can drop me off at any location that you're near, say Bermuda or the Caribbean?"

James rubbed his chin, thinking for a few moments, then nodded. "Okay, Dr. Saveroff, you win. My company has had a long, prosperous relationship with Zepheron, and I suppose I owe it to you for being so damn persistent, so I'll make the arrangements. You can be my guest for a few days, and I'll drop you off somewhere along the way."

She smiled and grabbed his hand, shaking it warmly. "Thank you, James. I think you will find our new offer very exciting."

"We'll see, Dr. Saveroff. We'll see. I'm a very determined negotiator, as you know." He then called over to a nearby crew chief. "Carlos, please escort Dr. Saveroff to Nicki's office and have Nicki set her up in one of our guest rooms. Dr. Saveroff will be accompanying us for a few days. I'm sure her previous room is still available."

James turned to Dr. Saveroff. "Figure something out with Nicki. I'll talk to you later."

"Thank you. I look forward to it."

James smiled and turned away. As Dr. Saveroff started to leave with Carlos, James turned back. "Oh, and stay away from any restricted areas of the ship."

She smiled. "You have my word."

[18]

Journey to Gough Island

A day later and five hundred nautical miles south of Long Island in the west Atlantic Ocean, the journey of the *Aquatarus* continued as it traveled swiftly through twelve-foot ocean swells in a southeasterly direction toward Gough Island. It was a cloudy day, but there was good visibility, and James and Alex were enjoying their morning together gazing out at the vast infinity of rough seas before them. They were just starting a relaxing breakfast when Dr. Saveroff joined them at their table.

"Hello, James. Hello, Alex." She turned to Alex and smiled. "Let me introduce myself. I'm Diane Saveroff, and I work for the Zepheron Corporation. James and I are in the process of negotiating a business arrangement that will benefit both our companies."

Alex put down her coffee mug and smiled. "So nice to meet you, Dr. Saveroff. I've heard about you too."

160

James gestured for Dr. Saveroff to take a seat, and she sat down. "I've heard so much about you from James. You're working on the ITUS Project in the Canary Islands, right?"

"Yes, I work on the island of La Palma."

"Dr. Saveroff, please help yourself," said James. "My chef loves to spoil us with his outstanding breakfast creations, so please indulge."

Nodding, Dr. Saveroff grabbed a plate and stared at the enticing mini buffet. "It all looks so delicious." She filled her breakfast plate with fruits, eggs, and thick English bacon. "So tell me, Alex, what exactly do you do for the ITUS Project?"

"Well, do you know anything about it?"

She laughed a bit. "I heard it has something to do with preventing part of the island from falling into the Atlantic Ocean."

Alex nodded. "That's partly correct. I've been working there as an engineer for the past four years. I'm a structural engineer, and work on the tunnel building and structural reinforcement projects."

James didn't interrupt. He loved hearing about Alex's work; it was a fascinating subject, and he's been meaning to visit the site to see the construction. The way Alex talked about it, it was like something out of a science fiction story.

"So why do they need these tunnels?" asked Dr. Saveroff.

"The Canary Islands are ancient volcanic islands that rose up thousands of feet into the air," said Alex. "Over millions of years, rainwater seeping into the mountains, along with erosion, caused the islands to become very unstable and dangerous. Geologists there have uncovered evidence of massive landslides that generated super tidal waves in the Atlantic Ocean. These tidal waves traveled thousands of miles and hit the coasts of Africa, Europe, and even America."

"Wow, that's amazing. And how high did these tidal waves get when a landslide happened?"

"They can get very high when they hit land," Alex said. "Ocean scientists predict that if a La Palma massive landslide happens, it will cause a tidal wave that will hit the east coast of America and be more than three hundred feet high. And there would be several waves that hit land, not just one."

"Oh no, that would be a disaster. So, what are you doing to prevent it?"

Alex sat up straighter and leaned forward, obviously excited to be talking about her work. "The ITUS Project has a team of over two thousand workers trying to prevent the island from splitting and sliding into the Atlantic Ocean. The project has several main goals. First, we built tunnels that drained huge amounts of water that had accumulated in the rock strata over millions of years. The water had caused weakness in the mountain rock structure.

"Then large tunnels were carved throughout the high mountains there. During that construction, they discovered a long fault or crack that was forming that would lead to a future landslide. And now we're in the process of building structural reinforcements at the fault joint using massive amounts of steel and concrete to stop any further movement."

Dr. Saveroff frowned. "I didn't realize that a La Palma landslide was in the process of happening. When would this landslide have happened if nothing was done to prevent it?"

"Good question," said Alex, "But we're not really sure. If you traveled to the top of the mountains there, at eight thousand feet altitude you'd see a long rift thousands of feet long. This is actually the start of the landslide, and earthquakes over the past hundreds of years caused this rift to increase in size. Geologists theorize that several more of these earthquakes could cause the rift to let go and cause a massive landslide that would create a mega tsunami."

"So what you're doing there is critically important and could save the lives of millions of people along the coasts of the Atlantic Ocean," said Dr. Saveroff. She looked between Alex and James. "Why haven't we heard about this in the news?"

"The governments of the world don't want to scare people. If you go to Wikipedia or Google, you won't see it mentioned there much, either."

James chimed in. "Alex joined me here on this work cruise because they let the workers on the ITUS Project off for a month." He grabbed Alex's hand. "I'm glad she got some time off to be with me."

Diane turned to Alex. "Why did they give you all a month off?"

Alex shrugged. "We're not exactly sure why, but we heard that they're bringing in some special equipment from South Africa to help out on the construction. I'm just glad to get the month off so I can be with James and traveling on this cruise."

James patted her hand affectionately. A galley attendant came by with a carafe. "Fresh coffee, anyone?"

Dr. Saveroff picked up her coffee cup. "I'll have some, thank you." The attendant filled her cup, then those of James and Alex, removed a few empty plates, and then left the area.

Dr. Saveroff wore a very nice ring, something Alex noticed when she reached for the coffee. It looked expensive and highlighted her attractive appearance.

"You mentioned some special equipment from

South Africa. Do you know where from in South Africa?" inquired Dr. Saveroff.

"Unfortunately, no, I don't. I don't even know what they're bringing in."

Dr. Saveroff set her cup down. "That's interesting because I'll be heading to South Africa just after I leave this ship. We have a manufacturing plant outside of Cape Town."

"South Africa," Alex said wistfully. "I've never been to South Africa. I've always wanted to go there on a safari." Alex faced James. "James, wouldn't you love to go on a safari there?"

James smiled. "I'd love to go on a safari with you. We'd have a great time."

He turned to Dr. Saveroff. "By the way, what does the Zepheron manufacturing plant make in South Africa?"

She picked up her coffee cup and took a sip. "They manufacture various materials for the defense industry," she said casually.

"What kind of materials?"

"Mostly chemical products for various weapon systems and explosives."

Alex raised her eyebrows at that, but James didn't miss a beat. "And you're heading there right after we drop you off in the Caribbean?"

"Yes, that's what I'm scheduled to do. I have to attend a special meeting there, so it'll be an interesting trip for me."

"You certainly get around the world, don't you?" said James. "Anyway, regarding our little business matter, how about we meet right here at three o'clock to go over your new business proposal? Will that work for you?"

"Yes, of course, James. That will be perfect. I really think you'll like all the new incentives that we're including in the contract. I'm sure I can convince you to sign this time."

"We'll see, Dr. Saveroff. We'll see."

***

Later on that morning, while James was working in his executive office suite near the bridge, Nicki came in to see James about something important. "James, you were supposed to contact our Abaco headquarters about the findings on the *Hydra* accident."

"Ah, sorry, Nicki. I completely forgot about that since I've been so frigging busy."

"Well, I have them on the phone right now, so I'll transfer it over to you."

"Okay, thanks."

James's phone rang, and he picked it up. "Hello?"

"Hi, James. How are things going on the *Aquatarus*?"

James immediately recognized his employee's voice. "Hi, Bobby, how are you guys doing down there at Abaco?"

"Everything's going good down here. We've been on schedule getting our ships out for their contract assignments, and the manufacturing lines have been on schedule as well. Luckily, we haven't had any issues."

"Good, glad to hear that. I know that I was supposed to call you guys about the *Hydra 3* accident."

"Yes, that's what I'm really calling you for. We're still dealing with the sub accident, and I just wanted to fill you on what we've found so far."

"How are the families of the pilots doing?"

Bobby sighed. "Not good. We're dealing with that the best we can, but they're basically just getting by. We're doing everything we can to help them."

"When I get back, Alex and I will visit with them when we can."

"I think they'll appreciate that, James."

"So what did you guys find out about the accident?"

"Well, we went through the all the telemetry recordings of the *Hydra 3* during its test dive and found that the most likely cause of the accident was a faulty ballast tank coupling valve. Apparently, it failed, and the ballast tank was unable to hold air, which caused the sub to sink till it hit crush depth."

James swiped a hand over his face in frustration. "What would have caused that valve coupling to fail?"

"We don't know, but we're looking into that. Apparently, that part was manufactured by a company in England, so I've sent one of our staff there to investigate what went wrong with that part."

"Good thinking. Let me know what you find out."

"I will." He paused for a moment. "James, there's something else."

"What is it?"

"We went through the manufacturing logs of the *Hydra*, and the employee who installed that part and that section of the sub quit a few days after the accident. When we looked into his employment background, we found out he used to work for a company that was owned by the Zepheron Corporation before he worked for us."

James sat up straight. "What? That's really strange."

"It is, and we're investigating that angle. It could just be a coincidence."

"Yes." James frowned. "Keep me informed, Bobby. What a strange situation. Just to let you know, we're not going to be back to Abaco for another week or so. We're heading down to the South Atlantic on a special request for help from a client friend, so let headquarters know. If you need me, just call or email Nicki, and she'll let me know."

"Okay. How's Nicki enjoying the trip?"

James laughed. "Loves it, she's having a great time on board and she's keeping our contractor friend Dr. Saveroff occupied and out of the way. She's been a big help on this trip."

"How's the contract going?"

"Good so far. I'll know if we're still partners with Zepheron in a day or two. I'm dropping her off, probably in Puerto Rico or the Virgin Islands as we head south, and she'll be out of our way after that."

"Okay. Good luck to you guys, and I'll keep in touch."

"Keep an eye on everything there at headquarters till we get back."

"Will do. Bye."

As James put the phone down, Nicki came into the room. "Did you find out what happened to the *Hydra*?"

James leaned back in his chair. "Yeah, it looks like it was a mechanical failure of the ballast system. But there may have been something else going on with one of the workers who constructed it."

Nicki shook her head in puzzlement. "I hope you find out what caused it."

"We definitely will. I'll see to that."

"Oh, on another matter, Rebecca wants to talk to you right away about some new AUV data recording that they found below the ocean."

"Really? Okay, I'll head there right now. Tell Alex that I'll be belowdeck in the dive control center, and we'll do lunch when I get back."

[19]

Deep Sea Marine Creatures

It took James several minutes to get to the dive control center, since it was located several floors below the executive offices. As he arrived, Rebecca smiled and greeted him. "I've got some surprising news for you. We received more data from the Electric Fish AUVs."

"That's great. Where were these hits located?"

"Amazingly, these recordings were taken off the coast of West Africa and further west toward the central Atlantic Ocean."

"That's crazy. What the hell are they?"

"I think we have an idea what they are, but first I want to show you something on the large monitor here."

Rebecca directed James's attention to the LED screen, which displayed a map of the Atlantic Ocean and the locations of the AUV hits recorded by sonar. "Now, you can see here that all along the west coast of Africa that extends south to Angola and north to Senegal, we found deep-sea movements of some type of very large marine life that we can't explain."

James nodded, waiting for her to continue. He knew she was particularly excited about something.

"But there's more," she said. "We also saw movement of these marine creatures west and away from the coast of Africa, going all the way over to the Sargasso Sea toward the Bahamas. And look where it passes by." She pointed. "This area right here."

"That's where the *Scorpion* wreck is."

"That's right. And we're not talking within several miles. It's right in this location." Rebecca tapped on the location at the edge of the Sargasso Sea.

"How many AUV hits did you get?"

"Over the past few months, we've tracked and recorded thirty-nine separate sonar hits that were recorded by the AUVs."

"How deep are you finding these creatures?"

"They tend to move deep, somewhere between seven thousand to ten thousand feet. And we've also found evidence that they may be moving in groups."

James shook his head in astonishment as he stared at the screen. "So what do you think they are?"

Rebecca looked down at the table, where she had her notebooks of data readings, and then back at James. "Well, one thing we do know is that these marine creatures are not like anything that has ever been identified before in the ocean. And we do know that these creatures are very large."

"How do you know that?"

Rebecca smiled. "We actually have a sonar image recording from an AUV that was traveling

169

down at about nine thousand feet when it collided with one of these creatures. Before it hit the creature, it took this real-time sonar imaging video of the water in front of it."

Rebecca pushed some keys of her laptop and suddenly a window appeared on the screen, displaying her AUV sonar video recording. James and Rebecca instinctively leaned toward the screen with intense interest. As the video started, Rebecca described the video setting. "What you're going to see is taken from the front of the AUV as it's traveling down at an angle. The image is a bit blurred and dark, but you can make out the deep ocean, its movement, and what it's about to hit. It's coming up in just a few seconds."

As they gazed at the video image, all they could notice was a gray-bluish dynamic movement and the aquatic sound of traveling underwater. This went on for several seconds until all of a sudden, the image changed and shifted slightly. In the background, a long, narrow dark body could be made out moving slowly.

As the video progressed, the long black body continued to increase in size, getting larger and larger until it struck the organism and then bounced off with a loud thud. The video and audio feed went black for several seconds and reactivated, and then all that was observed was the similar gray-bluish dynamic movement and the same aquatic sound of traveling underwater.

Rebecca rewound the sonar video to the point just before the apparent collision and paused it on the long black body of the underwater creature. She looked at James, raising an eyebrow. "This is what we have been tracking for months. We got lucky with this sonar image."

James walked up to the screen and stared at the long dark body of the mysterious creature.

170

He turned to Rebecca. "What is this thing, and where the hell did it come from?"

"We think that these creatures have always been down there. Probably for millions of years. It's just that no one's ever gone down searching for them. It was only recently that we had the technology to send down our AUVs. No one would ever have suspected that animal life could exist down at these depths, but we were obviously wrong. The more we search, the more unknown marine life we find that exists and thrives down there."

"So how big are these creatures, and what do they eat?"

"That's a good question, and unfortunately we can only speculate. We think by looking at this video and other data that these creatures are at least thirty feet long, probably longer. And as far as what they feed on, we're still unsure because down at these depths the amount of marine life is somewhat limited. But there are other creatures living there that we haven't identified yet."

James shook his head in wonder. "This is mind-blowing stuff."

"There's something else I want to show you. Take a look at this other screen over here." She led him to another area of the room.

James looked at what Rebecca was indicating.

"This is a graph showing a statistical zoological analysis of the discovery of large marine creatures in the world's oceans throughout the decades. You can see that this graph starts on the left and keeps going up toward the right side of the graph. It shows that the number of large underwater marine creatures keeps on rising as ocean scientists search the oceans. This number has not gone down yet."

"So what does that mean?"

"This graph projects that scientists in the

near future will find and identify at least ten new large underwater sea creatures."

James looked at her, surprised. "So what you're saying is that there are more unidentified deep-sea creatures down there, and this is one of them."

"Correct. We expect more discoveries like this one in the future, so don't be surprised if we discover more unimaginable creatures deep below the ocean."

James rubbed his face and peered around the room. He looked back at Rebecca after thinking for a bit. "Very good work, Rebecca. Keep me informed as to what else you find with the AUVs."

"I will. I'm going to try to enhance the AUV video to see if we can make out anything else that we're missing."

"Okay, good. Oh, I may need you when we get to our next destination. I want you to accompany us when we go down in the submarine there."

"Where are we heading?"

"I don't want to say right now, but you'll find out in the next few days."

"Okay." She smiled. "I do love a good mystery."

James nodded. "I'm heading up to the bridge, so I'll chat with you later."

She nodded back, and James left the room. Rebecca looked around and wondered why they would be diving down in that location. She became a bit anxious.

What was going on, and why wouldn't James tell them where they were going?

***

Later on that same day, James went searching for Alex. He had something important to tell her, but he couldn't seem to locate her after checking her private quarters and the executive offices.

172

After checking for her in the ship's gym, he made his way onto the upper promenade to see if she was there. As he walked toward the bow along the starboard side he noticed her gazing out at the sea all by herself. Excited to see her, he called, "Hey. There you are! I've been searching for you."

As James neared, she ~~embraced him lovingly and~~ hugged him in a blissful moment of tenderness.

She smiled up at him. "I'm so glad I'm here with you. I just love being on this gorgeous ship."

"I was looking for you everywhere, and I couldn't find you. ~~Were you hiding from me?~~"

With a big smile, she said, "I've been here for twenty minutes just looking out at the sea. It's just so beautiful looking out into the vast void of endless ocean. I thought I saw a ship way out in the distance over there, but I'm not sure. It's just so relaxing and peaceful being here all alone, ~~just~~ listening to the beautiful sounds of the wind and ocean waves. I could do this forever."

James moved slowly to Alex and gave her a warm kiss and then searched her eyes. "I'm so glad you're here with me. This is what we're going to be doing in the future, Alex, just you and me sailing the open oceans, traveling the world and exploring the planet."

"That sounds like fun. I think I'm going to have to go on a lot more of these work cruises with you."

He moved his head back from her a bit. "Hey, I've got something to tell you."

"It has something to do with Dr. Saveroff and the Zepheron contract, doesn't it?"

James smiled. "Yes, it does, and guess what? They're offering us an eighty-percent profit offer along with an additional twelve million bonus up front for renewing the Electric Fish contract with them."

Her jaw dropped slightly. "So what are you going to do? Are you going to sign on with them again?"

"I actually think I have to. It's a no-risk, total-reward situation. And I won't have to deal with all that political crap trying to get politicians involved with the Navy and their budgets."

"That's great! We'll have to celebrate tonight."

"I'm already ahead of you. I let my galley staff know that it's a special occasion for the both of us. We'll dine in the reserved private dining room."

"What are we having for dinner?"

"Anything you want, Alex."

"How about prime rib?"

He swooped down dramatically while holding her hand. "Very good, madam," he said in a fake accent. "I'll let Hans know that you requested prime rib tonight. Hans makes a very good prime rib with mashed potatoes with a scrumptious gravy."

Alex giggled at his silliness. "Oh my God, that sounds so good. I'm getting hungry already."

"Good. You're going to love it. I think I should invite Dr. Saveroff to have a drink with us tonight to celebrate the contract. Is that okay with you?"

Alex frowned slightly. "I guess so, but... I don't want her to stay for dinner. I just want you and me to have a nice private romantic dinner together. I'm having such a good time so far on the *Aquatarus*. We've got to make use of our time together."

"I don't want her to stay for dinner either. I'll tell Nicki to escort Dr. Saveroff to our table before we eat, and we can all celebrate with a few drinks. Then Nicki and Dr. Saveroff can have dinner together in the main galley next door."

"That sounds perfect. How do Nicki and Dr. Saveroff get along?"

"They get along quite well, and they actually go for walks on the ship together a lot. I didn't know how this contract thing was going to go, and I told Nicki to make her feel at home. They're kind of friendly now."

"That's great that they get along, but I'm not so sure about that Dr. Saveroff. There's something about her that I just can't put my finger on that seems odd."

James furrowed his brow. "Hmm, it's interesting that you say that because I thought there was something about her that's unusual too. But anyway, I'm going to sign the contract, and let's just enjoy the rest of the day together, and we'll celebrate tonight. Shall we go catch a cup of coffee and hang out in the observation area?"

Alex grabbed James's arm. "Sounds like fun. Lead the way."

They both walked away smiling and chatting arm and arm in the direction of the ship's stern.

[20]

Celebrating the Contract

The sun was about to set as the *Aquatarus* headed south of the coast of Florida toward the island of Puerto Rico. James and Alex were relaxing in the private dining room enjoying some hors d'oeuvres, observing the beautiful fomenting sunset playing out in front of them. One of the galley attendants entered the room and announced the arrival of Nicki and Dr. Saveroff.

James nodded. "Yes, please let them in."

Moments later, Nicki entered the spacious elegant dining room followed by Dr. Saveroff. James graciously welcomed them. "So glad you're here. Look how nice you both look. Please take a seat, and let's celebrate!"

Both women wore nice form-fitting evening dresses. Nicki's dress was purple and Dr. Saveroff's was red, black, and very sexy. They also had on fine necklaces and jewelry that adorned their attire in a comfortable but elegant way. Alex smiled at them and noticed their excitement to celebrate this special occasion of the contract signing.

As the ladies sat down, James requested four bottles of the finest champagne from his staff in attendance. As the bottles popped and the glasses were filled with the bubbly nectar, James rose his glass high into the air and proposed a toast.

"I would like to thank our business partner Zepheron for teaming up with my company again in this contract. A contract that will benefit both our companies. And I would like to thank Nicki for accompanying us on this amazing voyage through the Atlantic. And to my new good friend, Dr. Saveroff, for reinvigorating this contract deal. Thank you, Dr. Saveroff, for all you've done."

Everyone drank from their champagne glasses and cheered with much elation. Dr. Saveroff rose from her chair, walked over to James, and whispered something in his ear. Then she kissed him on his cheek and, grinning, grabbed his hand and shook it. Alex watched as she winked at him, thinking that appeared almost seductive. Irritated, she followed Dr. Saveroff with her eyes as she walked back to her chair and sat down. Although annoyed, she didn't want to spoil the moment, so she kept quiet but told herself she'd have to have a little talk with James in the near future.

Later on, when James and Alex were alone, an amazing dinner of prime rib with mashed potatoes, gravy, and other chef-prepared specialties was laid out for them. Alex smiled as she ate and told James that she wanted to thank Chef Hans personally. James summoned the chef to their table, and when he arrived she thanked him for the wonderful dinner. When asked how he learned to cook prime rib that good, he said, "I learned it from my wife, who can cook better than me." They all laughed and shared a drink as the evening went on.

After dinner, James and Alex strolled along the upper-deck promenade for a late-night walk to view the stars and to hear the enchanting waves. As they headed back and prepared to retire to their private quarters, Alex thought to herself, *I'll leave that talk for another time.* With what she had planned for them next, she was sure Dr. Saveroff would be the last thing on his mind.

* * *

The *Aquatarus* traveled on steadfastly for three days through mostly calm seas and headed south through the turquoise-colored Caribbean Sea. They arrived at the island of Puerto Rico to refuel the ship and to drop off Dr. Saveroff. Before she left the ship, Dr. Saveroff said goodbye to James and Alex and invited them to tour the Zepheron manufacturing facility in South Africa.

When the ship finally left Puerto Rico, they traveled on for another five days and were now deep in the southeast Atlantic Ocean, south of the equator and about six hundred nautical miles north of the very isolated Gough Island.

James was in his executive office when Alex came in to see him, carrying some papers. "I know you've been busy, so I went and checked on some things on the internet."

"What is it?"

"I've been reading all about Gough Island. It's a very isolated and mysterious island."

"I know a little bit about it, but what else can you tell me?"

"Well, it's a very rugged place that was first discovered in 1505 by a lost Portuguese explorer who was searching for a new route to the Orient."

"Interesting."

"Yeah, but there's way more. The island was later claimed and renamed Gough Island by Captain Gough of the British Navy in 1732. He was the one who rediscovered it."

"Is there anyone living on the island now?" asked James.

"No, there's no inhabitants on the island, but there is a permanently manned weather station there that's operated by the South African government."

"Yeah, I knew about that," said James. "The weather patterns there in the South Atlantic travel from east to west, so they can track the future weather patterns that way."

"Yes, that's right, and the nearest land area is Tristan Island, located two hundred and fifty miles north of Gough."

"Those islands there are some of the most isolated islands in the world. How big is the island?"

"It's about nine miles long and five miles wide, and it does have a few small islands off shore. There are some mountain peaks on the island that get up to three thousand feet in altitude."

"What else is on the island besides the weather station?"

"Not much, but there is some wildlife on the island consisting of many different bird species and several types of penguins. Mice are on the island from visiting ships and are causing many problems to the bird populations by attacking the bird eggs."

"That's not good for the bird population."

"No, it's not, and the University of Cape Town

has some ecologists that visit the island that are trying to eradicate the mice problem there. It seems that there having some success."

"Interesting how invasive species can cause so much trouble."

Alex's expression turned serious. "So what are we going to do when we get there?"

James hesitated a moment, debating how much he should tell her. "We're going to find out what's going on south of the island."

"What do you mean?"

James pulled out some paper documents that were on his desk and a large map of Gough Island, including the greater Atlantic Ocean area. He placed his index finger on a location on the map and said, "Look here, this area located about seven miles south of Gough Island is where the CIA contact said some type of nuclear device testing may be going on."

"Do you think that the South African government is involved?"

"We're not sure, but it's possible. It could be that the weather station is part of a cover for those involved with what's going on there."

"Hmm, I see. Are you going to go down in the submarine to investigate?"

"I have to, Alex. That's what the CIA wants me to do for them. I'm their cover to find out what's going on down there. We have to appear as inconspicuous as possible."

"Are you sure this is safe?"

He smiled reassuringly. "There's nothing to worry about. I've gone down in the *Sagittarus* many times. Right now, it's our best and safest deep-diving sub, so I'll be all right. I'm going to go down with Scott and Rebecca."

"I want to go down with you. I don't want you to go down without me there."

James frowned. "What? No, you're not going

down with us," he said, shaking his head. "You don't have any experience doing a deep dive, and you might get a panic attack and freak out. I've seen that happen to people before; in people you wouldn't expect."

"James, I'm worried about you, and I don't want anything to happen to you."

James moved closer and placed his hands around her shoulders and looked her in eyes. "Alex, I'll take you down another time in the sub, but not this time. If there is nuclear testing going on down there, then we'll have to collect data, take samples quickly, and get out fast. I don't want you involved with this right now. There'll be a lot going on, and something could happen that's not expected."

Alex stayed silent for a few moments before sighing. "All right, but just be careful. I know the CIA is paying you a lot of money to do this, but for God's sake be careful. And come back up as quickly as you can."

James smiled. "Don't worry. I'm not planning to hang out thousands of feet below the ocean in a submarine in a highly radioactive environment."

Alex looked at him with a worried expression. She felt uneasy and didn't know what to think.

***

The journey aboard the *Aquatarus* continued for two more days. Their progress slowed when they hit a storm the night before, which shook the crew up and caused some minor damage to the rigging and cranes. James had been summoned to the bridge by Captain Hayes due to an unusual sighting by the crew.

The captain handed James a pair of binoculars. "Take a look. We've spotted something due northeast at twenty-seven degrees latitude."

Both James and the captain peered through their precision nautical binoculars. "Yes, I see it, Kipp. What is it?"

Hayes put down his binoculars. "It's a ship. It's been following us for the past seven hours. We think it's the *Ososcelos*, the same ship that was following us in the Atlantic two weeks ago and the same one that caused us that problem aboard our ship."

"Why?"

"I don't know, but it sure seems odd that here we are closing in on Gough Island, and it's following us again."

James took a deep breath and slowly peered around the vast ocean expanse along the port side of the ship. He looked to Hayes. "When do we arrive at Gough Island?"

"About six hours."

"Okay, I want the crew prepared to launch the *Sagittarus* from the moon pool. Be as inconspicuous as possible. I don't want us to attract any attention from anyone on the island or the weather station. I also want armed guards stationed about the ship with concealed weapons in case we get any hostile visitors aboard during the night."

Kipp nodded. "I'll take care of it."

"Did anyone get back to you on Callum Namesbury?"

Hayes shook his head. "We're still looking into him. He apparently has a checkered past and is part of a banking cartel. We'll find out more on him soon."

James cursed under his breath. "I'm going to check with Nicki and get ready for the dive. Keep me posted."

"Will do."

"Thanks, Kipp," James said, patting him on the back. "I'll talk to you later."

James returned to his office suite and saw Nicki walking back to her desk. She looked up as he came in. "Hey, you're back. I just got off the phone with Professor Aldridge. He wants to talk to you about those items you sent him a few weeks ago."

"Great, Nicki. Tell you what, I've got some time now. Get him on the phone."

Nicki nodded and got the professor back on the line. She handed the phone to James.

"Hello, Professor, so glad to hear from you again."

"Likewise, James. I've got some good news on those items you sent me."

"Fantastic. So, tell me, what did you find out and what did you think of them?"

"Well, I had them examined by my good friend who runs the archaeology department at Cambridge. He and his associates were gobsmacked."

"How so?"

"The items were from a ship that was from a very ancient time period." James could hear the excitement in the professor's voice.

"How old, Professor, do they know?"

"No, they don't know yet, but they suspect it was pre-Graeco-Roman. Definitely not Egyptian or Phoenician. They said they have never seen anything like it before. They want to attempt to do carbon dating on the items, but they have a lot of work to do removing the concretions that have encased many of the items. But before they start, they need to have your permission."

"Yes, of course, Professor."

"Good, then. They have taken pictures of the items, and they're going to email you those along with a manifest of the items, including a contractual arrangement giving them permission by you to study and catalog the items that they separate. Is that acceptable?"

"Definitely. They have my permission to do all that."

"Oh, and they did find a few things that they could already identify. This included some ancient silver jewelry, some broken ceramic amphoras that were exquisitely decorated. And get this—gold medallions that have unique in-scriptions on them."

James chuckled at the glee in his tone. "Amazing, Professor."

He lowered his voice then. "They want to know more about that sunken ship that they were extracted from."

James chuckled inwardly. Of course they did. "Well, Professor, I'm not willing to divulge the location of the ancient wreck just yet, but I will have Rebecca chat with them about how we found the ship and any other details about the state of the wreckage."

"Jolly good job, James. You and Alex have certainly earned the right to celebrate tonight with a good round of bubbly."

"Thank you, Professor, but unfortunately I'll have to stay sober because we have something very important scheduled tonight. But I will tell Alex about what you said. I know she'll be very happy to find out what was discovered."

"Indeed, she will. I look forward to meeting up with you and Alex sometime."

"After we complete our current expedition, Alex and I will fly up to meet you there in England. We'll all have a good time."

"That would be brilliant, James. Do take care, my good friend."

"Goodbye, Professor. We'll keep in touch."

James handed the phone to Nicki and stood there silent with his hand on his chin, thinking quietly.

"What is it?" she asked.

"I want to tell you to keep the information about those discovered items confidential."

"Of course. I already have."

"Good." He looked at Nicki with a frown. He was regretting bringing Alex along. "We're going to be arriving at Gough Island very soon, and there's the potential for danger, either on the island or that damn ship that's following us. Keep an eye on Alex for me, okay?"

The color shifted in Nicki's face, and a bit of tenseness entered her gaze. "Okay, James. I'll look out for her. We'll be careful."

"Just keep her relaxed. I don't want her to be worrying about me."

Nicki nodded. "I will. I promise. I'll keep her entertained and distracted."

James placed his hand on her shoulder softly. "Thanks, Nicki. I appreciate it. Oh, and one other thing."

"What's that?"

"After dinner, don't go walking around the deck with Alex. She may want to go. But with that ship following us, it's possible we'll have another intruder on board. I'll have armed guards on the lookout, but I want to be careful."

Nicki frowned. She peered around the room with a worried look. "We'll definitely stay inside tonight." She laughed nervously. "You're scaring me."

"I just want you and Alex to be safe, that's all. Everything will be all right. I've gotta prepare for the dive now. I'll be down in dive support if anyone comes looking for me."

James started to leave, but Nicki called out to him. "James."

He stopped and looked back. "What is it?"

"Please be careful."

James smiled at her and winked. "Thanks. We'll be all right." And then he left the room.

[21]

Deep Dive off Gough Island

It was late in the day with just a little bit of sunlight left in the sky when the *Aquatarus* sailed within sight of Gough Island. The crew of the ship had been at sea for more than one week without seeing any land around them. But now virtually everyone on the ship caught sight of the landmass that rose out of the brisk sea before them as they passed the south side of the island.

Alex followed Nicki as they hastily left the executive offices and headed for the doorway that led to the port side of the ship. They had heard the clamor of the crew chatting about the sight of the mighty island. As they entered the connected promenade, they quickly noticed the prominent jagged landmass.

"Wow...what a strange-looking island," said Nicki.

"Yes, it's beautiful, isn't it?" said Alex.

There was a strong cool wind blowing past them, which provided some ambient sound to their discussion. It added to the surreal experience of being in one of the most isolated spots in the South Atlantic Ocean as they peered at a massive monolithic structure rising prominently out of the dark-blue sea. Both women took some time to take in all the features of the island and its robust colors and landscapes.

"Look at those mountains behind the shoreline. They have such a stunning hue to them," said Nicki.

"Yeah, it's almost like a purple slate-blue color. It's kind of dreamlike."

"I wonder how high those mountains are?"

"I was reading about Gough Island on the internet, and they apparently get up to three thousand feet high."

"Could you imagine climbing up those mountains?"

Alex peered at Nicki. "Yes, I could. I'd love to climb up to the highest peak. I think it would be exciting, and James would love to climb it too. But we'd have to bring a bottle of wine with us to celebrate the occasion."

Both women chuckled lightly over that thought.

Alex whipped out a pair of binoculars and scanned the island. Nicki noticed other members of the crew along the promenade, taking the time to enjoy the wondrous view.

After a short while, Alex called out, "I see a white building alongside the south side of the island."

"Where about?" asked Nicki.

Alex handed her binoculars to Nicki and pointed toward the structure she noticed. "Right over that way."

Nicki peered through them. "Yes, I see it. Do you know what it is?"

"It must be the weather station, the one that's permanently manned on the island."

"Yeah, it looks quite large, and I can see a dock right below it on the shoreline. I guess that's how they get to it."

Nicki put down the binoculars and looked at Alex with an intuitive gaze. "Could you imagine staying in that weather station for months? I wonder what that would be like."

"Probably dreadfully boring," said Alex with a laugh. "It must be a very peaceful and spiritual experience that you'd have to get used to."

Nicki was glad to see that Alex was relaxed and not thinking about James and his nighttime dive. It was coming up in a few hours. "Would you like to go to the ship's cafeteria and get a cup of tea and watch the sunset?"

Alex thought for a moment. "Sounds perfect to

me. Let's do it. It should be a beautiful sunset tonight."

The two women left the railing and headed back to the interior doorway to the ship. Just before they entered, Alex looked back at the magnificent island that was now slowly disappearing in view. "I still can't believe that I'm this far out in the ocean, south of the equator and a thousand, eight hundred miles from the nearest landmass," she told Nicki.

"Me too," Nicki said. "But I'm having a great time, and I'm really glad that I came on this trip."

Alex agreed as they both headed into the ship to see the sunset from the cafeteria. They were experiencing a voyage of discovery that they would not soon forget.

***

James, along with several members of his crew, were present in the ship's dive command center, preparing for the submarine dive that was to take place in just a few hours. Rebecca and Scott, who were going to join James in the nighttime excursion, were by his side, checking out a map of the Gough Island archipelago system. Kent was also present, along with other dive control technicians to help with the planning and safety protocols. James turned to Rebecca and Scott. "Are you guys ready?"

"I'm ready. It should be a really cool dive," said Scott with an anxious smirk.

"What about you, Rebecca?" asked James. "Are you ready?"

Rebecca smiled with a confident grin. "You bet. I'm psyched. You're not going to talk me out of it."

James shook his head and laughed. "You are

one ballsy girl. I'm so glad you work for me."

Both were dressed in official navy-blue dive jumpsuits adorned with patches and the large OECI logo embroidered on the right-upper side of their chests. They had been prepping for this dive and were studying maps of the undersea area south of Gough Island.

"I have to warn you that tonight's dive is different and potentially more dangerous than usual," said James. "This area that we're going to be searching may have been used for nuclear testing and could be contaminated with radiation. How do you feel about that?"

The faces of both Rebecca and Scott were studious and serious but unflinching. James nodded. They understood the dangers of deep-sea marine exploration and had made many dives with him in the *Sagittarus*. They were experienced and enjoyed the challenges and adventure of deep-sea exploration. And they were the best sub pilots he could ever want to operate his submarine.

"Okay, we're ready to go? So what do you know about this area so far?"

Rebecca directed her hand over to the map laying on the discussion table in front of them. "I've been going over all the maps of the area south of Gough Island, and unfortunately there's not a lot of information about the bottom of the sea here. But I did find some maps that were useful that were made by the British Navy back in the nineties."

"Good. So what's the bottom of the ocean like down there?"

"That area is very deep and is part of an undersea rift system that goes on for more than a hundred miles. There are some steep drop-offs in the ocean floor that appear like canyons, and there's also some undersea mountains down there too. It's a very geologically varied bottom because it's part of the mid-Atlantic ridge system, which stretches all the way from Iceland to the Antarctic."

James nodded his head, taking in the information. "I guess that's why Gough Island is here, because it was formed from the undersea volcanos along the ridge?"

"That's right, and the ridge is actually an area where the Earth is forming new bottom crust all the time. That splits the floor apart about an inch each year."

"All right, so we're going to have some interesting terrain to look at when we go down."

James turned his attention to Scott. "How's the condition of the *Sagittarus*? Is it ready?"

Scott smiled. "It's all ready to go. It's working perfectly fine."

"Great, then we should have a very interesting dive. I want the *Sagittarus* set up so it can take some environmental samples when we go down. We'll be taking some water samples and some bottom sediment samples too, so make sure you have all the attached service pods stacked with sample containers when we want to take a sample."

Scott nodded. "Will do. I'll load them up, and then we'll be ready to go."

"Rebecca," said James, "Make sure we have the underwater radiation scintillation counter installed on the sub and properly calibrated. We're definitely going to need that tonight when we go down. Let's just hope we don't run into any high levels of radiation."

"Okay. I'll get that installed right now and get it calibrated."

James glanced at his watch. "Good, then it looks like we'll be all set. I'm going to check in with Kipp one more time. We'll board the *Sagit-*

tarus and then start the dive. Just go through the dive checklist one more time to see if we forgot anything."

Scott nodded in agreement while Rebecca shot James a smile and gave a thumbs-up. "I'll check one more time, but I think we have everything we need."

"Okay, I'll be back soon."

James headed for the door on his way up to the bridge. He looked out to the sea through the large windows and noticed that the night had come fast, and it was now jet-black outside. He scanned the horizon to see if he could spot anything but could only make out the waterline of the boundless ocean. He searched around the bridge and found the captain by the radar screen, staring at the big black screen lit up in bright neon green.

"There you are, James. I was just going to call you. Look at this here on the radar screen," said Hayes. The captain pointed to a green blip on the left side.

James appeared perplexed. "What is it?"

Hayes took his eyes off the target and looked at James. "It's that damn *Ososcelos* ship again. It's been tracking us and is now just two miles behind us. It seems to be following our every movement now."

"Son of a bitch. Why the hell is it following us? What do you think is going on?"

"I don't know, but apparently you'll have company tonight when you make your dive."

"That's not good."

"And there's more. I got a call on our ship's radio from that weather station on Gough. They spotted us and wanted to know what we're doing in their waters."

"What did you tell them?"

"I told them that we have a team of marine

scientists onboard from Stony Brook University who are studying the various marine species living around the mid-Atlantic Ridge islands."

"And what did they say after you told them that story?"

"They wished us luck and told us to be careful because of the many hidden shoals located around the island. They also said that we should have notified them that we were going to be in their waters because the islands here are part of British territorial waters." He smirked. "Guess we should have requested permission before we came."

"I'm surprised they said that."

"I told them that we were just going to be staying the night and that we would be leaving soon."

"Did they buy that?"

"Yeah, they did. They seemed to accept our presence here, and we ended the conversation in a lighthearted note."

"Good. I don't want them to suspect that we're here for a different reason."

"I have something else to show you," said the captain. "Come over here."

"What is it?"

Hayes walked James over to the chart table and pulled over a large photo for James to see.

"This here is a recent satellite photo of Gough Island area. I was looking it over and I noticed that there seems to be something hidden below the surface, right around that small island located to the south."

"Really? Show me."

Hayes pointed, and James examined the photo carefully. "Yeah, I see it; it's fairly large and appears to be some type of man-made object. What do you think it is?"

"I don't know. It could be some type of under-water vehicle or submarine."

"You're right, it could be a submarine of some kind. It definitely isn't a natural object."

"That's for sure," said Hayes with a frown. "James, I'm very concerned about your safety with this dive since that mysterious ship is near us, plus there's this object. We'll be monitoring all the undersea activity using our systems, and we'll be in constant contact with you during your dive. If we spot any trouble, we'll let you know."

James nodded. "Good idea. I'm a little concerned myself. Something doesn't seem to be right here, and we know that that damn *Ososcelos* ship is nothing but trouble."

Hayes put his hand on James's shoulder. "We'll be watching everything. I'll also have some tactical watercraft in the water with armed sailors aboard, ready to respond if necessary. To protect you."

"Okay, Kipp, that's a good idea. Well, I better get down to the moon pool now and get aboard the *Sagittarus* with my crew. We have a long night ahead of us."

Hayes stared at James for a brief moment and then said, "Good luck, my friend. If you run into any trouble, come to the surface as quickly as possible."

James appreciated the concern, but he really didn't think it would come to that. "Everything should go well. We'll be in touch during the dive."

As he was leaving, he peeked out through the windows of the bridge again. All he could see was blackness out there, and that gave him a weird and eerie feeling. He was a bit unnerved by the news about the *Ososcelos*, but he had to get on with the dive. At this point he was committed, and he had taken a personal interest in finding out just what was going on here. He made his way down to the moon pool beneath the ship.

[22]

Descending in the Moon Pool

James walked out of the dive-prep room and into the large moon pool center located deep below the ship's stern, followed by Rebecca and Scott. All three moved onto the steel tarmac surrounding the full glowing moon pool. Their navy-blue suits made them almost appear like NASA-trained astronauts as they moved toward the *Sagittarus*.

Rebecca carried a small canvas bag containing the technical materials she needed for the dive and some assorted food goodies that Chef Hans had prepared for them to enjoy during their excursion. Kent was waiting on the tarmac near the entrance to the submarine to help supervise the launch of the *Sagittarus* along with his team of dedicated crew members. James walked up to Kent, smiling. "We're all set to go, is everything ready?"

Kent flashed a contented grin. "She's all prepped and ready."

"Good, we're good to go right now, but I want you to do something while we're down there."

Rebecca and Scott began boarding the submarine as they talked.

"What do you want me to do?"

"I want you to send out the *Dolphin* to the shoreline area by the island. We saw something submerged near that area that appears to be a possible underwater vehicle of some kind. I want that area sonar scanned to find out just what it is."

"Sure, I'll get right on it."

"And definitely keep an eye on that damn ship following us. Kipp told me that it snuck up on our ass and is only a mile or so back. I want to know what the hell they're doing out here."

"Don't worry, we'll keep a lookout on that ship, and we'll stay in constant contact."

They turned at the sound of footsteps on the tarmac. It was Alex coming to see James off. James smiled, and they waited as she moved toward them. They hugged for several moments before he looked into her eyes. "Come to say goodbye again?" He chuckled and kissed her. "I gotta go. We've got a long dive planned, and they're waiting for me."

"Please be careful, James. I don't want anything to happen to you."

"We'll be okay. I've done this many times before."

Kent approached and put his hand on James shoulder. "Gotta keep on schedule, buddy. They're waiting. Everything's ready for the launch."

James nodded and released Alex, still keeping his eyes on her as he approached the submarine hatch. He turned and gave her one last smile and a wink and then entered the submarine.

The crew closed the hatch and secured it from the outside. Several technicians moved around the perimeter of the moon pool to ensure the

Sagittarus would descend properly.

Alex moved closer to the *Sagittarus* and stood there, amazed at the beauty and sophistication of the craft but also with a feeling of anxiety. She thought the abstract cartoonlike image of a bold-looking seahorse on the side of the sub looked really cool as it descended slowly.

As James took his seat and joined his fellow undersea travelers, he peered out through the large forward bubble window and saw the crew assisting in the launch. One of the technicians gave the all-clear.

The craft was now complexly untethered. James reached for his headset and put it on. He put his left hand on the top of the headset and gave the voice command. "*Sagittarus* all clear and descending."

The speakers in the interior of the craft crackled, and the voice of the dive controller sounded, "Roger, *Aquatarus*, you are cleared for descent. Godspeed to you all, and good luck."

"Roger and out," said James.

$$* * *$$

Back in the moon pool Kent, Alex, and some of the dive technicians watched the slow descent of the *Sagittarus* through a large wall-mounted video monitor. An underwater camera tracked the movement of the craft as it departed.

Alex's anxiety over James's descent was temporarily displaced by amazement as she watched the sub drop away into the abyss. "Wow, they go faster than I expected."

Kent agreed and nodded. "Yup, she's totally James's baby. He started designing this sub shortly after he graduated Stony Brook years ago. It was a dream of his turned into reality. All of us wish we could go with him."

The *Sagittarus* was a twenty-seven-foot-long underwater vehicle made of pure molybdenum steel and titanium that sported a lustrous metallic-gray finish. It had a wide neon-green stripe that ran across the midsection, making the craft easy to see. The sleek aqua-nautical craft had smooth elegant fins that protruded from the rear of the craft that assisted in the stability of its movements. Two high-tech stainless-steel propellers moved the machine forward, using an advanced electronic drive-control system.

The craft was powered by a hybrid fuel-cell system that incorporated a silver-zinc battery-storage module, giving the ship a cruising range of more than one hundred miles. The fuel-cell system had an additional benefit in that it generated its own oxygen supply so the craft could travel below the surface for extended periods without having to resupply its interior atmosphere generators.

Alex watched as the craft drifted down into the deep sea until it was barely visible on the monitor. Then, as time went on, the visual image had completely blended into the background, and James and his crew were on their own. They were now in the province and watch of Poseidon, the legendary god of the sea.

***

The craft had been descending for more than twenty minutes and was now reaching the mesopelagic zone of the ocean, the area where visible light could no longer reach.

James and Scott were seated side by side in the front of the craft while Rebecca was seated directly behind them. The ship could carry a crew of four in normal missions, but there was an auxiliary seat near the back where a fifth could sit if ever needed. James had only wanted a minimal crew on this mission, since it was potentially risky and they had never been in this location before.

As they descended, they noticed small fish and jellyfish that were common in these waters. James grinned, excited to find out what else was below them.

As the craft entered the twilight zone, Scott maneuvered some knobs and switches. "It's getting dark here, guys. Putting on the forward lights."

The ocean lit up, illuminating the area around them.

James could feel Scott's excitement radiating off him. "Let's take a look to see what's swimming around us now, shall we?"

As they continued down, they peered outside for several minutes, searching. Then Rebecca called out, "Look! What's that?" She pointed to the upper left side. "Over there, ten o'clock."

James and Scott eagerly peered out and spotted the creatures. "Wow," said Scott. "We've got a beautiful school of fish out there now. Rebecca, can you identify them?"

Rebecca, who had extensive training in marine biology and ichthyology, analyzed the shapes and colors of the fish swimming by. "They appear to be angelfish. Oh, and I also see a few white hawkfish too."

James smiled. "I knew you'd know what they were."

"Well, the angelfish around here have a bit of a different appearance than those found in the northern Atlantic."

"Whoa!" Scott cried. "Look at that!"

Everyone anxiously peered outside to see what Scott had spotted—a big gray monster of the ocean.

"Holy shit... that's a huge frigging shark!"

Rebecca peered up at the large monster in awe as it swam by. "Great white."

Scott turned to her. "You sure? I didn't think that great whites could go to this depth. We're at over three thousand five hundred feet."

"Oh, yeah, great whites are often found this deep. Some have been spotted all the way down to seven thousand."

"Very cool. Definitely don't want a close-up with those things."

She laughed. "Yeah, you wouldn't want to get near that."

"It's amazing how these creatures are being found deeper and deeper in the ocean."

"Yes," agreed Rebecca. "The further we search the deep, the larger the creatures we find down there. You have to wonder what undiscovered creatures are living way down in the deepest parts of the ocean."

"All right, guys," said James. "Let's get focused here. We have to search for any evidence of any nuclear testing in this undersea area. Scott, activate the radio-scintillation counter."

"Okay," said Scott, flipping a switch. "Scintillation detector activated and scanning."

James tapped his knee nervously. After only a minute, he couldn't hold back. "What do you have? Any readings yet?"

"No readings detected yet."

"All right, that gives us a baseline." James turned. "Rebecca, what's sonar indicating at this point?"

Rebecca turned to read the green-glowing sonar scanner. "We have varied terrain below us that levels off at five thousand feet. There appear to be some small mountains bordering our position here."

"Okay," said James. "Let's just keep going down

from here, but keep monitoring the bottom terrain and the radioactivity levels. I want to see what the hell's been going on here the last few years."

***

Back on the *Aquatarus*, Captain Hayes was notified by one of his bridge crew of a disturbing development.

"Captain! We've got something going on with the *Ososcelos*."

Hayes moved to his crewman near the radar screen. "What do you have, Andy?"

"Something that appears to be metallic and fairly sizable is moving near the *Ososcelos*."

The captain peered at the screen. "What the hell could that be?"

"I don't know, Captain. It could be a small ship or maybe even a submarine."

The captain's face reflected his anxiety as he moved about in place, thinking for a few moments. He glanced over to the front bridge windows and saw the dark mysterious sea. "I don't like this. We have to do something."

The captain turned to Andy. "Contact the helidrone pilot. Tell him to launch the helidrone and have him fly over the *Ososcelos* to find out just what the hell is going on there. Have him check the whole ship if he has to."

"Will do, sir."

"And have him fly over the that small island south of Gough to see if anything is going on there too. I don't want any damn surprises. You got that?"

"Yes, sir."

***

Back on the submarine, all was going well with the crew as the craft reached a depth of five thousand feet. They had just completed a radio conversation with the *Aquatarus*, letting them know their current status. Then something changed on their sonar screen.

"James, we're entering an area where there's some jagged outcropping of ledges below us, so we have to be careful. Sonar is also indicating that we're nearing the entrance to a large oval-shaped vertical cavern of some kind."

"All right. Rebecca, slow our descent a little so we—"

Suddenly the sonar collision-warning alarm went off, emitting a loud, high-pitched shriek. Before Scott could react, the ship collided with an underwater object, causing everyone to be jolted and rolled about in their seats.

"Son of a bitch!" barked out Scott. "What the hell did we hit?"

James's experience kicked in. Maintaining his composure, he searched about the craft and calmly surveyed for any damage.

The submarine had stopped descending but was still moving slightly in a sideways motion. All inside noticed the weird metal grinding sound on the exterior.

"All right, guys," said James, "let's check for any damage. Look over your instruments and see if there's any leakage inside."

All of them knew exactly what to do and had past involvement with underwater collisions. Those past encounters had not been serious, but they all knew that any collision could lead to a deadly situation.

Several nervous moments passed as they monitored the conditions and state of the sub's interior.

"All instruments indicate a normal status," Scott announced with a more relaxed tone. "And I'm not detecting any interior leakage anywhere."

James turned. "What about you, Rebecca? Do you see anything back there?"

"Everything's fine back here."

"Good, thank God everything's all right. We're going to have to be more careful now as we proceed down. But right now, let's concentrate on getting off this damn ledge before we tumble off it and hit something else."

James looked at Scott, who had his hands on the ship's controls. "Give it a go. See how she moves."

Scott took a deep breath and firmly placed his hands on the double joystick propeller drive controls and attempted to propel the craft off the ledge.

Instantly, the craft powered up and forward as they rose off the rock ledge. As the vehicle picked up speed, James gave a command. "Stop the sub and turn it around. Let's see what we hit."

"Roger."

As Scott carefully slowed down their momentum and maneuvered the vehicle a hundred and eighty degrees around, the bright forward lights of the vehicle lit up the underwater rock formation they had collided with.

"Wow! It's a ledge formation that extends out from the cliff face," said Rebecca.

"Unbelievable. We could have gotten stuck in those large boulders sitting on that ledge. Thank goodness we didn't get stuck in those babies," said Scott with a stunned grin.

"Rebecca," asked James, "what's sonar indicating below us?"

After a slight pause, she said, "We've got several thousand feet of clear sailing below us. Just as long as we stay away from that cliff face, we'll be all right."

"Do you see any more ledges?"

"No... I don't see any at all. We've apparently entered into a giant undersea crater that's roughly two miles wide."

Scott turned to James with his eyebrows

raised. "Wouldn't this be the perfect place to test a nuclear weapon? Nobody would ever know."

James nodded in agreement. Maybe there really was something going on in this strange area of the ocean.

As time went by and they continued their descent, they noticed another change in the environment around them, which made Rebecca uneasy.

"You know, I'm a little concerned we're not seeing the deep-sea fish population that we normally would at this depth."

"What's our depth now?"

"We're approaching eight thousand and two hundred feet now," announced Scott.

"I agree, we're barely seeing anything now. Just a few deep-sea fish and worms but not much else."

"About a minute ago I noted a big red squid, and—" Before she could complete her sentence an alarm went off again.

The crew jolted into action, fearing they were close to hitting another rock formation, but Rebecca was very familiar with that unique alarm tone. "It's our radiation alarm. It's detected radioactivity in the water here."

"What's the reading?" asked James, his voice tense.

"Whoa! We've got a reading of twenty thousand becquerels per cubic meter."

Even though that was why they were there, the numbers shocked James. "Damn, that's a fairly high level. That's definitely not a normal reading at this depth."

"No, it's not," said Rebecca. "Background radiation around this part of the Atlantic Ocean would be about three becquerels per cubic meter. Ten thousand becquerels is indicating a major release of radioactivity."

"But from what and where?" questioned Scott.

"That's what we're going to find out," said James.

James turned to Rebecca. "I want you to take some underwater samples. Take a bunch as we travel deeper at regular intervals."

Rebecca jumped out of her seat. "I'm on it." She moved to the back of the sub near the technical service console.

Analyzing the moment, James thought about how strange it was that they were traveling thousands of feet into an unexplored undersea canyon with dangerous levels of radiation. In all his years of deep-sea diving, he had never come across anything like this. It made him feel a bit tense, but he knew he had to keep it inside and put on a brave face for the crew.

He turned to Scott. "Let's proceed down cautiously and keep an eye on the sonar situation. I'll monitor the radiation levels now that Rebecca's busy."

"Okay. I have to say, I'm a bit uneasy. This is a really weird canyon."

"I understand, but just keep your mind focused on our mission and the instruments. We're going to be okay."

Scott took a breath and nodded his head in agreement. James had never seen Scott this anxious on any of his previous missions. But he knew that Scott had what it took to get through this.

[23]

Flying to the Ososcelos

It was pitch black outside, and a light rain had begun to fall as the helidrone traveled steadfastly toward the mysterious *Ososcelos* ship. It was carrying a crew of two, which included Chester and his assistant pilot, Jason. They had been in the air for twenty minutes, and Chester was having difficulties locating the *Ososcelos*.

"Damn," Chester cursed through his radio link with his copilot. "It's not going to be easy for us to find that ship since they have no lights and there's no moonlight around. But we should be near it right now, according to my readings. Go ahead and check that area over with your binoculars. Southeast."

Jason was seated in back of Chester and was holding a pair of infrared binoculars that was able to see objects in very low levels of light using thermal imaging technology. He scanned the area while the helidrone hovered in place.

Disappointed, Jason sighed. "I don't see a damn thing out here. This rain isn't helping, Sea's getting rough now."

"I'll fly around, so just keep looking. It's got to be around here somewhere."

"All right."

Jason scanned the murky sea, searching for anything that resembled a ship. Every now and then he thought he saw something, but it always turned out to be nothing.

As time went by, Chester was getting antsy. His fuel gauge decreased to just below three-quarters, and he still had to fly over the small isolated island to check that out, according to the captain's orders.

"All right," he said, clearly disappointed, "I'm going to give you one more minute to look for that damn elusive ship. We're getting low on fuel, and we've got to head over to the island."

"All right, let me give it one more try."

Again, he searched the shadowy waters. As he was about to give up, his eye spotted something unusual that appeared to be moving just below the water, emitting visible heat. It was big and ghostly and had an arrowlike shape to it. At first he thought it was a whale, but as he focused he noted details that no living creature would display.

"Holy shit!" he cried out. "There's something below the water, moving fast toward the *Aquatarus*."

"What is it?"

"It's gotta be a submarine of some kind. It's a weird-looking thing."

"All right, I'm going to take us down near the water to get a better look."

Chester skillfully flew the craft down, fast and hard. Jason felt the quick surge downward, and his stomach almost flew out of his mouth. As they hovered just twelve feet above the waves, both men stared in amazement. Something dark gray and metallic was traveling fast in the general direction of the *Aquatarus*.

"Holy Christ, this must be the thing that the captain spotted on the radar. We must be near the *Ososcelos*."

"So what are we going to do?" asked Jason.

"We've got to get out of here and radio the captain of what we found. And then get over to the island."

"Okay."

Chester nailed the throttle, and the helidrone shot up like a rocket. They were now on their way northeast toward the island, which was about eleven miles away. As they sped away, Jason yelled, "I see the *Ososcelos* now! It's about a half mile from us."

"Do you see any other ship near it?"

"No, it's just sitting out there all by itself, and it's not moving."

"I'm going to call it in and let them know that they've got an underwater bogie heading their way, and it could be trouble."

"What are they going to do?"

"Don't worry. The captain knows what he's doing. He's been in military conflicts since he was a captain in the Navy."

***

Back in the *Sagittarus*, the situation was really heating up. Scott had piloted the submarine down to a depth of ten thousand feet, just narrowly missing another rock outcropping. Their sonar system was sounding out alarms, so they had to be extra careful since the pressure at this depth could cause their ship to implode if they collided with any strata formations. Their radiation detection system added to their uncertainty as it was detecting increasing levels of radioactivity.

As they continued down, they maneuvered the craft so they were facing the canyon wall with their observation lights blaring. Staring out the window, James gasped.

"Rebecca, come here," said James.

She was busy labeling sample bottles but was quickly at his side. "What is it?"

Then she peered through the sub's front window and saw it immediately. "Oh my God! What the hell happened here?"

The canyon wall had obviously been mangled and distorted by some unknown force. Large fractures, ripples, and gouges raked across the stone, as if it had been ripped apart by a force of unimaginable intensity. The smooth rock surfaces they had observed from the beginning of their descent were gone and now replaced by a bizarre distorted surface.

"The only way for this kind of extensive damage to the rock strata to occur is either a volcanic blast or some other kind of explosive force."

James shook his head. "I don't even know how to describe what we're seeing. I've never seen anything like it before."

"I guess it could be what geologists would call high-impact shock-synthesized formations. They're not very common."

"All right, let's get a sample of that to take back to the ship. I want to know what caused it."

"Okay. I'll use the manipulator arm to get it. Just hover the sub close enough to the wall."

Scott called out, "You ready now? I can hover right here for you to get your sample."

Rebecca headed to the back area of the sub. Out of the three of them, she was the most experienced at using the manipulator arm.

James continued looking at the wall, the pieces falling together. "You know, with the evidence of high radioactivity levels and a huge explosion, it's gotta be a nuclear detonation of some kind."

Scott glanced at James nervously. "Damn straight it does. Are we almost done? I'd like to get out of this frigging hellhole."

James stared out at the cliffside. "You and me both."

***

At the surface, the *Aquatarus* continued to carefully monitor the *Sagittarus*. A sailor approached Hayes, looking somewhat alarmed.

"Captain, that unidentified submarine just passed one mile south of our position, and it's starting to dive down."

Hayes had taken protective countermeasures to protect the ship and its crew, but now he realized that the rogue submarine was most likely diving down to the *Sagittarus*. "Notify the *Sagittarus* immediately that they have a potential threat heading their way. Tell them to protect themselves if they can."

"Yes, sir."

Just then, Kent and Alex entered the bridge and immediately noticed the worry on the captain's face.

"We just heard the news that a submarine from the *Ososcelos* was approaching our ship," said Kent. "Is this true?"

Hayes sighed with frustration and tilted his hat with his hand. "Yeah, I've got bad news. The helidrone pilots spotted a sub heading toward our ship from the *Ososcelos*. But we just found out that sub, or whatever it is, is now diving into the crater, presumably heading toward the *Sagittarus*."

Alex placed her hands over her mouth. "What?" she cried. "What are they going to do? Oh my God, what's going to happen to James and his crew?"

Kent patted Alex, trying to calm her down. "Alex, take it easy. It's a big canyon down there, and it's not likely that they'll be able to find them there."

Alex put her hands to her forehead and frowned. "I told him not to do this, but he wouldn't listen to me. Oh my God, what are we going to do now?"

"Alex," said Hayes, "James is very savvy. I know he'll figure out a way to get out of any trouble. We're notifying him right now of what's happening, and we'll be working with him to get him and his crew to the surface safely. You just have to trust us."

Alex looked at Hayes with glassy eyes and a disheartened stare. But the captain did not waver from his stern, poised appearance of confidence and hope. This gave her some assurance that James would make it back to the ship all right. She nodded in affirmation.

"Alex, let the captain do his work here," said Kent. "Let me take you down to dive control, where you can monitor what's going on with James in the sub. Okay?"

Alex agreed but was obviously still numb. Kent guided her to the doorway of the bridge. As they were about to leave, the captain said, "I'll keep you informed."

Alex stopped in place and gave a quick glance back at the captain, then continued out of the bridge.

After they left, Hayes turned to his crew and gave an order. "Track that bogie and relay its position to the *Sagittarus* at regular intervals. And contact dive control and find out what the *Dolphin* found near that small island. Let's get on this, people. We have a serious situation, and we need our full attention to keep the *Sagittarus* safe and get her back on this ship."

***

After Rebecca was done with her extraction, James instructed Scott to immediately return to the surface. Now that they had possible evidence of a nuclear detonation, it was time to head back to the surface to get the samples analyzed. Then the news of the sub came in, which set them all on edge.

They were coming up fast and had reached the seven-thousand-foot depth when a voice came over the radio. "*Sagittarus*! You've got trouble heading your way. That submarine is now navigating over toward your position."

"How close?" asked Scott.

"It's looks like they're at two thousand feet and moving down directly above you."

James surveyed the situation. The rogue sub was now a hostile threat, and they had to take measures to protect themselves. He glanced at Scott and then Rebecca. They both looked scared. "How are you guys doing? Are you okay?"

"I'm all right," said Rebecca, "But I have to say that this is really freaking me out."

"I can't believe this," said Scott. "Who the hell are they and why are they threatening us?"

"Just relax and concentrate on the navigation. We're going to get through this. Just be alert, and we'll make our way up to the surface."

Scott sighed and nodded his head as he held the controls.

A minute later, dive command gave another

update. "The sub has descended further and is closing on you fast. Take immediate action."

"Roger that," said James. "Scott, take us toward the canyon wall. It shouldn't be far from here. We can try to find a ledge or a crevice to hide in."

"Okay, but I hope you know what you're doing. Those rock outcroppings are treacherous and unpredictable."

"We don't have a choice. Do it now."

Scott maneuvered quickly in the eastward direction toward the canyon wall. James reached for the sub's forward light switch to see what was before them. They had been off so as to not give away their position, but they had to see. As the lights flashed on, all three of them screamed.

"Holy shit!" yelled Scott as he slammed the throttle backward.

They were on a collision course with a huge rock outcropping. As they all watched in horror, their sub slowly started to reduce its speed but was still moving forward, now just feet away from the canyon wall.

"Brace for impact!" shouted James.

They all held their breath and tensed up, grasping their seats. Fortunately, the craft's velocity had slowed fast enough to avoid disaster, and they softly jarred into the outcropping, leaving them shaken but unharmed.

"Whew! That was a close one," said Scott.

Rebecca unwound her grip on her seat and rubbed her forehead, breathing with a sigh of relief.

James realized that this was no time to celebrate and ordered Scott to duck the *Sagittarus* under the ledge that they had just bumped into. After some precision maneuvering, they were safely tucked away under the ledge and up against the canyon wall. He flicked off the lights again.

At least now they were hidden and not easy to see with their lights off. The *Sagittarus* was now positioned with the back of the sub to the wall so they could see what was in front of them.

An uneasy calm overcame them as they peered out into the midnight-black water. The fear that an unidentified submarine was out there somewhere, attempting to hunt them down, had their hearts pounding.

After a few quiet moments of getting their senses settled, Rebecca whispered, "How long are we going to stay here?"

"We're going to have to ride this out. It's best we just stay hidden here for a while until we get word that they left the area."

James could see that she appeared a bit confused and shocked, but he knew that she would be all right. He turned to Scott. "How are the fuel cells doing?"

Scott glanced down at the control panel readouts to get a reading. "They all look good. We have more than sixty hours of fuel and air supply available."

"Good. We'll wait a few minutes and then check in with dive command. That goddamned submarine should be gone by then."

"I hope so," said Scott, sounding anxious.

∗∗∗

Deep within the *Aquatarus*, the atmosphere was tense in the dive control center. Captain Hayes, Kent, and several senior members of the dive command team gathered around the mission planning table, calculating a strategy to help get the *Sagittarus* back on the ship safely. There were some heated discussions as to the best

215

course of action. Technically, Kent was next in command, but all the ship's high management left the critical decisions to the captain. They knew James always relied on the captain's viewpoint in making important decisions.

Kent slowly looked around the table at each member and then settled on Hayes. "What you think we should do? What're our best options?"

Hayes shrugged and peered back at Kent with an anxious frown. "We don't have a lot of options right now, but let's move the *Hammerhead* down into the canyon to get a better view of where that damn submarine is. Maybe we can distract it so they can get up to the surface without being spotted."

"That's a good idea, but that drone has an explosive charge in it. It's one of our demolition drones. If it went off, it could take out the *Sagittarus*."

"True, but we could also use it to defend the *Sagittarus* if we denotated it near that sub."

"Yeah, we could do that."

Kent and the team members mulled around the use of the *Hammerhead* and quickly reached a joint consensus.

"All right, we'll use the *Hammerhead*. Let's get on it, guys."

Kent turned away from the captain and could already see the crew heading toward the moon pool to prepare and launch the *Hammerhead*.

Kent gazed at Hayes. "It should only take a few minutes. We'll get her down there fast."

The captain nodded, praying inwardly. *My God, they're in a damn serious predicament now. James, I hope you figure some way out of this.*

[24]

Escape from the Deep

An hour had gone by since the launch of the *Hammerhead*. It was well on its way toward the *Sagittarus* to help guide them up to the surface safely, away from the threatening submarine that was lurking below. The crew aboard the *Sagittarus* had not moved from their previous location up against the canyon wall. Luckily, they had not been spotted, and they had just received a radio transmission from dive control letting them know the *Hammerhead* was nearing their location.

"Roger on that drone assistance, *Aquatarus*. We need all the help we can get. Over."

"We'll feed you readouts from the drone when it's in position near your location. We're going to get you guys out of there one way or another. Over."

"Good work, *Aquatarus*. We're ready to move out of here as soon as you give us a clear path. Over."

217

"Roger, will do. We're almost there. Over."

"Over and out," said James, and he placed the mic into its resting slot. James grinned at the others, and their faces brightened with hope and some renewed energy.

"Damn glad to hear they're giving us some help," said Scott, holding his water bottle.

"We'll be out of here, hopefully soon. It's a big canyon, and we're not easy to find."

Just then, a radio transmission crackled out a garbled message. All three crew members looked at each other uncertainly. Although they couldn't understand the message, they could tell that it wasn't good news.

"Did you hear what it said?" asked James.

"No, I couldn't make it out, but it sounded like a warning—Oh God," said Rebecca, pointing in front of the submarine.

Out in the darkness before them, a distant light moved slowly in their direction. They couldn't make out any shape or contour, but they knew that it had to be a light from the rogue submarine.

"Holy shit," James whispered, as the terrible realization sunk in that the intruding submarine was so close.

"Do you think they spotted us?" said Scott, confused and worried.

"We'll soon find out," said James.

All eyes were now nervously fixed on the nefarious glowing object in front of them. The strange light seemed to be moving very slowly as it approached. It moved in one direction for some time and then stopped, changed directions, and moved in another. This went on for a few minutes as they all pondered what it was doing.

"They must not be able to see us because we're hidden in this crevice," said James.

"Maybe we should try to get out of here before

they spot us?" blurted Scott.

"No, not right now," said James. "We might have to make a run for it if they get too close. But right now, let's just stay still and quiet."

Scott moved his hands to the controls, ready to accelerate.

"I'm ready to go with your order."

Suddenly, the radio came alive and a clear message was heard. "*Sagittarus*, *Sagittarus*, do you read us? Over."

James grabbed the mic. "This is *Sagittarus*, we hear you loud and clear. Over."

They waited anxiously.

"We have sonar signatures of the *Hammerhead* and another object that's near your last position along the east wall of the canyon. What's your location? What's going on? Over."

"That unidentified object is in fact a submarine that's down here looking for us. We're hidden in a crevice up against the east wall. Over."

Seconds went by.

"Understood, *Sagittarus*, we're moving the *Hammerhead* closer to your area. We have it fixed on that sub, and we're going to track it and attempt to distract it. The *Hammerhead* is near your area, so hang in there. Over."

"Thanks, *Aquatarus*. Relay any information you receive. Over."

James put the mic back in its slot and took a deep breath. He made eye contact with his crew. "What's going on out there now?"

"The light disappeared," said Scott. "It looks like it moved away from us."

"Good. We're going to wait here one more minute, and then we're going to make a run for it to the surface. When we break from this location, I want you to head out a hundred feet away from the canyon and then head straight up to the surface. Go as fast as you can."

"We might be too close to the canyon wall if I only go out a hundred feet. We could collide again with the wall."

"That's a chance we'll just have to take. We might be spotted and may have to duck for cover up against the wall again. We don't know what capabilities that sub has, so we have to play it this way."

"Okay."

They all sat there staring into the dark void, knowing that they were about to venture out where they could be spotted and attacked. Scott was sweating and appeared uneasy.

James waited a bit longer and was ready to the give the order. He glanced back at them. "Are you guys ready?"

They nodded almost reluctantly. "Let's get out of here. Go!"

Scott nailed the drive motors, and they whined with electric power as they moved forward. Scott kept the ship's lights off so they wouldn't be seen, and they proceeded swiftly. All three felt strange knowing the submarine was out there somewhere, lurking in the darkness. And now they were making a lot of noise and could be detected by sonar.

"How's she handling, Scott?"

"Pretty good. I rarely get the chance to drive it this fast, and I have to say it really moves nicely."

"Good. We should be able to get up to the surface in no time."

Scott glanced at James and nodded. "I'll feel a lot better when we get back on the *Aquatarus*."

***

Back in dive control, Kent and two of his crew were watching the sonar tracking screens.

"Look, we've got a new bogie on the screen. It must be the *Sagittarus* heading up to the surface."

"Yeah, I see that," said Kent. "It looks like them. Come on, guys, get to the surface." He clenched his fist.

"Wait a minute!" said the dive control officer. "It looks like that sub knows where they're going. And they're following them. Holy shit, they've got trouble now."

The officer looked at Kent, his face a mask of worry. "It's going really fast, and it's gonna catch them before they get to the surface. We've gotta do something."

***

Back in the *Sagittarus*, a frantic radio message came in. "Warning, *Sagittarus*! Alert! You've got trouble coming your way. That sub is heading directly your way and will intersect your position in a minute or two. We advise you to take evasive maneuvers now!"

James turned abruptly in his chair and yelled, "Scott, change course and move us in a zigzag manner. Do it now!"

Scott immediately jolted the sub in a new direction and let it rip at top speed, driving erratically in random directions from time to time. This went on for some time.

James monitored the controls of the sub, checking for any sign of the rogue sub nearby. They were all wired up and tense, clearly concerned about being attacked by the enemy nearby.

Then they heard a unique sound they had not heard before. James searched around, looking for what it could be. After checking his controls, he realized it was coming from outside of the sub. "Son of a bitch. It must be that goddamned sub coming toward us."

"Change direction again!" he shouted at Scott. "It's near us! Do it!"

Scott turned the sub sharply, and all aboard were forcefully jostled about. There was no avoiding it, though. The *Sagittarus* was in a fight for its life, and if they did not respond accordingly, they would all be dead.

"Keep it in a zigzag pattern," said James. "We can make it!"

Rebecca was scrunched up in her seat, her eyes wide open. She placed her hands over her face and waited.

As bad as the situation was, it all got worse. Suddenly, their submarine was struck by a forceful impact on the lower port side, which knocked everyone out of their seats and onto the floor. A jarring metal-on-metal sound screeched through the interior, ringing in their ears. They all scrambled to get up from the floor, as the sub was still moving, though now they were headed in a different direction due to the impact.

James got up slowly, determined to get control, and managed to get into the pilot's chair. "I'll drive. Get in my chair and hold on."

James glanced back at Rebecca and saw she was still on the floor, trying to get up. He turned to Scott. "Go help Rebecca."

Scott shot up and held on to whatever he could, making his way toward Rebecca. When he finally got to her, she was half standing near the service modules in the back of the ship. He noticed she was bleeding from a gash on her face.

She looked at him and shouted, "We've got a water leak by the rear hatch!"

Scott looked down and saw water puddling on the floor near the hatch. "All right, let's see what we can do."

They waded toward it, fighting the unsteadiness of the sub's movement.

James had heard her shouting about the leak, but he refocused on piloting toward the surface, knowing they would have to deal with it.

James managed to steer the craft steadfastly without interference for a short while and made it to a two-thousand-foot depth. All seemed to be going well, and it appeared they would be free of the attacks from the intruding submarine.

But that all changed when they heard the ominous whining sound of the enemy submarine approaching them again.

James swiftly turned the craft in a different direction, hoping to throw off the nearby intruder. It didn't work, as the sound gained in intensity.

"Son of a bitch!" shouted James. "They're right on our asses. They must have some kind of sonar tracking system."

Scott and Rebecca were fiddling with the hatch. Rebecca glanced at James as he frantically changed directions trying to avoid another collision. It was all a blur, like a bad dream come true. She looked at Scott, deflated, on the verge of tears. "I don't think we're going to make it out of this alive."

Scott put a hand on her shoulder and squeezed reassuringly. "We're going to get out of this. Just hang in there."

She nodded and tried to distract herself, going back to helping Scott tighten the hatch.

Through all the commotion, James managed to catch a breath and called back to them, "How's the water leak?"

"We think we fixed it," Rebecca yelled back. "Just get us to the surface."

Immediately after, they were struck again. The sound of the collision was unbearable and harsh and knocked them around. Rebecca thought to herself that the next strike could penetrate the sub's venerable metal skin. Then, as they were getting back on their feet, the *Sagittarus*'s drive motors stopped, and they were dead in the water.

Scott quickly made his way to the copilot's chair to assist James, trying to get the sub's motors back on. "What happened? Why isn't it moving?"

"I don't know," James said, trying not to panic. "The electric drive just suddenly died, and I don't know what the hell's going on with it."

Scott scanned the gauges and digital read-outs. No one knew the operations and inner workings of the sub's systems better than Scott, so James left him to do his checks.

"I see what it is. Our fuel cells got knocked out by the collisions. We're on batteries right now, so we don't have a lot of power."

"Damn it!" cried James.

Scott activated some of the control switches. "I can get our fuel cells started again, but it's going to take a few minutes."

"Can you at least get us moving using the batteries?" asked James.

"Yes, I can, but we can't go fast until we get the fuel cells back on."

"All right, get us going," said James, unable to hide the fear in his voice.

Scott pushed a button and hit a toggle switch, and instantly the submarine started moving again, albeit at a reduced speed. His frown told the story of his frustration.

James took a breath and grabbed the steering joystick. "Well, at least we're moving, but we're like a sitting duck here at this speed."

Scott shook his head. Their chances of getting safely to the surface would be zero if they took another hit.

Amazingly, they made progress, moving slowly upward, and were now only at a thousand and eight hundred feet from the surface. James was determined to get to the surface, trying not to think about their odds. All three of them felt some encouragement by their progress, but just when things seemed to improve, an ominous sound was heard by all aboard the ship, and they all tensed up.

"Shit!" said Rebecca. "It's that damn submarine. They're gonna hit us again!"

Scott shot James a terrified grin. "It's looks like we're screwed."

James focused on the controls, not acknowledging the looming threat. But as the sound got louder, it started to affect him. He looked up and around, searching for the direction of the submarine. His eyes bulged and his jaw dropped when he realized—they were going to be rammed again.

Then, totally unexpectedly, an explosion boomed outside of their sub, which jostled them around, but it was noticeably different from the previously attacks. They realized that they were not being attacked at all, and some type of explosion or collision had occurred in the ocean nearby that did not involve them.

As the silence went on, James finally said, "Think something happened to that submarine?"

"It sounds like it got hit or exploded," said Rebecca, relieved. They were still alive.

Then a broadcast came across the speakers. "*Sagittarus… Sagittarus*, are you all right? This is the *Aquatarus*. Please report your position. Over."

James took the mic, glad to hear their voice but confused as to what had occurred. "This is the *Sagittarus*! We're alive, but we barely survived a series of attacks from an attacking sub. We've sustained some damage and our fuel cells have been knocked out. Please tell us what's going on out there. Over."

"Roger, *Sagittarus*, we've been monitoring your movements and the attack on you by that enemy sub. We took action and detonated the *Hammerhead* drone into its hull. We were concerned that we impacted you, but we're glad to see we got the enemy knocked out. It's apparently drifting now and may be attempting to escape to the surface. Over."

Relieved to hear they were now more or less safe, James wiped the sweat from his forehead and sighed. Scott and Rebecca grinned at each other and high-fived.

James squeezed the mic. "Roger, *Aquatarus*. We're glad to hear of your assistance. We're moving up toward the surface. Please let us know if it's safe for us to proceed. Over."

"Roger, *Sagittarus*. You have a clear path to the surface with nothing in your way. We have several armed watercraft waiting to assist you when you get there. You have a very anxious girlfriend waiting to see you, James. She was worried but very happy to hear you're all okay. Good luck and enjoy the ride. Over."

Realizing the path was clear, they started to unwind and reflect on what had transpired. They took time to enjoy the view outside the forward bubble window and noticed how the light penetrating the ocean became brighter as they approached the surface. They settled down even more when they noticed the colorful fish and other aquatic creatures in the ocean environment around them.

Rebecca reflected on the tense moments they had just survived. *I can't believe what we just went through. My friends aren't going to believe me when I tell them what happened.*

As the *Sagittarus* finally made it to the

surface, they all savored the final moments as the craft penetrated the water line. Waves crashed into the window, sending a wonderful feeling of elation that they would never forget.

When the hatch popped open, Rebecca was the first to look outside. After taking in a few deep breaths of fresh air, she noticed several fast boats manned with armed guards heading their way. James and Scott spotted them as well through their sub windows. It was a welcome sight after all they'd been through.

Then off in the distance, only a hundred yards away, something large and gray pierced the ocean water and rose above the sea. It was big and had a sleek wedge shape to it. Astonished, James cried out, "It's that goddamn submarine. It must be in trouble."

The crew aboard the boats shifted in the direction of the enemy sub with their machine guns blazing, blasting away indiscriminately.

Rebecca quickly bolted back inside the *Sagittarus* and slammed the hatch shut. The three of them watched as the boats moved in closer and continued to let loose on the sleek dark-gray craft. Their assault was brutal, and some of their bullets ricocheted off. They could hear the pinging sound even from inside. The enemy ship sank back into the sea.

"Wow, they blasted that fucking sub to smithereens, didn't they?" said Scott.

James laughed. "They got what they deserved, those bastards."

"Do you think there're people in that submarine, or is it a drone ship?" asked Rebecca.

James shook his head. "I guess we'll never know. But we're going to find out who and what was behind this attack when we get back to the ship."

At that point, one of the boats had made its

way back to the *Sagittarus* and started towing it in the direction of the *Aquatarus*.

When they were finally anchored to the *Aquatarus*, Alex, Nicki, Kent, and the captain were waiting for them. As James made his way up the deck, Alex ran into his arms and they hugged and kissed. Alex cried and smiled at the same time, squeezing him so tight he pretended he couldn't breathe.

Finally, after letting him go, she looked him in the eyes and said, "I'm so glad you're all right. I was so worried that something bad was going to happen to you."

James wiped away her tears. "It's okay. We made it back safe. And we're together again. That's all that counts, sweetheart."

He turned to Nicki, who winked and shook her head at him, letting him know he was in trouble for his crazy exploits. She would give him an earful later.

That night, they all celebrated as the chef and his staff prepared a wonderful celebration for the three members of the *Sagittarus* who had returned alive and well.

During the delightful dinner, with Alex by his side, James thanked everyone who had assisted in getting them back to the surface. James recounted the frightful events that they went through during their dangerous descent.

After some time, James said goodnight, and he and Alex made their way to his suite, totally drained and in need of some well-deserved rest. As he fell into bed, his mind flashed with images of their amazing journey into the darkness and the unknown.

Just before he dozed off, he pondered the nefarious activities that had happened around Gough Island. The *Ososcelos* wasn't far from his mind either.

[25]

South Africa

The next day, the *Aquatarus* was once again on the move, sailing northeast on a course to Cape Town, South Africa. They needed to refuel ~~the ship~~ and get some supplies, and Cape Town was the nearest port available, even though it was over a thousand miles away.

James and Alex strolled into the cafeteria totally refreshed and rested after a deep sleep the night before. They enjoyed a relaxing breakfast together and shared some quiet moments viewing the open ocean, enjoying the colorful cloudscape. Alex marveled again at being together on the *Aquatarus*, traveling to new unexplored reaches of the oceans.

While sipping her morning coffee, Alex turned to James. "What's your favorite part of the ocean that you've ever traveled to?"

"My favorite? Hmm. That's not easy to answer because I've been to so many places around the world and seen so many lovely sights. I guess a few would include the Patagonia region along the south coast of Chile and strangely enough the southeast coast of Greenland."

"Greenland. That's interesting. Why there?"

"Oh, it's a beautiful area. They have one of the largest fjord systems in the world with floating icebergs and magnificent mountains everywhere. Wonderful area to visit by boat."

"It sounds great. I'd love to go there with you someday."

James smiled. "We'll do it, ~~Alex,~~ and I know you'll love it. We'll sail up one of the long fjords and go hiking around the seaside mountains there. It's so bold and beautiful. It's hard to put into words."

"Are there any polar bears there?"

"Oh, yeah, for sure. But if we went there, we would go with a tour group. They have special- ized crews to keep you away from any danger, so we wouldn't have to worry."

"~~I'd love to do that.~~ Let's do that trip this year sometime." *Sounds great.*

"Definitely."

As Alex put down her coffee, she noticed the captain entering the dining area, accompanied by Kent.

"Hi, Kipp. Hey, Kent," said Alex.

"Good morning, Alex. James," said the cap- tain, nodding his head to both of them.

"Hey, good morning, guys," said James ~~with a happy glance~~.

"Kent and I thought that this would be a good time to go over a few things with you," ~~said the captain~~. "If it's okay with you and Alex, I mean."

"That's fine with us. Alex and I were just finishing up."

"I see you're back to your normal relaxed self after that mess from yesterday."

Kent chuckled at the captain's unprompted humor.

"Yeah, I'm getting back to normal," said James. "What a crazy day that was. I hope Rebecca and Scott are putting it behind them."

"That's what I want to go over with you."

Alex frowned up at the men, concerned. "Please have a seat."

After they sat down and were served some coffee by the attendants, Kent looked at James. "We got those underwater samples analyzed."

"Already? What did you find?" asked James.

"Our lab found very high levels of radioactivity. They also found that the levels increased the deeper that you guys went into that canyon."

"Ha, just what we suspected. Did they determine what type of radiation was being emitted?"

"They detected high levels of alpha, beta, and gamma radiation emitted from residue radionucleotides present in the deep areas. And get this, they also found very high levels of neutron-induced radiation."

"Wow, that's a telltale signature of a nuclear detonation."

"It certainly is. The lab's still working on identifying which radioactive isotopes are present, but they expect to find strontium, cesium, and probably even plutonium."

"Yeah, I'll bet," said James, thinking for a moment. "Okay, so it's safe to assume someone was testing nuclear devices deep in that canyon for some reason. Who could possibly be behind this? And how does this tie in to Gough Island and that frigging *Ososcelos* ship?"

"James," said Captain Hayes, "I had my military contacts look into Namesbury, and it looks as though he has a bit of a shady past."

"Shady, how?"

"Well, he's a very wealthy billionaire who was

born in South Africa. He runs the Stonus Financial Group, which is one of the largest financial firms in the world. It's based in Europe and has a track record of being very secretive and predatory."

"What do you mean predatory?"

"They like to do leveraged takeovers of other well-established companies and then sell off their assets and lay off the workers. They also had trouble with the law and were indicted on fraud and extortion charges several times and had to pay fines to regulators well in the hundreds of millions."

"Anything else?"

"Yes, now this is interesting, and ties it into Gough Island and South Africa. He has several residences around the world, including a lavish estate on the outskirts of Cape Town, South Africa. Nicki searched his financial holdings, and guess which company is one of his holdings?"

James shrugged. "I can't think of any right now."

"How about Zepheron Corporation?"

James's jaw fell open. "Namesbury is the owner of *Zepheron*? As in, the company we just signed a contract with?"

"Yup, that's the one. He's a major shareholder of Zepheron and hides this from public view by having the shares issued in shadow-company stock."

"Holy shit," James murmured. He took a few seconds to process the information. He knew this was big, and they were now on to something important.

Alex glared at both the captain and James, a look of betrayal on her face. "Isn't it convenient how Dr. Saveroff was on this ship, and she works for Zepheron, *and* she was seen spying around restricted areas?"

"That definitely looks very suspicious, doesn't it?" said Kent.

"Wait a minute," said James. "We can't be sure that she's involved with this Gough Island nuclear testing."

"Yeah, but it's possible. And you better be careful with what you do and say around her," said Alex with a suspicious stare.

James mulled that over for a moment, thinking. "Zepheron has a manufacturing facility in Cape Town. I wonder if that facility has anything to do with nuclear materials or weapons?"

"We should look into that," said Hayes.

"Dr. Saveroff actually invited me to visit the Zepheron manufacturing facility if we were to be in Cape Town. I might as well take her up on the offer."

James turned to Alex and smiled. "Care to visit the Zepheron manufacturing plant while we're were in Cape Town?"

Alex chuckled. "Sure. Just as long as you take me out on the town while we're there."

James grabbed her hand. "You bet, ~~darling~~. We'll have a great time ~~there~~."

He turned to Kent. "Have Nicki contact Dr. Saveroff to get us a tour of their facility. We might as well visit one of our business partners while we're in town, don't you think?"

They all grinned at his suggestion.

After the others left, James and Alex strolled the promenade, taking in the views of the endless rolling sea that the isolated area provided. The views were so bold and breathtaking that Alex stopped and gazed in the direction of Gough Island. Endless rows of waves traveled in nearly parallel lines in the direction toward the ship. The sky was checkered with white and gray clouds moving quickly from west to east with breaks of blue throughout. The cool wind blew past her face with a force almost touching her inner spirit. And there it was, far in the distance, now a small speck of landmass surrounded by the endless mysterious sea. It all blended together to induce a kind of hypnotic trance on them both.

During the walk, Alex's mind wandered, and she thought about the last few days and the coming visit to Cape Town. She was excited but a bit unsure about the next destination.

$$***$$

After breakfast, James headed to his office suite to go over business matters with Nicki. He had a lot to get done, catching up on his companies' activities and chatting with his personnel back at headquarters on Abaco Island. He also sent an email to his CIA contact on what was going on around Gough Island and on what they discovered, using a secure server address. This was important, and after all, he was getting paid a very large sum of money for his surrogate CIA activities. After James completed his email with the CIA contact, he noticed a paper note that Nicki had left on his desk the day before. Call Professor Aldridge when you get a chance.

He was still holding the note when Nicki pranced into his office and sat on his desk in front of him.

She folded her arms and looked at James with a glare. He sighed.

"James," she said, "You were very foolish diving into that crater. You put the crew's lives in danger and your own. I think you better start being more careful in the future."

James glanced up. "You're right, Nicki. We're getting ourselves involved in some serious stuff. So I'm going to need you to look out for us in the future. I know you see things that I maybe miss."

James could see that she was worried. The last few days had been stressful for them all.

"You know, Nicki, maybe I shouldn't have brought you on this journey. I didn't know things were going to unfold this way."

She put her hand on his arm. "No, James, I'm glad you invited me to come. I just don't want anything to happen to you. But you have Alex on board, so don't get into any situation where something could harm her or you. All right?"

James nodded. "You're right. I'll be more careful. I'm glad I have you on board looking out for us. Are you having a good time?"

Nicki smiled. "I am. Maybe I'll join you on more of these trips in the future. They're fun and certainly exciting."

"How're your kids and mom doing back home?"

"They're good, and Mom's taking care of them. Everything's fine, I just miss them."

"We'll be back soon enough. When we get to Cape Town, we'll all celebrate and tour the town. Take some time off and enjoy yourself."

"I will. I'm looking forward to it."

"It's a big beautiful city right on the coast with a lot going on in the town."

"Oh, I got an email from Dr. Saveroff. She said you're welcome to tour the Zepheron facility in Cape Town. She's going to be leaving in a week, so I let her know that you and Alex are going to visit their facility in a few days."

"Great. Thanks. Oh, I saw that I got a call from Professor Aldridge yesterday."

"Yeah, he said that he has some interesting news for you."

James nodded. "I'll talk to him later today when I get a chance. I wonder—"

Before James could complete his sentence, one of the bridge crew officers ran into his office.

"Hey, there are whales alongside the ship! You've got to see them."

Nicki gasped. "I've never seen a whale." She looked at James. "Let's go."

James followed Nicki out of their office and ran down the hallway to the door that led to the promenade. A group of people were already viewing the whales, crying out excitedly.

Nicki was in awe as she spotted one. "Wow, they're humongous. This is unbelievable!"

Nicki watched a school of large gray whales moving swiftly a hundred yards off the starboard side. They were easily keeping pace with the ship, staying right alongside. Then, totally unexpectedly, one of the gigantic creatures launched into the air in a vertical manner so that all but its tail was above the water. As the massive creature slammed down into the water, it made a magnificent splash of water spray.

All present oohed as the whale submerged again.

Nicki was totally blown away. "That was amazing. I can't believe that I got to see whales. I've got to get a picture of this."

"Don't worry, Nicki," said James, "Someone else is taking pictures. We'll get them to you."

They all continued to watch the whales, some of which were vaulting into the air every now and then.

"What kind of whales are they?" asked Nicki.

"They look like humpbacks. You can tell by their long pectoral fins and their knobby heads."

Nicki hung out for a while, watching the vast ocean expanse even after the whales had disappeared from view. She felt the sea breeze, the smell of the salt water, and admired the color of the cloudy horizon. The ocean had the power to transform an ordinary person into a new being, reaching into their emotions and soul. They were never the same after their senses got a full dose of its beauty. James was happy to see that she'd had the opportunity to experience it.

"Come on," he said. "Let's head back."

As they made their way back to the office, Nicki went to get them both some coffee. James leaned back in his chair and noticed an email response from his CIA contact.

He clicked on it.

Dear James,

Thanks for the information on what you found around Gough Island. Sorry to hear about the trouble you had and glad you're all safe and sound. We suspected that nuclear weapon testing was taking place there, and now we have confirmation.

Be very careful on your trip to Cape Town and your visit to Zepheron. Just play it cool and act normal. Callum Namesbury is a very dangerous character, long associated with financial crimes and funding terrorist organizations around the world. He's also suspected of being involved in several unsolved murders and would stop at nothing to get you out of his way. Proceed very cautiously and be on the lookout for trouble. I'm alerting our CIA operative in Cape Town to look out after you.

Your assistance to us is essential and much appreciated. Do not be a hero. If you feel threatened at any time, just get out and leave. Thanks, and stay in touch.

David

[26]

Cape Town

It was a beautiful sunny day as the *Aquatarus* sailed ~~with pride and distinction~~ into the sprawling harbor of Cape Town, South Africa. They had a rough night approaching the city, as they hit a storm, and the rough seas had rattled the ship and caused many an uneasy sleep. But now all on board enjoyed a relaxing, smooth ride through the large harbor, surrounded by magnificent views of vast mountains.

A sleek aluminum Harbor Master watercraft skillfully guided them into their waiting dock slip and helped them finalize their secure docking. They were now set for a nice stay and ready to be resupplied with fuel and provisions.

While James was busy with the captain, Alex and Nicki eagerly stood on the viewing deck and took in the gorgeous views along the harbor.

"My God, this is a mighty big city."

"Yeah," said Nicki. "I never expected Cape

Town to be this big and beautiful."

"You know, you hear about faraway cities and places like this, and you picture them in your mind, but you can never really do it justice," said Alex.

"Exactly. I would have never thought that Cape Town was such a cool place."

They took in the vast views of the city. In front of them, to the north, was a huge downtown district with many modern glass-faced skyscrapers and other multistoried commerce buildings. To the east, up on a hill sat a large stadium with a silvery dome that covered part of the opening to the sky. Over to their left, the city faded into the harbor, and past that was a large barrier island. To the north and east of the city, well in the background, there were the mountains. They rose high above the city like sentinels, with a well-defined ridge that housed many pinnacles. High along the right side of the ridge was an extended flat section that gave the mountain its name: Table Mountain.

After James had completed his business in the bridge, he gathered Alex and had his personal Land Cruiser readied for them to tour the streets of Cape Town. As they watched and waited for their vehicle to be set on the dock, James grinned at Alex. "So what do you think of the city?"

"I love it," she said. "I didn't think it was going to be this big and modern."

"It's a big city with three million people. I actually flew here a few years ago to check out some business, but this is the first time I came by ship."

At that moment, one of his crew shouted up to him, "Your vehicle is ready, sir."

"Good. Let's go, Alex."

They proceeded down several flights of stairs and walked across the gangway that connected the ship to the dock and continued a short distance to his shiny silver SUV. They were excited to ride around and see the sights. Just as they were about to enter the vehicle, his cell phone rang.

Wondering who it could be, he looked at Alex before he answered it.

She smiled. "It's probably Nicki. Maybe you forgot something."

He laughed and took the call. "James, where are you going? You just can't take off like that without telling me what's going on."

James grinned at Alex and covered the phone. "It *is* Nicki. She's like my mother." He took his hand off the phone. "Hi, Nicki, sorry about that. Alex and I are going to take a ride around the city and stop for lunch somewhere."

"Okay. You guys have a good time, and *be careful.* Stay out of trouble. Call me later on if you go somewhere just so I know where you guys are."

"All right, I'll let you know. Thanks for looking out for us. Bye."

They got into the cruiser, and James drove through the streets, taking them into the modern downtown section. They toured the downtown district, just driving around and taking it all in.

"This is a very nice city. A lot of restaurants and shopping around here. Do you remember your way around from your last time here?"

"A little bit. It's definitely changed somewhat since I've been here."

James recognized a main thoroughfare and swiftly guided the vehicle onto it.

"This road will take us up to Table Mountain. It goes up to the mountains. We can get some great views of the city."

"Sounds exciting. Let's do it," said Alex, flashing a smile. James could tell she was excited to finally get away from the boat and explore something new.

As they headed farther away from the downtown area, they started to head uphill, and the area became less populated. The roadway twisted and curved on and on for five miles until James suddenly slowed down and quickly made a left-hand turn onto a single-lane roadway.

"I remember driving up this road with one of my clients the last time I was here. There's a great view in a few miles."

Alex was holding on to the handhold above the doorframe as the twists and turns of the roadway jostled her around in her seat like a doll. "Don't go so fast. You're making me a little dizzy on this curvy road."

James chuckled. "Sorry, I guess I'm a bit excited being back here. It's such a cool place."

A few minutes later, they could see the end of the road nearing as James slowed down. The road was suspended along the side of a massive mountain. James slowed to a crawl and stopped at a parking area.

"Let's take a look at the view," said James, beaming.

Alex got out and walked around to James. They walked hand in hand the short distance to an overlook. No one else was around, and James put his arm around her as they gazed out into the elevated expanse before them.

"It's amazing up here!" cried Alex. "The city looks so small."

"About a hundred miles or so south of here it turns into the Indian Ocean."

"Just totally awesome. I love it."

James pulled out a compact pair of binoculars and looked through them in the direction of the city. "I see it! I see our ship. Here, take a look."

Alex grabbed the binoculars and gazed down into the city metropolis, trying to spot the *Aquatarus*. She took some time to view the various sections of the city. There was so much to look at. Finally, she spotted the harbor and the ships. Then she noticed the scarlet-red color of their home ship with its beautiful white lines and the large OECI logo on the upper-front side.

"I see it! It's the best-looking ship in the harbor. I can't believe we came in that thing."

"You better get used to it, sweetheart, we're going to be doing a lot of this in the future."

She beamed at him. "I love it here."

James cupped her face with his hands and their lips touched in a tender kiss. They smiled, their foreheads touching, and they turned to scan the horizon's near endless beauty.

Alex thought to herself about how happy she was and how exciting it was to be on an extended vacation with her soulmate.

＊＊＊

A few hours later, they were enjoying a marvelous seaside lunch in a restaurant overlooking the Cape Town seaport. They were exhausted after their drive around the city, taking the time to visit several shops and museums. And now they had a chance to sit back and enjoy some of the local foods and share a nice conversation.

Alex looked at James, a light smile playing at her lips. "I'm having a great time here. I'm glad that I got the time off to come with you."

"Isn't this great? Traveling around the world, exploring unknown places?"

"Yeah, it is. I'm looking forward to working with you in the future and going on more of these trips."

As Alex sipped on exquisite local wine and

feasted on her delicious lunch of fresh sea bass, she gazed out into the harbor. The blue water stretched out far and wide with boats and ships docked along the side of the many holding slips. She noticed many modern seaside condo complexes intermingled with floating homes and dockside shopping districts. The *Aquatarus*, which was docked on the northeast side of the harbor, dwarfed the other ships nearby.

"So, when do you have to go back to work?" asked James.

"It looks like it will be in a few more weeks. They just gave most of the employees a temporary extended vacation. My friend Debbie had to stay, and she told me that they had to bring in some special equipment. Said we'd just be in the way."

"What did they have to bring in that was so special?"

"She's not really sure. It apparently has to do with the machines for tunneling out the mountain."

She put down her fork and frowned at James. "She said that they're being very secretive about it and only a few of the upper management are allowed to be in the areas where they're doing the work."

"That's kind of weird, isn't it?"

She shrugged. "It's because they've never done anything like this before. Debbie said she's going to sneak into those areas sometime and take a look at what's going on."

Just then, James's iPad alerted him to a text message that came in on his phone.

"Oh, Nicki just texted. We have an appointment to visit the Zepheron facility tomorrow at ten a.m. She said Dr. Saveroff will meet us there and introduce us to the management."

James looked up, away from his iPad. "I know a manufacturing plant isn't as glamorous as shopping in Cape Town, but I really need to do this."

She looked at him and leaned in and lowered her voice. "Do you really think the facility here has anything to do with the nuke testing?"

"Well," said James, "we know that Namesbury character is bad news with a long history of trouble, and he *is* an owner of the company that happens to be the owners of a ship stalking us. So yeah, I think it's possible."

"Well, who needs shopping when I can find out what's going on? Hey, wouldn't it be something if we *see him* there tomorrow?"

"That would be something, wouldn't it? Here we have a company that I'm doing business with that may be involved with setting off nuclear weapons underwater in the middle of the South Atlantic."

"I always knew you were a man of danger," said Alex with a mock grin.

"Yeah, ha-ha, very funny. Well, anyway, sweet-heart, that's not till tomorrow. You and I have the rest of the day all to ourselves to just relax and have fun."

Alex smiled as she picked up her glass of wine. "Let's toast to a wonderful time here in Cape Town."

James picked up his glass and clinked it with Alex's. She leaned in again, this time with a sensual, teasing look on her face. "James, have I ever told you that you are a very handsome man?"

James laughed and smiled back. "Yes, you have. I take it you want to have dinner in our suite tonight."

Flashing a naughty smile, she winked at him and sipped her wine.

They both laughed and enjoyed the rest of their lunch, eager to get back to their accommodations by the charming seaside harbor.

[27]

Zepheron Corporation

They arrived at the Zepheron facility the next morning as scheduled and pulled up to the security gate. It had taken them almost an hour to get to the facility, the trip having taken them over the mountains and into the country, northeast of the city. After showing their identification to the security officers, they proceeded to park their vehicle. High razor-tipped security fencing ran around the facility, with more security guards positioned on the side and rear of the building.

"I'm surprised by all the tight security here," said Alex.

"No kidding," said James. "Gated facility. Armed guards around the perimeter."

As they opened the doors of their vehicle, they were immediately welcomed by a young, nicely dressed woman who came out to greet them.

"Hello, Alex and James. We've been expecting you."

"Hi there. Interesting facility you have here," said James.

The Zepheron rep held out her hand, and James shook it. "My name is Aletta, and I'll be taking you on a tour of our company today."

"Nice to meet you," said Alex. "You have such an interesting accent."

Aletta smiled and chuckled. "Yes, I'm a native South African, and we have our own unique pronunciation of the English language here."

Alex shook her hand as well, and it did not escape James's notice how polished and confident she appeared.

"Tell me, Aletta, why all the intense security around the building?"

"We manufacture many products for the defense industry for many countries around the world. We take our clients' security concerns very seriously, including yours," she said, patting his arm lightly.

"I must say, I'm very impressed so far."

Aletta grinned at them and signaled for them to follow her. "Shall we get started?"

As they approached the walkway up to the facility, James looked around. The facility extended as far back as his eye could see. A flagpole displayed the South African national flag. The yard was nicely manicured with bushes and flowers, and the building was an off-white concrete structure with a rough exterior. There were large windows at the front of the building, which was presumably for the business office, but there weren't any for the rest of the manufacturing facility.

They entered a large glass door with the Zepheron logo positioned above the entryway. As they made their way through another security checkpoint, Dr. Saveroff and another company executive approached.

"Hello, James and Alex. So nice to see you guys again."

"Well, hello, Diane," said James. "I wasn't sure we would ever meet again."

"Glad to prove you wrong," said Dr. Saveroff as she shook his hand with a glowing grin.

Dr. Saveroff's smile, along with him calling her Diane, made it clear to Alex that they were a bit more familiar with each other than she'd have liked.

"Oh. I'd like to introduce you both to the chief operating officer of this facility, Eon Valstrand."

James and Alex smiled and cordially shook his hand. He was a tall, slender middle-aged African man in a crisp business suit.

"Welcome, both of you, to our South African headquarters. We are very proud to be a business partner with your company, James, and we would like to show you our facility here while you're in town."

"We'd both love to see what you make here," said James. "We just happened to be doing some work down here and had to make a supply stop here in Cape Town. And then I remembered Dr Saveroff telling us that she would be here for a while."

"Tell me, what do you think of Cape Town?"

She smiled. "Oh, it's a very beautiful city. I'm amazed at how big it is."

"Yes, most visitors who come here don't expect to see a city this modern and large this far south on the African continent. Some actually love it so much they stay and become citizens. You'll find that we have a very diverse ethnic population here, with people from Asia, Europe, and of course, locals."

"We had some time yesterday, so I took Alex up to Table Mountain to see the city from the mountains."

"Yes, the view from the mountain is very enchanting. I go there often myself. Sounds like you had a nice time in the city?"

"We loved the city. And lunch was fantastic," said Alex.

"Excellent. Well, I think we can get started on our tour, so follow Aletta into the visitors lounge, where you will be briefed. Aletta will escort you around our facility. After you complete the tour, if you have any questions, just stop by my office."

"Will do," said James.

"Just one thing we ask of all visitors," said Valstrand, "and that is to please keep everything you see here confidential. We manufacture very high-tech equipment for militaries around the world. They require strict confidentiality and secrecy. During the tour, we will not tell you anything that will jeopardize our clients' security, and don't be surprised if we can't answer some of your questions. You understand, right, James?"

"Of course."

As they followed Aletta into the visitors lounge, Dr. Saveroff said, "I'll catch up with you guys later. Enjoy the tour." She walked away with Eon as he headed into the office area.

They made their way into the lounge and were offered coffee and refreshments during their briefing. When they were done, Aletta announced they were now ready to take the tour.

"I'm going to give you both a pair of safety goggles to wear when we enter the manufacturing areas. It's unlikely that you will come in contact with any flying particles, but it is possible. These will protect your eyes if any are present."

Alex flashed James an excited grin. They followed Aletta down a hallway until they came to a large room with many people sitting at computer workstations.

Aletta stopped and announced, "This area is part of our research and development department. This is where we work with our clients on developing the features and systems that they require. We use the latest computer-aided design to develop the systems from the ground up."

James eyeballed the manned computer workstations, marveling at how modern and sophisticated they appeared. He noticed a strange table in the background that had intricate metal pieces on it with various shapes that were being bombarded with different-colored laser beams. Puzzled as to what it was, he asked, "What are you doing with those lasers on that table?"

"Ah...that is a new process we are using to measure and design system components for manufacturing. It is a laser-based system that is directly integrated into the milling machines that produce metal or plastic components with exceptional quality."

"Oh, yes, we're starting to use those systems at OECI too. It's amazing how it reduces steps in the manufacturing process."

"Yes. It saves time and money and improves the overall quality. Let's move forward, we have a lot to show you."

They continued through the design area and then entered a new work area with a very high ceiling.

"Wow, this place is bigger than it looks from outside," said Alex.

"This is the start of the many manufacturing lines that are all linked by our assembly-line delivery system. It's a computer-controlled robotic actuated system that delivers the necessary parts to the manufacturing stations and then delivers the completed parts to the next assembly area for production."

"Fantastic," murmured James as he marveled at the system. He searched the complex production line, spotting a series of cavernous work rooms that were all intersected by a central hallway. It consisted of heavy train-like delivery cars that each contained automated arms that could pick up, move, and manipulate metal objects in a precise manner for additional manufacturing.

James studied the work areas and noticed well-placed signs on the walls describing the workstation areas and the hazards present, along with specific work area requirements.

"I'm very impressed with your delivery system."

Aletta smiled proudly. "Yes, this is a state-of-the-art manufacturing line. It makes our products very cost-competitive."

"Yes, I can see that. What exactly do you manufacture here?"

Aletta stopped and thought for a moment, clearly trying to decide what she could divulge. "Here we manufacture precise metal components for aircraft, battle vehicles, some marine craft, and..." She hesitated a bit and continued almost reluctantly, "And we make some parts for weapon systems."

"Interesting. What type of weapon systems?" asked James, obviously interested.

Aletta gazed at James with respect and smiled apologetically. "I'm sorry, James, but I am not authorized to answer that at this time. Come, let's proceed further into the building."

As they moved forward, both James and Alex shared a look. Aletta led them into a new connected work area, where some small electric-powered vehicles were parked. She walked up to one of them and said, "Okay, we're going to use this electric car to tour the rest of the plant. It's quite a long walk, so this will save us time. Go ahead and get in."

After they were all seated safely, Aletta turned the key and hit the throttle, and they were off. Except for a mild whining sound from the electric motor, it was a smooth and quiet experience.

"This place is huge." said Alex.

"This facility is probably the largest manufacturing facility in South Africa," said Aletta with a self-assured grin.

"I don't doubt that."

As they rode on through several interconnected manufacturing zones, James's eyes searched all about the intricate manufacturing lines and the people stationed in their work areas, all wearing blue company uniforms. Many were using specialized devices to assist them in their various jobs.

"These areas here are additional manufacturing locations," said Aletta as she drove. "But coming up ahead are our quality assurance and testing areas."

Aletta slowed down and allowed James and Alex to get a better look. They drove on for several minutes and were amazed at the efficiency being applied to test and examine the manufactured metal and composite materials. Finally, they arrived at what appeared to be the end of the building, where the manufactured items were boxed and readied for shipping, and Aletta stopped the vehicle.

A doorway led to an additional section of the building. Boxes of materials near the entrance had radioactive symbols on them, which James found interesting. "What's in this area here?"

"That is a restricted area. You are not permitted in that section."

"What do you make in there?"

"I'm afraid that's proprietary. I'm sure you understand."

James nodded, but he wasn't about to let it go completely. "Tell me, Aletta, do you use or manufacture any nuclear materials here?"

"No, we do not," she said, smiling tightly. "Well, I think it is about time for us to head back to the office area. I can answer any additional questions there."

There was no mistaking the tinge of anxiety in her voice. James and Alex shared another look as Aletta turned the car around and headed back the way they came. It took a full ten minutes for them to arrive back at the office section of the building. She dropped off the car and led James and Alex to the visitors lounge.

While there, one of the office workers approached them. "Mr. Sebring, you have a call waiting for you in our courtesy room. If you'll come with me, and I'll take you there."

"Oh, okay, I wonder who's trying to get me? Alex, wait here. I'll be right back."

"Okay," said Alex, already in a conversation with Aletta.

The Zepheron employee guided James to a secluded area within the office complex where the courtesy room was located. She left him near the entrance, and he entered the room. As he walked in, he noticed a wall-mounted monitor and a phone placed on a small table near a comfortable couch. He was monetarily confused by what he saw, and then he felt a pair of hands touch his body from behind.

"Diane. What are you doing here?" He smiled but dropped it when he saw the serious look on her face.

"James, I have to talk to you about something."

"What's that? Is something wrong?"

"On your voyage down here, did you happen to stop on an island?"

"Yes, we made an overnight stay off the coast of Gough Island."

"You did. Oh..."

"Why do you ask?"

"I don't know how to say this, but you apparently upset some people who are connected with that island."

"What are you talking about?"

She looked nervously about the room for a few moments and then gently grabbed his waist and pulled him toward her. "There's something going on with people associated with this company and Gough Island. I can't tell you everything about it right now, but you did something there that got their attention."

James tried to step back a little, but she held on tight. "What is it that we did?"

"I'm not sure, but I found out through a friend."

James look at her, confused. Could she be any more vague?

"I just wanted you to know that you're dealing with very nasty and dangerous people, and I don't want anything bad to happen to you."

James shook his head. "What's going on here that they don't want us to know about? Tell me!"

She placed her hand over James's mouth to quiet him down. She then ran her fingers slowly down his chest all the way down to his waist, touching him in a way that was more than friendly.

James was both startled and stirred by her strange warning and her intentions, but he wasn't going to be so easily distracted.

Unexpectedly, the door to the room jerked open, and Aletta walked in. James stepped back from Dr. Saveroff, trying to act calm and inconspicuous.

"I see you completed your call... Well, hello.

Dr. Saveroff. I didn't realize you were in here too."

Trying to act the part, Dr. Saveroff thought of something quick. "I left my cell phone in here, and I had to retrieve it, and James and I were just chatting." She nodded at James. "I'll catch up with you guys later before you leave."

"Okay, see you then." James could feel Aletta's gaze on him, so he turned to her. "Alex is waiting for us. Shall we go?"

James started to walk out but not before he noticed a video camera mounted in the corner of the room, pointed in his direction. Had he and Dr. Saveroff been seen together by security guards? It all made him a bit wary. He'd have to be a lot more careful.

As they were escorted through the office area of the building, Aletta asked if they had any questions before they left.

"No, I don't think we have any right now," said James.

"I'm totally impressed with your facility," said Alex.

"Yes, thank you," said Aletta. "I've really enjoyed meeting you both and taking you on a tour. Before you leave, I just wanted to bring you back to Mr. Valstrand to say goodbye. He told me a lot about what you've accomplished in the ocean engineering and defense industry. He wanted to know your impression of our manufacturing facility."

"Sure, let's go. I'd be happy to let him know what we thought."

Aletta smiled and walked them deep into the heart of the office complex, passing by secretarial staff, conference rooms, and offices. After making their way through a long hallway, they entered a spacious, well-decorated office with floor-to-ceiling windows and a view of a pond surrounded by a manicured garden.

Mr. Valstrand was standing next to another well-dressed individual, who James assumed was another high-ranking corporate officer. They were engaged in a conversation while examining a large map on the rectangular office table in front of them.

Mr. Valstrand looked up at them. "Well, hello again."

Valstrand walked over to them, his associate close behind. "Let me introduce you to one of our corporate investors. This is Mr. Callum Namesbury. He's on the board of directors and just happened to be visiting today."

James was shocked when he heard the name, but he played it cool. "Well... so nice to meet you, Mr. Namesbury."

"Likewise, James, I've heard about you. Your company has quite a reputation."

Knowing the man's questionable past, James found it interesting that Namesbury looked rather ordinary and nonthreatening. He was of average height, thin, and somewhere in his sixties.

"Thanks. Let me introduce my girlfriend and business associate to you. Alex."

Namesbury grabbed Alex's hand and held it firmly. "It's a pleasure to meet you, Alex. You're a very pretty lady."

"Nice to meet you, too," said Alex, pulling her hand back with apprehension.

"So, what do you think of our facility?" asked Valstrand.

"We're very impressed with everything," said James. "You have the most modern manufacturing area I have ever seen. And I was amazed with your automated robotic delivery system."

"Thank you. We take pride in our products and our workers, and we strive for constant improvement. That's why we were very happy to have continued our partnership with your company."

"Yes, we are very happy about that too. It took some time to iron out the details with Dr. Saveroff, but we're happy it all worked out."

"Yes, indeed, it was a good arrangement for both our companies, and as you know, working with defense departments is always a tricky process."

James laughed. "You're right about that. That is probably my least-favorite part of the business."

James looked to Aletta. "Well, I think we've taken up enough of your day. Thank you again for showing us around and giving us the tour."

"It was a pleasure," said Valstrand.

"How long are you visiting Cape Town?" asked Namesbury.

James started to answer, but he noticed an odd look on Namesbury's face. He looked toward Alex. "I... I think we're going to be leaving in a day or two. We had to refuel the ship, grab some supplies, and give my crew a rest. We'll be heading north, probably to the Canary Islands."

"Canary Islands? What's going on there?" asked Namesbury.

"Just a quick stop," said James, smiling awkwardly. "Alex has some friends there and a few other things going on."

"Well, have a safe trip," said Namesbury with a smirk.

"Thanks," said James, wondering what that was about.

Aletta gestured for both of them to follow her out of the room. As they were about to leave the building, Dr. Saveroff came rushing up to them to see them off.

"Thanks for visiting, and have a safe trip back on the *Aquatarus*," she said.

256

"We had a nice time," said Alex.

James was about to turn and leave with Alex when Dr. Saveroff mouthed some words to him quietly. Remember what I told you.

Alex saw it too and wondered what it meant. Minutes later, after they entered their SUV, James and Alex looked at each other, the same things on their minds.

"So, what do you think?" said James.

"I can't believe that we met Namesbury. What's he doing here?"

"Yeah, it's very coincidental to see him here, especially after what we went through."

"What was Saveroff saying to you on our way out? That was odd."

"She was giving me a warning. She told me, before Aletta came into the private room, that we got their attention because of what we did at Gough Island."

"So there's no doubt this place is involved in the nuke testing going on at Gough Island."

"They're definitely involved. But I still don't know why. What are they trying to hide?"

"Yeah, and what are they planning to do with those nukes they're testing?"

Rumbling sounds caused them to look up at large trucks leaving the facility grounds and entering the highway.

"Look at those trucks," said James. "They all have radioactive transportation symbols on the back."

"I wonder what they're carrying and where they're going?" Alex asked.

"Last night Kent told me that Zepheron has several uranium mines and a processing plant located north of here."

Alex's eyebrows shot up. "How did he find that out?"

"Nicki did some research."

Alex frowned. "You know they're hiding some-thing in that back manufacturing area. The restricted area."

"Yeah, it probably was a nuke assembly area."

James started the vehicle, hit the gas, and proceeded in the direction the trucks had gone in.

"Where are we going?" asked Alex.

"We're going to follow those trucks and see what the backcountry looks like."

Alex grinned. "This should be interesting."

While driving, James nervously looked in the rearview mirror at the facility. He sure hoped he was doing the right thing.

[28]

Into the Desert

They followed the convoy of trucks for over an hour, driving over mountain ranges and isolated valleys, heading northeast into the high plains desert. They had passed by some small villages a while back but were now in an isolated and remote province that James told Alex was home to several mining operations.

James was getting tired and was about to turn back when he noticed the trucks were turning onto a side road, heading into a secluded valley. He slowed to a crawl but continued to follow them, trying to not give away his intentions. As he did, he noticed in the mirror a dark-blue van behind them at a distance.

Alex was getting antsy and hungry and wanted to head back. "James, how much longer are you going to do this?"

"I just want to see where they're heading. Like I said, I know from the map that we're very near the uranium mines and processing plant."

"Okay, but we don't want to be doing this all afternoon."

"All right, hun. I'll turn back soon."

After following the convoy a few more miles, the trucks turned into a large gated industrial complex that contained many large buildings and storage yards. James pulled over onto the shoulder of the road and watched as the trucks proceeded through a checkpoint, stopping for an inspection by the guards.

James used a small pair of binoculars to watch as each truck was searched and certified to proceed through the gate. He failed to notice the same blue van he spotted earlier had stopped thirty yards back.

"Wow, whatever this place does, it certainly has strict security measures," said James.

"Yeah, I see that," said Alex, a bit unnerved. "Maybe we..." Alex was about to say they should leave when she noticed a security camera mounted on a nearby pole. It was pointed right in their direction. "James, we're being watched. Look." She pointed to the camera.

He looked up. "Damn it. All right, I'll pull up to the gate and make it look like we got lost."

"What? Don't do that! Then we'll have to go up to the checkpoint." As James pulled back onto the road, she threw her arms up in exasperation.

"Don't worry, I'll just play it cool, and maybe I can find out what the hell they're making here."

James drove his vehicle slowly into the driveway toward the guard gate. As he approached the checkpoint, men dressed in black uniforms approached from both sides of the SUV. They had pistol holsters on their belts, and one carried a clipboard.

James rolled down his window as a large

burly guard wearing a hat came to his side "Hello, what's the purpose of your visit here, sir?"

"Oh, we're tourists visiting this area, and we apparently got lost. Maybe you can help us find our way back?"

"I'll need to see some identification from both of you, sir."

"What? Why? No need to do that. We're just going to turn around and head back."

"I'm sorry, sir, you'll have to provide some identification."

He noticed the guard on Alex's side move up to the window with his hand on his weapon, searching inside.

Alex, who James was sure was totally freaking out, just stared at the guard on her side.

Then other guards came out of the checkpoint office and approached his vehicle, walking in a very determined manner. How could all this be happening? James wondered. Just because he pulled up to the entrance? It seemed excessive. And very strange.

James turned to the guard on his side. "By the way, what do you make here?"

"We're not permitted to discuss that," the guard responded harshly. "Now show me your identification...now!"

James tensed. He weighed his options frantically, looking around.

"All right, get out of the car," the guard yelled. "BOTH OF YOU, GET OUT OF THE CAR NOW!"

The car jostled, and Alex shrieked. Guards on both sides were attempting to open the doors. Luckily, they were locked. Realizing he had to do something, James thrust the stick into reverse and hit the gas. Alex screamed as the vehicle sped backward and away from the guards, obviously startling them. As he maneuvered the car around, some of the guards pulled their guns out of their holsters and pointed their weapons at the SUV.

"Get down!" James yelled at Alex.

Alex lowered her body, trying her best to hide as James floored the vehicle, making it to the roadway rather quickly. He turned right and sped away, his heart pounding.

Alex sprang back up from the seat. "Holy shit, James, why did they do that? What's going on?"

"I don't know. It's almost like they knew who we were and wanted to get us."

That was when James noticed in his rearview mirror that same blue van that he had spotted earlier was approaching them rapidly.

James nailed the gas and turned to Alex. "I don't want to freak you out even more, but we're being followed."

"What?" yelled Alex as she turned to look. "What are we going to do?"

"Open the glove compartment and pull out my pistol."

Alex took a deep breath and did as he ordered.

"Give it to me."

She carefully handed it over to him. James grabbed it and placed it between his legs, checking the mirror every now and then. Alex kept looking back too.

As they raced away, James thought over his options and saw that the roads were deserted, and not one car had passed them by. The van following them was now starting to catch up.

It turned into a chase as the van managed to get closer to James's SUV. As they rounded a long curve, the van accelerated and managed to pull alongside their SUV, even though they were both tearing down the highway.

Alex nervously peered at the vehicle and saw that the front-seat passenger was holding a pistol. She screamed as the window of the van rolled down and shots rang out. Everything was a horrible blur as bullets flew, and they swerved on and off the highway. Thankfully, neither of them was hit. As James recovered and steered back onto the highway, Alex screamed again. "They're moving back alongside us. Do something!"

James shot a quick glance at the van and reacted quickly as it pulled alongside again. He swerved the steering wheel hard and rammed his vehicle into its side. It veered to the right but quickly recovered and managed to stay on the road. Alex screamed—the man was aiming his gun at them again, trying to get an accurate shot. James rammed his car into them again. It worked, and this time the van was knocked to the right and skidded into the desert, where it ran into the sparse terrain and eventually came to a stop.

They sighed with relief. James was just about to celebrate, but then their vehicle started to lose power.

"Son of a bitch!" James yelled as their vehicle eventually lost all power and started to slow down.

"What happened?" cried Alex.

"One of their bullets must have done something to our engine. I have to pull over."

Alex shook her head and covered her face with her hands. She looked back at the van off the road and noticed that it was now backing out of the desert. They'd be on them at any moment.

"Oh shit, they're coming back onto the road. They'll be coming after us. What are we going to do?"

James thought quickly, and then he noticed something. A deserted group of buildings off to the right, away from the road. He quickly steered the vehicle onto the side of the road, stopped, and grabbed his gun. "Quick, get out. We have to run."

They got out and scuttled into the brush, away from their car. James grabbed Alex's hand and said, "We have to make it to those old buildings over there. It's our only chance."

Even though Alex was in shock, she kept a cool head, knowing that their lives depended on getting away from those thugs. They ran as fast as they could in the direction of the old buildings; they were about a third of a mile off the road. While they were running, they noticed a dirt road leading to them and got onto it, which made it easier for them to move.

After a while James felt comfortable enough to stop and look back to see where the blue van was. It was moving slowly along the highway, apparently searching for them in the brush.

He glanced at Alex, who was out of breath like him. "Are you all right?"

She just stood there looking terrified and shook her head, breathing intensely. She flashed a pitiful grin at him. "I just hope we can get out of this alive."

"We'll make it, baby." He grabbed her hand and squeezed it reassuringly. "Let's get to those buildings. We're almost there."

They bolted in the direction of the buildings again, running at a reduced rate because they were getting tired. As they got closer to the structures, James could see more detail—it appeared to be a long-abandoned mining camp. A large old wooden building stood with several smaller wooden dwellings surrounding it, along with a huge elongated factory-type building with a somewhat rusted corrugated roof. There was a tall brick chimney attached to the building that had partly broken apart and fallen to the ground. An old railway system ran through the property, presumably for trains that had once delivered materials to the various structures.

"Wow, this mining camp must be from the early 1900s," said James.

Alex was finally able to catch her breath. "We better find a place to hide. They could catch up to us at any minute."

James turned to gaze back toward the road. They were now on a rise in the terrain and could get a clear view of where they had come from. He immediately ducked down. "Shit, you're right. They're coming this way."

They took off toward the largest building, jumping over the old dilapidated railroad tracks. They moved up a ramp that led up and into the building and took a look around. It was completely empty, with a hallway running through the center of the building with many rooms off to the side.

"Come on, let's go toward the back of the building."

Alex nodded, and they marched around, their footsteps echoing through the old structure, unnerving them. The building went on a long way, and as they traveled deeper into its mysterious interior, it got darker and gloomier. James slowed down and moved carefully so he did not run into anything. Alex was nervous and stopped to catch her breath and get her bearings. As she turned to catch up with him, she ran into a large spiderweb. She screamed. "Holy Christ! James! Get it off! Get it off me!"

James quickly came to her aid, using his hands to swipe away anything that was attached to her face. He saw the spider and whacked it off. He was startled by how large and weird it looked.

"I got it, you should be okay now."

Alex rubbed her face and head, feeling for any remnants of the spiderweb. Satisfied it was gone, she huffed out a breath, her heart pounding.

"That was terrible, let's go," she said.

They kept going and wound up near the back end of the facility, near where the old brick chimney was located.

James stopped and sighed. "All right, stop here. This spot looks as good as any to hide out. We can hide in back of this dilapidated equipment, and we've got an exit point out that doorway if they come this way."

Alex breathed slowly, trying to get her heart to calm down. She gave James a weak grin and said, "Okay." She trusted him.

"Sorry I got you into this mess, but I didn't—"

"It's all right," she said. "I mean, these aren't the same people at the checkpoint, are they? I can't believe they shot at us. Evil bastards."

"Yeah, real psychopaths."

James pulled out his pistol and cocked it. "You know, I was warned by my CIA contact that Namesbury could do something like this."

Alex's eyes widened. "You think they work for him?"

James shrugged, then looked at her seriously and held out the gun. "If something happens to me, I want you to protect yourself. I know you know how to use it. Okay?"

Alex glared at him, not wanting to think about that possibility. She nodded her head, affirming she would deal with that situation if she had to.

They both startled at a sound in the distance that seemed to originate from inside the building. When nothing else happened for several seconds, they frowned at each other and focused on the dim foreground from where the sound had come from.

James lowered his voice and whispered, "This could be them. If I see them, I'm going to take a shot."

Alex tensed up and appeared ready to run. They watched and waited, and then more sounds were heard radiating throughout the aged wooden building. James steadied himself on a wooden beam and took aim with his pistol, ready to fire if he could get a clear shot.

Footsteps echoed, coming closer and closer to their location. James could tell that there were two of them. He then heard some muttering. Alex clamped her hands over her mouth in terror, and then there was nothing but silence.

James was alert and ready for the moment he had to react. He spotted them, tensed up. He aimed his pistol and took a shot.

The men cursed and shouted as they took cover. Then all hell broke loose when they returned fire. Alex and James ducked under an old metal machine beside them and waited for the shooting to stop. Bullets flew over their heads and all around them whizzing as they went by, then went quiet as they reloaded.

James knew that it wasn't safe where they were, and he had to do something quick. As soon as the shots stopped, he grabbed Alex and fired two rounds in the direction of their attackers. "Let's go, we've got to get out of here."

They rose up and bolted for the doorway that led outside. Just as they cleared the doorway, gunshots pinged and resonated in their direction, but all of them missed their target. *they all missed.*

They wasted no time and ran as fast as their legs could carry them. James spotted another building nearby and decided to go for it. They didn't have many options, but at least he still had more ammo left in his gun. Just as they were about to enter the building, James turned and saw two cars parked off in the distance that had come from the highway. Were there more than two thugs after them? He kept that thought to himself, not wanting to alarm Alex any more than she already was.

As they made their way up a small flight of stairs into the building, he peered around for a good place to hide. He didn't see any right away and knew the assailants were right behind them, so he kept moving. The building appeared to be an office and didn't have a lot of hiding places. They walked quickly through the mostly empty building, dodging dusty furniture that dotted the inside.

They finally saw an exit point where a wall had collapsed. They were about to make their way over the scattered debris when a shot banged in their general direction. They ran quickly over the loose debris of wood and brick. Alex's foot got caught on the corner of a collapsed wood wall, and she stumbled to the ground. James quickly helped her up, and they both checked back in the direction of the shots and then hopped over the remainder of the building materials in their way.

Suddenly, they were out of the building again. James swiftly steered Alex over to a wall to rest for few seconds. He assumed that the thugs would be coming out from where they'd just been, so he grabbed her hand and followed the contour of the building till they reached the corner and then hid around the side, where they couldn't be seen.

With his gun in his hand, he slowly looked back around the corner of the building to see what was happening. One of their attackers exited the building, crouching with his gun drawn. He stopped and circled around.

James hurriedly ducked back behind the

corner, keeping his pistol up and ready to fire if needed. As least from this position, he could take both of them down if they approached, and he had cover this time. He got antsy and peeked again to see where they were. Both men were standing near the fallen wall, holding their guns, searching.

Then as he ducked back down, a torrent of shots tore through the air in a near endless barrage, and Alex jumped beside him, covering her ears. He couldn't imagine what was happening, and after a minute of silence, he somehow gained the courage to look at what was going on.

His mouth dropped open. The two assailants who had been stalking them were lying on the ground dead in a pool of blood. Someone had killed them both, but who could it have been? He saw no one as he continued to peer around the corner.

Alex grabbed James, wondering what was happening. Then as he continued to survey the death scene, he spotted two mysterious figures approaching the bodies very slowly with their guns drawn, ready to fire, their backs to James. One of the figures walked up to the dead assailants and kicked them both, apparently checking for signs of life. Satisfied that they were dead, they started to search the area. He was shocked to hear his voice being called and looked at Alex in amazement and confusion.

"James! Are you out there? James! You can come out now. It's safe to come out!"

Then one of the figures turned around, and he couldn't believe his eyes. It was Dr. Saveroff, accompanied by a tall man. He contemplated what to do. Could they trust her? He decided that it seemed safe enough and marched out into the open slowly so he could be seen.

As she spotted him, she came running up to him with her handgun down by her side. "Are you all right? Where's Alex? Is she okay too?"

James just stood there in shock, shaking his head. "I can't believe what's happened to us in the last hour. What the hell is going on? Why are you here?"

Dr. Saveroff approached, put her gun back into her thigh holster, and rubbed her hand on his arm. "James, it's a long story. I'm just glad that you're all right. I work for the CIA, and we're investigating Callum Namesbury."

Just then, Alex came running up to them. She grabbed James, and he turned to hug her.

"Are you all right?" asked Dr. Saveroff. "I was worried about you both. I was afraid that Namesbury and his thugs had gotten you."

"How did you know we were here and how did you find us?" asked Alex.

"When you arrived at the Zepheron facility, my partner here placed a tracking device on your vehicle because we wanted to see where you would be going and to make sure you would be safe."

Alex placed her hand on her head. "I can't believe this. Thanks for saving our lives."

"You're welcome, Alex. I'm sorry for the deception, but I had to keep my cover and not give away who I really work for. I had to maintain my role here while I investigated what was going on with Zepheron and Namesbury."

"What did you find out? How are they involved with the nuclear testing at Gough?" asked James.

"I'll fill you in on the way back. With everything that's going on with Zepheron and Gough, it'll take too long. I want to get you out of here and make sure you're safe, so let's get going. We found your vehicle earlier, and it's dead. I'm just glad to see that you're not."

"We'd be dead if it weren't for you," James said.

She hesitated, then nodded. "That's what they intended to do. They were going to get rid of you both. You were in the way of their plans."

"And what's that?" asked James.

"Well, we're not completely sure, but I'll fill you in on what we know so far on the way back to your ship."

She searched the area for her partner and spotted him near the dead bodies. "Namesbury's guys will be checking around, so let's get going."

They got in her car and made a quick getaway out of the desert without any interference. On the ride back, they learned that nuclear weapons were being secretly produced at the Zepheron facility. Namesbury was behind everything, including the nuclear testing. He was developing specialized nuclear weapons for some nefarious purpose. Unfortunately, the CIA did not know exactly what that purpose was. She was still playing her undercover role, trying to find out what those plans were. She assured James she would let him know what they found out in the future.

Hours later, they were back on the *Aquatarus* safe and sound. They were tired and worn out, and Alex was still reeling from the trauma of their dangerous encounter.

Before retiring to his quarters, he ordered the captain to set sail north to the Canary Islands and had dinner along with two bottles of a nice Chianti sent to his room. It was time to relax and put their ordeal behind them.

[29]

West of Africa

Two days later, the *Aquatarus* was cruising north off the coast of Africa. James was set to drop off Alex at La Palma, where she was to visit with her friend for a few days and then return to work once her project started back up.

The *Aquatarus* was scheduled to head back to headquarters, where they had new jobs that he had to tackle. While checking his emails in his office, Nicki came in to chat. She sat across from him, staring daggers at him until he finally acknowledged her.

"What?" he asked.

"I can't *believe* that you guys almost got killed out there," she said. "What were you thinking when you pulled into that secret Zepheron facility?"

James looked at her, bewildered. "Uh..."

"Alex told me all about what happened," she said accusingly.

272

"She did, huh? What else did she tell you?"

Nicky crossed her arms over her chest. "She told me that when you decided to pull into that remote facility there, the guards wanted you to get out of the car and that you refused and started to drive away. Then they pulled their guns out as you were leaving."

"Did she tell you what happened next?"

"No, that's all she said, but she did tell me that you had car trouble in the desert after you left the facility."

James relaxed inwardly. He looked at Nicki, amused. "You know, I told Alex not to tell you these things, but she just doesn't listen to me. You always find out everything, don't you?"

"You can't hide anything from me, James. And now you know that I will always find out from Alex."

"Yeah, I can see that." They both chuckled a bit.

"Oh," said Nicki, changing the subject, "I was checking your emails and I saw that you got an email from Professor Aldridge."

"What did he say?"

"He wrote something about the items you sent him, and he still wants to have that chat with you. It sounds important."

"Oh, good. Let me check out his email now, and I'll chat with you later."

"Okay. Don't forget we have to set up that equipment manifest sometime soon so we'll have it when we return to Abaco."

"Yeah, yeah, we'll work on that soon."

Nicki left, and James searched for Professor Aldridge's email.

He found it and began reading it.

Hello James,

I know you are traveling around the Atlantic right now on the Aquatarus, and I hope that my email finds you soon. I just wanted to inform you that my friends and associates at Cambridge are continuing to sort through the remains of that ancient ship you sent to us. They managed to identify many new pieces, and the results are fascinating. It's not easy work, since the wreckage has been down there for many centuries.

One particular thing that has them gob-smacked is a long copper-like device that seems to extend into some type of intricate mechanism. At first they theorized that it could be an ancient telescope. But after further examination, they think that it's possibly some type of navigational computer because of ancient markings on the metal surface. They are in the process of consulting with other artifactual experts to determine what this item is.

All in all, it's a brilliant discovery that would shock the world if they were to find out. At this time, they cannot place these items from the wreck with any known ancient civilization, and so they believe it's possibly a new ancient civilization, just waiting to be discovered. I was careful to conceal just where this ancient wreck was found, but those involved were astonished to realize that this wreckage was found to be over a thousand miles west of Europe, in the middle of the Atlantic.

I've been informed that these items would be a cherished treasure in a museum setting and could fetch millions in a brokered transaction. You certainly have made the grade with this discovery, and I'm looking forward to showing you personally just how amazing these items are here at Cambridge. I attached some pictures of the items for you to view. Please plan to visit with me in the near future, and we'll all have a bloody good time!

All the best,
Ashton

James nearly jumped out of his seat after reading the email. His heart was racing. They had discovered a world-class ancient wreck site brimming with valued artifacts of antiquity. Geared up, he went for the pictures and opened them up, not knowing what they were going to show.

As he went through each one, he was left with increasing feelings of awe and bewilderment. Several exhibited pottery, metal jewelry, and other metallic adornments from a time long gone. There were coins, round and rectangular in shape, that displayed abstract markings that seemed to echo a forgotten ancient language and culture.

Then he noticed the mysterious long copper instrument that Professor Aldridge had spoken about. He wondered to himself whether another ship's captain from long ago had used it to navigate the ocean and where that captain had traveled to. It was exciting to imagine, and he thought about how wonderful that device would look in a glass cabinet in his office back on Abaco. Anxious to share the information with his crew, he summoned several of them to show them what an amazing discovery they had made.

After James displayed the pictures, they were blown away. After some time of celebration and conversation, everyone headed back to their duties aboard the ship except Rebecca, who stayed behind to discuss something important with James.

"I was checking out the Electric Fish data, and I wanted to tell you about a few things going on."

"Okay, what is it?"

"The first thing is we have a telemetry reading from one of our EF drones that has indicated that it went into extraction mode and is floating near the surface."

"Cool, where is it?"

"Not too far from our present location. We could potentially reach it in about twelve hours or so. Do you want to get it?"

"Sure, why not. But why did it go into extraction mode?"

"Not sure, but it could have collided with something down there and its internal sensors put it into a safety mode to protect the unit and the data."

"Okay, let's get it. We have a little extra time built into our schedule."

"We'll have to head a little northwest from here," she said.

"No problem, I'll let the captain know."

"Okay, great. Now the second thing. And this is really cool...we have some drones sending in data from just a few hundred miles north of here. I received telemetry that indicates large numbers of marine life on the move, heading in this direction."

Rebecca displayed the exact locations of the indicated positions on her iPad.

"Wow, what the hell is it? Do you know?"

"We don't know for sure, but it's very deep, around twelve thousand feet, and it seems to be of various sizes of creatures. And get this, there are some very large targets included in this travel mass. And they aren't whales."

"How do you know that?" he asked.

"We can tell by their sonar signature."

James looked around the room, perplexed, and gave it some consideration. Then he grinned at Rebecca. She knew just how to get him hooked on something.

"James, this could be a once-in-a-lifetime discovery for us if we were to go there and do a dive. What do you think?"

James took a deep breath and stared at her

for a few moments and then smiled. "All right, let's do it. Let's head to the deep sightings first, and then if we have time, we'll go back for the drone."

Rebecca smiled and clenched her fist in celebration.

"Send the exact coordinates to the captain, and he'll put us on a course to that location. I just hope that we can get there in time to find whatever it is."

"I think it will still be moving northwest but will probably be a little farther up, so we have a chance."

Rebecca started to leave the office when James said, "Oh, tell the dive officer to prepare the *Sagittarus* for another dive. I'm going to go down with you and Scott again if it's still present when we get there."

"Will do!"

After Rebecca left, he peered around his office suite in a happy mood, thinking about his life at sea and how he'd somehow started up a world-class company that was making amazing scientific discoveries deep under the ocean. He was proud to be aboard his ship with Alex. He had to share the recent excitement with her.

He got up and headed to the ship's lounge compartment, hoping to find Alex. She'd go bananas over the amazing pictures of the artifacts.

***

Twelve hours later, the *Aquatarus* arrived at the location where the mysterious deep-sea movements had been detected. The *Sagittarus* was prepped and had already started its dive. Rebecca, Scott, and James felt confident, despite their recent scare together. They had never been to this particular area of the Atlantic and were interested to see how this discovery related to the other Electric Fish detections they encountered.

They slowly descended and had shared several radio communications with dive control aboard the *Aquatarus*. Everything was going well when Rebecca unexpectedly spotted something on the sonar.

"James, I'm detecting some movements in front of us. Can you guys turn on the high-beam lights so we can get a better view?"

Scott, brimming with excitement, hit the switch. "I can't wait to see what's down here."

"Telemetry aboard the *Aquatarus* is showing the movement of marine animals this way. We just have to get to where they are."

James suddenly saw something and shouted, "There!"

Several marine organisms swam within their view, and they cried out in excitement.

"I see some small copepods swimming around here," James relayed back to the ship, "Along with some jellyfish and shrimp too."

As they continued down, larger creatures appeared. "That's a cuttlefish over there, and a few eels swimming around," said James. Over the years of working the sea he had learned much about the deep-ocean fauna and could identify many marine organisms. But Rebecca was an expert in that field, and James respected her knowledge. "Am I right?"

"Yep. Cuttlefish," she confirmed.

"They're kind of cute, aren't they?" said Scott.

"Some species migrate in cycles to the surface and then return to the twilight zone at night where it's safe for them from predators," said Rebecca. "That includes both eels and cuttlefish."

"Really? I didn't know that," said James.

"Marine scientists now believe that this is the norm for most marine species. And when they do, they deposit organic matter below the surface, which keeps carbon dioxide from escaping to the atmosphere for thousands of years."

"Interesting," said James.

"What's the bottom terrain like in this area of the Atlantic?" asked Scott.

"We're just on the west side of the Mid-Atlantic ridge, and there happens to be some underwater ridges right where we are. The only thing is that this area is largely unexplored, and our ship's sonar showed some rises in the sea floor, so we'll find out soon enough."

They continued to plunge into the deep and entered the final reaches of the twilight zone, where barely any light from above made it down. It was nearly dark outside, but their lights shone on creatures swimming across their viewing area. At first it was confusing as to what type of deep-sea animal could travel so fast.

"Wow," said Rebecca. "These guys are Humboldt squid. Look at how huge they are."

The squid swarmed in front of them, traveling in all different directions, displaying their quick speed and agility. Some of them attached themselves to the sub's front-arm actuators as if they were attacking the craft.

"Whoa, they're grabbing our sub. What are they doing?" Scott asked, sounding somewhat anxious.

They all felt the sub jostle slightly from the attachment of the large creatures.

"These squid are territorial animals. They're probably confused by our presence and the lights, and they're showing their aggression."

"These are some of the largest squid I have ever seen," said James.

"Yeah, Humboldts can get to over sixty pounds

and have been known to attack scuba divers."

"Do you think these squid could be some of the organisms that we're detecting with the drones?" asked Scott.

"Nah, they're not big enough, and we're not deep enough yet. Whatever the drones spotted are very long."

Scott nodded, then muttered to himself, "Hope *those* creatures don't get territorial."

James stayed silent, not wanting Scott to get any more wound up.

Time passed, and eventually the squid disappeared as they entered a depth that was totally void of light—the Bathyal zone. Time seemed to stand still and darkness prevailed. Some creaks and metallic sounds aroused the crew as the pressure on the craft increased, causing the metal machine to announce the strain.

All seemed to be going according to plan until they reached the six thousand-foot depth. An alarm sounded, causing Scott to slow their descent.

"We're nearing the top of an underwater ridge," Rebecca said. "Proceed slowly, Scott, and watch for any protrusions."

Scott maneuvered the craft and steered the pitch so they could get a better view of what was below them. Then they spotted what sonar had been detecting: a rocky bottom with huge boulders strewn about.

"You're doing good," said James. "Just keep it slow and follow the ridge."

Eventually, the ridge dropped off sharply and then fell off into a gentle slope, which they continued to track downward.

"This is probably the first time any human eyes have seen this ridge," said Rebecca.

"Yeah, what a marvel these underwater mountains are. There're thousands of miles of these submerged mountains that have never been explored," said James.

James leaned forward suddenly, having spotted some very unusual crabs moving about.

"Whoa!" cried Rebecca. "Those look like yeti crabs. There's got to be a hydrothermal vent around here somewhere."

They were all on the lookout, keenly focused on the areas lit up by the bright lights of the sub. They continued, slowly following the descending terrain for a while, seeing more crabs, huge clams, and bottom coral as they traveled along. Then there it was, right in front of them: the hydrothermal vent that Rebecca mentioned.

Scott slowed the sub into a holding pattern, as they were within fifteen feet of the large vertical thermal vent. He glanced at the thermometer—the outside temperature of the water had increased dramatically. The tall alienlike edifice rose twenty-five feet upward. Blackish smoke billowed from cracks in the mortarlike structure, especially from the top.

Hundreds of bright-red tube worms surrounded parts of the chimney, with many deep-sea crabs moving about, apparently consuming something around the tube worms.

"What a big, beautiful smoker this one is," said Rebecca, beaming with excitement. "I've seen a few small ones off the coast of Iceland, but this baby is magnificent. I'm going to take a picture." She moved to grab her camera.

"What are the crabs eating?" asked Scott.

"They're actually eating the bacteria that grow around the smoke and thermal water releases," said James.

"Yeah," said Rebecca. "These worms and crabs eat the bacteria that chemically synthesize nutrients from the mineral releases. There's no sunlight down here, so they have to survive on that."

A radio transmission from the *Aquatarus* abruptly crackled out from the speakers. "*Sagittarus, Sagittarus*... do you read me? Over."

James grabbed the mic. "This is the *Sagittarus*. We hear you loud and clear. Over."

"We've been tracking you on sonar, and right now you have a large mass of creatures heading directly your way, about seven hundred feet below your position. Over."

"Roger, *Aquatarus*, keep tracking us down here and give us updates on what you're seeing. Over."

"Roger, will do. Over and out."

James hung up the mic and looked at his crew. "Here we go. Are you guys ready for this?"

Both Scott and Rebecca nodded in agreement. Rebecca got up and moved toward the utility console. "I'm going to check on our front-mounted camera. I want to make sure that it's on and working."

"Good idea," said James. "This might be the first time any human has ever laid eyes on these deep-sea animals. Let's make history, guys."

Scott throttled the controls and picked up the pace of descent. The slope was getting steeper as they traveled down, staying twenty feet above the bottom. They were on a journey of discovery, heading for a certain rendezvous with the unknown. Only in their thoughts could they imagine just what lay ahead.

[30]

Creatures of the Deep

As they traveled deeper and deeper, a host of strange new deep-sea animals appeared around them. Many displayed a brilliant show of lights of various colors created by the creatures' bioluminescence. Others had unique features like large mouths and eyes to help them collect the rare nutrients present in the cold, high-pressure environment.

"Current's strong," said Scott, feeling the tug in the controls.

"Look at all the plankton in that current," said Rebecca. "I wonder why it's concentrated in this fast-flowing area?"

They continued calling out what they saw. Fanged-toothed fish, red jellyfish, some giant isopods, and the ghostly chimaera, whose shape resembled a flying scarecrow. These deep-sea organisms were expected to live in the Bathyal zone, but what surprised them was the number of creatures within this area.

"God, that chimaera is bizarre-looking," said Scott. "What are those spots on its face? It looks like its face was sewn together."

"Oh, those are sensory organs that detect electrical fields in the water. It helps him find his prey."

Then all of a sudden, many more large fish darted across their field of view. They all let out a collective "Whoa." It was as if they had entered a marine organism highway, with unique animals of all sizes darting by.

"What's going on?" asked James. "Why are all these fish so concentrated here?"

Rebecca gazed at them in wonder as they swam by. "I don't know. It's almost like it's a massive migration of some kind. I mean, it's possible they've been doing this for millions of years and we just didn't know about it until now."

"Holy shit," cried Scott. "Look at that frigging thing! What is it?"

A strange-looking large gray beast was right in front of them, looking mean and nasty, almost like it wanted to take a bite of their ship.

"My God," said Rebecca. "It's a shark of some kind. Maybe a frilled shark? This is amazing." She snatched her camera and took a picture of it. The fifteen-foot beast bent its body as it moved forward, its bloodred gills and curved scissor teeth giving it an appearance from an alien world.

The amount of sea creatures became so dense that some were colliding with their submarine, making bumping noises randomly.

Rebecca saw other large animals go by that she had never seen before, including the goblin shark, the demon catfish, and the rare and colorful swell shark. These were sizable sharks that were more than ten feet in length.

"It looks like there's a whole deep-sea ecosystem down here that these large sharks are following and feeding on."

"Yeah, but what's eating the sharks?" asked James with a puzzled frown.

A short while later, most of the horde of the marine animals had thinned to a trickle, allowing them to see further out in front of them. At this point Scott had stopped the sub's descent and was piloting the craft slowly in a southwest direction, opposite of the flow of the marine animals.

They weren't prepared for what happened next. Rebecca was fiddling around with her camera when she casually glanced up and saw something out the window and let out a blood-curdling scream. In all his years of working with Rebecca, James had never heard her scream.

"What is it? What?" he asked.

She just pointed, and at first he didn't know what to make of it, but he understood why it had Rebecca so freaked. It was the body of a creature so large that it nearly took up the entire view from the window.

"What the hell is that?" yelled Scott.

They all watched in horror as it gradually turned sideways, completely blocking their view inside the craft. It was grayish black, with occasional small discolored patches on its long, cylindrical body. It took several seconds for it to fully move across their path of vision, and as it finally did, they looked at each other in complete shock.

James took a long, slow breath and asked, "What is it? Do you have any idea?"

She rubbed her head, shook it, and said, "I don't know what it is. I have never ever seen anything like this in marine biology literature.

It's got to be a new creature of some kind. Totally undiscovered."

Then the radio blared out a loud message, which startled them, "*Sagittarus, Sagittarus!* What's going on down there? Over."

James clutched the mic. "This is the *Sagittarus...* Dive control, what do you guys have? Over."

It took a few seconds for the message to come back, and there was some weird static in the audio feed.

"We're getting confused by your sonar signal. We're seeing all kinds of movements around your position. What's going on down there? Over."

"*Aquatarus*, we're apparently in a current belt of some kind that's full of aquatic animals. What are you guys seeing? Over."

"*Sagittarus*, whatever is around you is really frigging big, and there's a whole bunch of them. You might want to think about getting out of there now. Over."

Scott didn't know what to think. He couldn't help looking out the forward window from time to time, but he dreaded what he'd see.

James searched for an answer on what to do. They were making history with what they had seen, and they might never get another chance to see this newly discovered species so close. But he was responsible for their safety and chose the more prudent thing to do.

"All right, let's head up," he said. "We really don't know just what's going on out there, and I think we're all getting a bit uneasy."

They thought they heard a sound from the speakers. It was a strange noise, almost like an elongated low pitch that seemed to come and go in repeated sequences. Rebecca looked at James worriedly and noticed him sweating.

"That sound is not coming from the speakers,"

she whispered. "It's coming from outside the sub. It must be from those things out there."

"More of those creatures are approaching!" Scott yelled as he pointed outside, looking terrified.

They all turned to the window.

"Oh my God!" cried Rebecca.

Out in the dark bluish water, several of the huge creatures slowly swam by. This time they noticed other parts of their body in more detail, including their heads and side flippers. They were utterly enormous and long in length, and it was obvious that they were feeding on the marine creatures.

Then one of the monsters approached them head-on, nearly colliding with the sub. They all freaked when they got a good view of its frontal area as it came near the viewing bubble.

"My God, look at the elongated head on that thing," said Scott.

"Yeah, and the teeth protruding from their jaws are enormous. It looks like its jaw may be double-hinged, just like some ancient predator species," said Rebecca, clearly mystified by the creature.

"Scott, get us out of here," said James. "This is getting a little too dangerous." He anxiously peered out at the creatures.

Just as the sub started to move up, they were shaken by an impact. The lights flickered and then went out and then came back on. An alarm went off, which sent Rebecca scrambling around to find the source of the trouble.

"Scott, do you still have power?" asked James.

"Yeah, I think I do," he said, fussing with the controls and checking his instrument panel.

Then they were struck again and moved off-kilter.

"Shit. We lost power again," said Scott. "I don't know what's going on, but we can't move."

They sat there, dead in the water, with all lights in the sub knocked out. Finally, the backup lights came on and illuminated the interior of the craft enough for them to check their controls.

Rebecca came up to the front to help assess the situation. The *Sagittarus* had little power and no propulsion. And, worst of all, the massive creatures were still out there.

Rebecca and Scott frantically worked to solve the power issue as the craft started to drift into the deep dark abyss. Sonar and radio were both out, and they had no idea what was below them.

"Try to reset the fuel-cell breakers," said James. "The VFDs could have gotten knocked out of phase by a power spike."

"I didn't think of that," said Scott, getting up to check. "Let me try it."

He rushed to the back console and checked

around, breathing heavily, high on adrenaline. He located the circuit for the VFDs and gave it a reset, pushing the breaker in and then out two times. Instantly, the lights and the fuel cells came back on as they heard its distinctive whining sound. It was music to their ears.

"We're back in business!" yelled Scott, wiping the sweat from his brow.

There was no time to celebrate, as the depth gauge reading said they had drifted down.

Scott jumped back into his seat and piloted the sub upward and forward, attempting to take them to the surface. The forward lights had also come back on from the reset, and as they traveled up, they again spotted a mass of marine organisms in the current. Just when they were almost out of the belt, they spotted something.

"Look! There's another one of them!" cried Rebecca.

They all nervously peered out the front window as one of the monsters swam right up to the front of their craft, clenching a large shark in its jaws, shaking it around in an attempt to kill it. Amazingly, the shark was still alive and was trying its best to escape. Then, incredibly, the freaky creature slammed into the front bubble window of the sub, creating a loud sound as the two creatures struggled with each other. Blood poured out from the massive injuries of the shark as it strained to survive. Then the shark went limp, and the monster moved away from the front of the sub. As it swam slowly by, they could see the detail in its dark-spotted skin and the intricate lines of its rear caudal fin. It was like a weird dream as they all watched, not saying a word, doing their best to get to the surface.

At this point they all had enough excitement and were relieved as they made it up a few thousand feet toward the surface. James felt safe enough to make a call up to the *Aquatarus*.

"*Aquatarus, Aquatarus*, do you read me? Over."

There was a slight delay, then light static. "Roger, *Sagittarus*. We hear you loud and clear. We tried to contact you a while ago and couldn't get you. Over."

"Copy that... We got tied up down here with a little problem, but we managed to fix it. We're heading up now and should reach the moon pool in about twenty minutes or so."

"Roger, your position is looking real good on sonar. We're looking forward to seeing you aquanauts when you get here. Oh, and there's someone standing next to me who wants to say something to you."

James smiled, knowing who it was. "Okay, put her on."

"James? James, are you there?"

"I'm here, Alex."

"I'm so glad you guys are all okay, and I just want you to know that we have a bunch of champagne here ready to go when you guys get back."

"That's why I love you, Alex. I think we can all use a bit of the bubbly when we get out of here."

"And we have quite a story to tell about our dive!" yelled Rebecca.

James hung up the mic and peered out from his chair into the gorgeous sea view before them. Light rays blared through the water and marine creatures swam by as they neared the surface, leaving them all feeling better.

As they approached the *Aquatarus*, James looked at his two sub companions and said, "You guys did a hell of a job on that dive, and I'm giving you a raise."

Rebecca and Scott cheered, making James laugh. They high-fived each other in celebration.

Rebecca smiled at James. "I won't say no to that, boss."

Scott laughed. "Shoulda got that on tape."

They all laughed as they entered the moon pool, looking forward to getting on board the ship.

Later, they entered the officer's section of the cafeteria, happy and excited and eager to share their stories of the monsters from the deep. The party went on for hours while members of dive control collected and prepared the data and visual images.

***

The next day, after they had rested and collected their thoughts, James invited Rebecca and Scott to review the data of their recent dive in his office. Alex was there as well. They were all stunned by the images.

"Oh my God, that creature is huge and monstrous-looking," said Alex.

"Yeah, we had a few frightening moments down there when we spotted them," said Rebecca.

"How long is it? It looks like it is more than fifty feet."

"Well, it appears to be at least sixty to seventy feet long by looking at the images and sonar readings."

"Do you have any ideas of what this creature is?" said Alex with a dumbfounded glare.

"I checked all of the possible large marine creatures known to the oceans, and it did not fit any of them. Now look here..."

Rebecca maneuvered keystrokes on James's computer, and images of giant creatures popped up on the large office monitor.

"Here we see a few possible candidates, and obviously none of these fit our creature."

Three large whale species were displayed on the screen.

Rebecca glanced briefly at Alex and then back at the screen. "These are the largest known sea creatures of the oceans—a whale shark, a fin whale, and a blue whale. The blue whale is the largest creature to ever have lived in the sea."

"So, what is it, then? What could it be?" asked Alex.

"I have some ideas," said Rebecca. "By putting several of the images together into a merged visual picture, I came up with a composite depiction of our creature. Here, take a look."

Instantly, the entire screen was filled by the image of the monster. They all stared at it in awe.

"Ugh, it's kind of nasty looking," said Alex.

"Yeah, that's our monster. She's beautiful," said James.

"Notice the long, narrow body, the paddle-like swimming appendages both front and back, and the elongated head with scissorlike teeth. This thing is evolved to catch and eat large creatures like sharks and other prey deep in the ocean."

"In other words, it's a killer," said James, shaking his head. To think they'd been that close to it.

"Now, check this out." Rebecca displayed images of prehistoric sea creatures that roamed the seas millions of years ago.

"Are these sea monsters of the past?" asked James.

"Yes, these are pics of what an ichthyosaurus and a mosasaurus appeared to look like for a comparison to our unknown creature. Our creature does not look anything like an ichthy-osaurus, but notice how it appears a little like a mosasaurus. Very long in length and similar paddle-like swimming appendages."

"Yeah, but our creature is narrower and has a completely different-looking tail fin."

"Yes, that's true, and our creature must be a gilled species able to extract oxygen from the sea since it lives so deep. The ancient mosasaurus, of course, was an air-breathing reptile that had to come up for air and only hunted in shallow water."

"But how could these large monsters stay hidden from scientists for so long?" asked Alex.

"More than ninety-five percent of the planet's oceans remain unexplored. It's completely possible for something to stay hidden all this time. Remember that our EF drones are the first sophisticated sensing probes ever to explore these deep-sea depths. There are a lot of new species just waiting to be discovered down below. And the fact that we found all those marine animals in that fast-flowing nutrient-rich current belt gives us a guide as to what's happening down there."

"What do you mean?" asked Alex.

"There're thousands of miles of deep-sea mountain ranges along the oceanic thermal ridges. These create nutrient-rich environments for marine animals to find niches within ecosystems."

"Are you sure that this creature is the one we've been hearing with our drones over the past few months?" asked James.

"Yes, I got up early this morning because I couldn't sleep and went through the sound data. They're a perfect match. We've been hearing them deep below and off the coast of Africa for quite some time, and this is our baby."

"So why is this creature down in these deep waters in the middle of the Atlantic Ocean?" asked Scott.

"My guess is it likes to hunt prey here. And

check this out. This current belt seems to flow very near the spot in the Atlantic Ocean where the *Scorpion* sank. Near that ancient wreck that we found."

Oh my God, thought James. "Are you saying there could there be some sort of association between those wrecks and the current belt and those large creatures?"

Rebecca looked a bit stunned. "I... I hadn't even thought of that. But it sure looks weird that those two wrecks are right in the location in the Atlantic where those sea creatures roam. I'll have to give it some more consideration."

Alex smiled and decided to change the mood. "So what are you going to name those new giant sea creatures?"

"Well, do you have any suggestions?" asked James with a lighthearted grin.

"How about we name it a *Saggasaurus* since you discovered it in the *Sagittarus* submarine?"

James chuckled and looked at Rebecca. She smiled, and they both nodded their heads in agreement at Alex's suggestion.

"Okay, let's name it the *Saggasaurus*. When we eventually announce it to the world, it will sound like a perfect name for a mighty deep-sea monster."

They all laughed and celebrated the moment. A moment they would never forget. Thanks to James and his crew, OECI was set to make their mark in the history books.

[31]

The ITUS Project

Two days later, the *Aquatarus* was well on its way to the majestic Canary Islands. They were back on a course to the island of La Palma to drop off Alex.

James and Alex were enjoying their morning ritual of a relaxing stroll around the *Aquatarus*, taking in the sights and sounds of the sea. As they rounded the bow onto the port side of the ship they noticed Nicki and Kent walking eagerly toward them. They looked serious, so whatever was going on had to be significant.

Nicki was nearly out of breath. "James, we've got an important message for you. You have to come to the office right now."

"What's the matter?"

"We got a call from Dr. Saveroff. She wants to talk to you immediately. She said that it has to do with the nuclear weapons and Zepheron."

"What? Did she say what?"

295

Alex just stood there looking concerned.

"Come on, there's no time to waste. You have to call her now."

James hesitated, glancing at Alex. Then they all took off hastily in the direction of his office suite. As he entered, one of the officers immediately handed him a phone. "Hello, this is James."

"Hello, James. So glad I got you. Listen, something urgent has come up, and we need your help."

"Who's we? What happened?"

"First, is there anyone else listening on this line? This is classified information."

"No, it's just me."

"Good. We found out some important information about the nuclear weapons that Zepheron was manufacturing and testing off of Gough Island."

"You did?"

"Yes. We knew they were developing these nukes, but we had no idea just what they were intending to do with them. But we just found out where they were shipped."

"Where did they go?"

A moment of silence stretched out. "James," she said finally, "The nukes were shipped to La Palma. To the ITUS Project."

James's jaw dropped. He looked at the others and lowered his voice so no one could hear. "But that's where Alex works."

"I know. But we confirmed it. They were shipped there a few days ago in a special hidden cargo directly to the ITUS Project."

Alex was right behind him. He turned to her and gave her a halfhearted smile. He couldn't hide it from her.

"Why would they send nuclear weapons to the ITUS Project?"

Alex paled when she heard.

"That's why I'm calling you. We suspect they're intending to use those nuclear weapons to cause a worldwide event."

"What do you want me to do?"

"I'm heading up to La Palma right now with a team of agents. I need you and Alex to meet us there to advise us on the facility. Alex knows it, and you just need to be there for her. Are you willing to help us?"

He looked at Alex, and she nodded. "I think she'll be willing to help, and I'll certainly assist in any way I can."

"Good. I'll send a helicopter to your ship to pick you both up. It should arrive in four hours, so get your things and be ready. They will radio your tower when they're near."

"Okay, we'll be ready."

"Thank you. You will both be briefed on the helicopter, and I will see you both when you get to the island."

"Very well, we'll see you on La Palma."

James hung up the phone and turned to Alex. Her forehead was creased with worry. She had heard enough to understand a little of what was going on. "Zepheron shipped weapons there?"

James nodded. "Come on, let's go get a cup of coffee and I'll fill you in."

As they were leaving, Nicki came up to them, looking concerned. She placed her hand on Alex's shoulder. "If you guys need any help with anything just ask."

"Thank you, Nicki," said Alex. "I'm going to have to pack a few things, so I may need some help. Could James and I have a bit of privacy? I'll meet you in my cabin."

Nicki nodded solemnly and turned to leave. James and Alex headed to the cafeteria. They could never have imagined they would be heading into another dangerous situation so soon after their last one.

***

Seven hours later, they were both approaching the island of La Palma aboard a US Navy S-61 Sea King helicopter. They had been picked up from the *Aquatarus* helipad and had been traveling over the Atlantic for three hours, making them anxious to get to dry land.

During the flight, they were briefed on the situation by Special Agent Garrison, who had been working the case with Dr. Saveroff. Also aboard the flight were three other CIA agents and a team of six Navy SEALs. All of them were disguised in plain clothes so as to not give away their cover when they arrived at the ITUS Project.

Special Agent Garrison was chatting with the SEALs when he noticed Alex, who was sitting across the aisle looking a bit uneasy. James was next to her, his hand resting on her leg. He went over to their bench and spoke in a loud voice over the sound of the engines. "Are you all right? We're going to land in about ten minutes!"

"I'm okay, but I'm looking forward to getting off this helicopter. It shakes around a lot!"

Alex and James were both dressed suitably, with Alex wearing tight black pants and a khaki-colored bulletproof vest.

He placed a hand on her shoulder and squeezed reassuringly. "You'll be all right soon enough."

Then he looked at James briefly. "We want to thank you for helping us out here. We don't know much about ITUS. I looked over a diagram of the facility. Those tunnels in the mountains are damn confusing."

"Don't worry," said Alex. "I know my way around there very well. I'll be able to guide you and explain the place."

The agent looked at them seriously. "Look,

this is going to be a potentially dangerous situation. We're dealing with very bad people who couldn't care a thing about your lives. We're going to do everything possible to protect you both, but I don't want you sticking your necks out. You got that?"

They both nodded their heads in agreement.

"Do you know how to use a gun?" he asked.

James smiled and lifted up the left side of his shirt, exposing a handgun.

Agent Garrison nodded. "Good. What is it?"

James pulled it out and handed it over to the agent. "Walther P99 compact."

Garrison examined the piece slowly and then handed it back. He turned to Alex. "What about you? Do you have a gun?"

She looked up nervously. "I know how to use one. I've shot with James before at the range, but I don't have one now."

One of the Navy SEALs called out, "Here, she can use this."

He handed it to Agent Garrison, who then handed it over to Alex. She examined it slowly and nodded her head briefly. "I hope I don't have to use it."

"It's good to have anyway," said James.

Garrison nodded. "We don't know what we're going to encounter, and it may save your life." He looked at her sternly. "Don't be afraid to use it."

She sighed and nodded again apprehensively.

The loudspeaker aboard the large helicopter crackled to life. "ETA, five minutes."

The crew started moving about, grabbing their possessions and bagged gear. The sound of the engines changed pitch, and minutes later, everyone aboard felt it bounce and then settle still. They had landed.

Agent Garrison placed his hand again on Alex and said loudly, "Okay, when we get off, we'll meet up with Agent Saveroff and the others in the task force." As Alex started to move, he winked at her. "Everything will be fine."

The exit doors slid open, and the agents and soldiers piled out. Garrison got up and waited for James and Alex to move forward.

"Okay, let's go."

Once out of the copter, they were directed to a gathering of people over to the far-right side of the small landing strip.

When they got close, they were greeted by Agent Saveroff. "Hey, guys, so glad you made it. Thanks for volunteering to assist us."

James took in her different appearance, as she was dressed in her official CIA attire consisting of form-fitting khaki-colored pants and a multipocketed black vest. "No short skirt and high heels today?"

She laughed and punched him lightly. "No, not today, I'm afraid."

Agent Garrison came by and said a few words to Saveroff. She nodded. "Okay, let's get in the vehicle, and we'll go over the layout of ITUS and what's going on there."

They followed the group into the transport van and took their seats. It was a large vehicle identical to the ones used by the engineers and construction workers who made the daily trek into the ITUS tunnels to get to work each day.

When the entire team was in, it took off and headed up into the mountains. They drove for a good twenty minutes, heading up toward the higher reaches of the large mountain ridges until they reached the entrance. Alex was used to the daily trek, but this was the first time for James, and he was itching to see it for himself.

The vehicle slowed and stopped at the security checkpoint. The driver and one of the CIA agents got out and spoke for several minutes with the security officials, flashing credentials. Other guards walked around the entire vehicle, checking for anything unusual. When they were finally cleared, the two agents boarded the van, and it took off in the direction of the entrance.

"Wow, the entrance tunnel is huge," said James.

"It has to be large to accommodate the construction and tunneling machines that work in the facility," said Alex.

The tunnel was bright, the sides and ceiling of the tunnel coated with a smooth white surface that reflected the LED lighting. There were trucks passing in the opposite direction and there were many side tunnel turnoffs. Occasionally, there were digital information signs that hung from the ceiling to update the workers on project matters.

The vehicle started to slow down as it entered a side tunnel. It went on a little farther and then pulled over to the side. Eventually, it stopped and everyone got off. They were in a terminal area, where workers would meet and catch their transport vehicles that took them to their various departments. They oriented themselves and headed into one of the side doors into a meeting room to regroup and go over their plan.

When they were all in and settled, Agent Garrison pulled out a large map of the ITUS facility and laid it on the table for all to see. Saveroff joined him.

Agent Garrison gazed across the table slowly. "Okay, I'm going to go over how we're going to proceed. We have identified the individual responsible for producing these weapons as a Callum Namesbury, one of the major shareholders of the company.

"Less than twenty-four hours ago, we discovered that a number of these weapons were shipped to this large underground facility. Why they would ship these weapons here we could only speculate, but recent intel indicates they intend to create a global event by detonating some or all of the weapons here at this facility."

Alex's jaw dropped. "*What?* You think they're going to detonate them *here?*"

"Yes."

James glared at Agent Saveroff. "You didn't say anything about them detonating the nukes in the exact place you were asking us to come to."

Diane shook her head. "We just learned this. I didn't know when I asked you to come."

"Save it for later," Garrison said sharply. "Now, Alex here is an engineer and has worked in this underground facility for a number of years. We brought her here to advise us on the facility since she knows the entire layout. Alex, what would happen if those nuclear weapons were to go off inside this tunnel system?"

Alex shook her head, folded her arms, and tried to stop herself from shaking. "Well, it would certainly set off a huge landslide. Roughly half the island would cascade down into the ocean. A landslide of that size would cause a series of massive tsunamis to strike the east coast of the United States and other areas. Without proper warning, it could kill many millions of people."

A buzz of chatter began as everyone tried to speak at once.

Garrison banged his hand on the table to get everyone's attention "All right, simmer down. We're going to have to assume that Namesbury's plan is to trigger a massive tidal wave that will kill millions of people. We're going to have to stop this from happening."

One of the agents who was from the Spanish government asked, "What is his motive?"

"He's a wealthy businessman and part owner

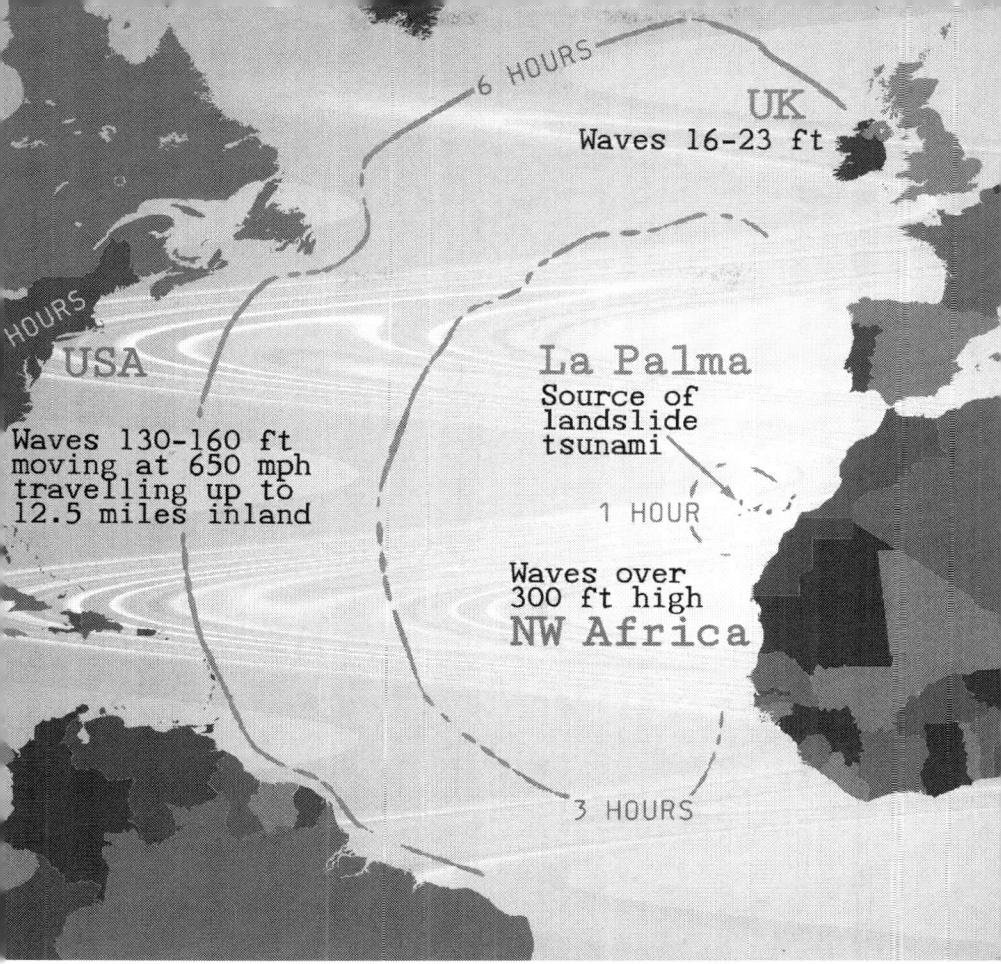

6 HOURS

UK
Waves 16-23 ft

HOURS

USA

Waves 130-160 ft
moving at 650 mph
travelling up to
12.5 miles inland

La Palma
Source of
landslide
tsunami

1 HOUR

Waves over
300 ft high
NW Africa

3 HOURS

of a well-known weapons manufacturing company that sells products to military organizations around the world. He's been indicted several times and actually spent some time in prison in Belgium. Why he would be trying to set off a deadly tidal wave, we don't really know yet. But I can tell you that there are agents combing through his offices and emails, trying to find out just what's going on. When we find out anything important, I'll let you all know."

"Now, Alex, I want you to come up here and take a look at this map of the interior layout of the area."

303

Alex moved over to the map.

"See if you can point out any potential locations where they would put these nukes. Let me know if you see any places that we could check."

"I don't really know because it's such a big facility, and there are a lot of places that they could hide them."

"I understand, but take a minute to study it."

Alex took a deep breath, sighed, and stared at the map. She knew she had to hurry.

After a few minutes of looking it over and moving her fingers over the map, she looked at Garrison and said, "Well, there would need to be a synchronized explosion to get the island to split symmetrically and fall with maximum force."

"What do you mean by synchronized?"

"I mean all of the nuclear devices would have to be exploded on a time-coordinated basis. A controlled demolition. They would all have to go off on a set schedule, controlled by internal clocks or by an interconnected, hardwired system."

"Okay."

"On the other hand, I don't think it would be an internal clock, since it would be hard to get it accurate enough. They're probably using a hardwired control system that they would have to conceal from the workers here."

"So where could they hide all that?"

"The most likely place would be in the utility and ventilation conduits."

She focused on the map again and pointed to the conduits that ran parallel to the work tunnels. "Here. This is where we should focus our efforts. I think this is where they would put the bombs."

James was impressed with Alex. She was cool as a cucumber, despite the situation.

"All right, everyone, we'll focus on the vents. We'll split into two groups and commence our search. If you find anything suspicious, radio it in, and we'll come to you. Our communication equipment should work since there are repeaters in the tunnels."

They packed out of the room and moved to the transport vehicle. As Alex and James were walking to the vehicle, Alex spotted someone passing by. "Hey, Debbie!"

Surprised to see her, Debbie ran up to her and hugged her. "Alex, what are you doing here? I was going to pick you up in a few days."

Debbie could see that she was accompanied by James and a group of odd-looking individuals who appeared to be some type of security force.

Alex glanced around awkwardly. "I'm uh... part of a team checking on something. I can't say too much, sorry."

Debbie seemed confused. "What's going on?"

Alex looked at Debbie seriously, clutched Debbie's arm, and whispered, "Tell me, have you seen anything suspicious going on here over the past month? Anything at all with equipment being moved around or anything else weird?"

Agents Saveroff and Garrison noted the conversation and came over to listen. Debbie glanced at them nervously.

"What? Umm." She hesitated a bit. And then it struck her. "Wait a minute. Yeah, remember when we spoke before, I told you that they had shut down the operation and were bringing in some large special pieces of equipment?"

"Yeah, what was going on with that stuff?"

"Well, they almost never do anything like that, so we all thought it was really weird."

"What did they do with it, and where did they put it?"

"I don't know exactly. They shut down the

entire facility, and we weren't allowed to go in."

"Do you have any idea what they did?"

"I did see something strange when I was working in Tunnel 19."

"What?"

"I saw a group of people working there that I didn't recognize. They were working in the service conduit, and they were all wearing blue jumpsuits and green hardhats. They didn't even acknowledge me. Then days later, I noticed those same people working in some of the other conduit tunnels along Tunnel 21 and 23. They seemed to be hooking up some type of wiring system. I didn't know what to make of it, and I just figured that they were installing new monitoring equipment."

She looked around again. "Can you tell me what's going on?"

Agent Garrison had heard enough. "Let's go! We have to move, now!"

As everyone moved to the transport van, Alex gripped Debbie with both her hands. "Listen, Debbie, go tell all your friends here to get out. Don't hesitate, just do it. Tell everyone to get out!"

"What's wrong? Why are you saying this? You're scaring me!"

"This place might blow up! Get out of here now! I have to go."

She turned and marched quickly onto the transport van. Agent Garrison got in behind her.

Debbie watched as the van sped out in the direction of the main tunnel, heading for Tunnel 19. Alex's frightening words left a terrifying ring in her mind. She didn't know what to do or what to think. She took off running.

She had to warn the others.

[32]

Tunnel 19

As the van traveled deeper into the massive underground complex, everyone on board became increasingly anxious and uneasy. Some had pulled out their weapons, checking them over. Others were chatting with their team members and going over their procedures and planning. They had all seen combat, but this was the first time they had to stop someone from detonating nuclear weapons intent on wiping out millions of people.

Alex and James were terrified, but they knew they had to follow through. There was no way they could ask anyone to escort them back. They needed everyone. As the tunnel followed a long bend, Alex called out, "That's Tunnel 19 straight ahead!"

Garrison acknowledged Alex's call and stood up and spoke loudly so everyone would hear. "Team One will get off here and search the tunnel. Alex will guide us. You know what to do if you spot anything suspicious. There could be some civilian workers around, so don't shoot unless you're sure."

The van moved slowly past the sign indicating Tunnel 19, then it stopped.

Agent Garrison glanced at his watch. "All right, Team One... go!"

The door opened, and several members piled out of the vehicle along with Garrison, James, and Alex. They assembled near the Tunnel 19 entrance.

Agent Saveroff stayed in the vehicle and shouted "Good luck!" as they departed. She was leading Team Two, which was heading to the other tunnels of interest.

Garrison looked over his team and nodded. James and Alex stayed in back while they scouted ahead. When it was clear, Garrison motioned them forward. "Okay, let's move. Alex, lead the way."

Alex stepped forward and led the way into the tunnel. There were regularly interspaced side hatches that led into parallel conduits. These carried the utility lines that supplied the electrical and communication wires necessary for the entire ITUS Project.

As they headed deeper into the complex, Alex said, "All right, we're approaching a system interface area, and we might see some ITUS workers. This is where Debbie saw those strange workers that were installing wiring."

Garrison nodded to Alex and then to his men. James followed close behind and whispered for her to be careful as they neared the opening.

Alex approached a hatch that was already open and entered the conduit. The area was unattended, so she turned and said, "It's unoccupied, come on."

Several members followed Garrison and James into the service conduit while others stayed outside to stand guard.

"I'll take you to where Debbie saw the new wiring system being installed."

Alex walked down the passageway, passing side hatches that led off to other service rooms.

"Is there anybody in these side rooms?" Garrison asked.

"There could be, but I don't think there's anyone in them now."

Garrison looked behind at his men following and said, "Keep your eyes open."

One soldier stopped. He opened a hatch and peered inside to find a long room that contained piping and wiring along with assorted mechanical equipment. Satisfied there was no threat, he caught up with the others.

The service conduit bent up ahead, obscuring their view.

"Okay, we're here. This is where Debbie saw the strange equipment being installed."

Garrison signaled to his men to open the hatch as everyone stood aside. One of the team tried to open the entrance but was unable to do so. He tried it again with the help of another, but it was stuck.

Garrison turned to Alex. "It's locked."

"What? They never lock the entries here. Are you sure?"

Garrison nodded to his men. "Go ahead, try it again."

The men tried again with more force but failed to get it to move.

Alex looked baffled. "I don't understand. There's no reason to lock these areas."

"Unless they put something in there that they don't want anyone to see," said James.

"All right, we're going to burn it open."

Garrison signaled to his men, and two of them immediately went to the door hatch. One of them removed a small backpack and took out some thin puttylike wads of clay-colored material and pressed it on the hinges and securing mechanism.

"All right, everyone stand back."

"Does this make an explosion?"

"Just a little one... You'll see," said the demolition expert.

The agent pressed a small transistor-sized igniter into the putty and moved back. Within seconds, there was a spark and then a rapid burning sound with smoke. The entire wad lit up in a glowing, hissing, burning haze that penetrated the metal like melting butter.

"What is that stuff?" asked James.

"It's thermite, made from metal powders and incendiary composites. It's deadly shit," said Deo, the demolition expert.

"Oh...yeah, that stuff is nasty. You wouldn't want to get it on you," said one of the Navy SEALs standing alongside.

Deo looked back at James. "It'd burn right through your arm."

The entire metal hatch sheared off the doorway and fell onto the floor with a clang. Smoke and haze filled the immediate area. The soldiers stood guard on each side of the hatchway, searching for anyone who might have heard the noise. They had their pistols drawn, ready for an altercation.

One of the other agents quickly moved inside the conduit with his pistol out. He checked about and said, "It's all clear."

Garrison gave a nod and several agents followed, with Alex and James behind them.

Everyone moved about, checking around the entire long tunnel space. Alex spotted something. "I see something here."

Garrison came to her with an agent and James right behind.

"There's a thick cable here that I've never seen before."

Garrison signaled his nuclear weapons expert to assist in the examination of the cable.

They both gazed at the one-inch blue cable and noted that it ran the entire length of the room. They followed it up and saw it continued beyond what they could see.

Alex turned to the nuke expert. "Have you ever seen this kind of cable before?"

"No, I've never seen it before, but it could be part of an IIS."

"What's that?"

"An integrated ignition system. The military uses IIS cable systems for controlled demolition situations."

"Like what?"

"Blowing up bridges, enemy fences, and other large structures that get in their way."

"Can we follow it up and see where it goes?"

They continued through the narrow conduit, passing by several other side hatches as they searched. The others followed behind, providing support and protection. At one point they heard voices near one of the hatches. Everyone froze, and Garrison ordered one of his men to check it out. A team member managed to open the hatch and looked around with his gun hidden from view. Several men were stopped in a truck outside in the tunnel, apparently doing some kind of routine work. Alex peeked out and relaxed a bit. She recognized them.

She turned back to the team. "It's okay, I know them. They're just regular ITUS tunnel workers doing their job."

She closed the hatch and the group carried on, following the path of the cable.

After tracing the mysterious cable for fifteen minutes more, they stopped. The cable had disappeared from view.

Alex and the nuke specialist stopped and searched around, confused.

"Where did it go?" said the specialist.

"There's a side room up here just ahead. Let's check in there."

Alex went up to the hatchway that led into the utility room. "Damn, this one's locked too," she said as she wiggled the hatch handle.

Garrison again signaled for the hatch to be opened.

His demolition man quickly maneuvered, placing thermite putty around the handle of the hatch and adding the ignition source. It rapidly went up into a hissing blaze of smoke. After a few moments, the handle fell to the ground and they were able to enter the room.

Alex entered and stopped in her tracks. Motioning upward, she said, "Look at that. The blue cable comes into the utility room right over here, then it enters this metallic boxed-in area."

"What is this thing?"

"I don't know. I haven't seen anything like it in these conduit rooms. It looks new."

"All right, I'll take it apart and see what's inside."

With Alex by his side and James and the others observing, the nuclear specialist carefully removed a section of the metal covering. As it slowly came off it exposed a portion of the contents inside.

As soon as he was able to get a good look, he whistled low. "Holy shit. Look at this thing. It's a nuke all right."

James cursed under his breath. He should never have agreed to let Alex come. The tension in the room immediately became stifling.

"Before I do anything, let me take a radiation scan."

He pulled out a small orange electronic pack and extended a small metallic coil. He turned it on. The unit made sounds as the scan began, and then he checked the readout.

"Yeah, we've got fucking trouble."

"What's the matter? What is it?" asked Alex.

He turned to her with a scowl and wiped his forehead. "This thing is unique. Custom built. I've never seen anything like it."

Garrison moved near him. "What kind of a bomb is it?"

"It's a plutonium bomb with an integrated detonation timer attached."

"Can you disable it?"

"Maybe. Maybe not."

"What's the problem?"

"The problem is that it's probably linked to the other devices in the service conduit and they're connected by that blue cable. If I try to disable it, it could have a tampering system that sets them all off."

"We'd never be able to get out in time," said Alex.

"Yeah, we'd be vaporized," said James.

Garrison tousled his hair in frustration. "Look, we don't have a choice. Disable it now."

The specialist took a breath and wiped the sweat beading on his forehead. The fate of the world was in his hands.

Garrison's radio chirped just then. "Tango Niner to Iron Hawk... Do you read? Over."

"This is Iron Hawk. Over," Garrison said.

"We located a fireball in a utility room off Tunnel 21, not far from Tunnel 22. They appear to be connected by a blue cable running through the conduit. Over."

Garrison raised his arm and spoke near it.

"Roger, Tango Niner. We also located a fireball here. Disarm if possible. The fireballs are connected, so proceed with caution. Over."

"Roger on it... We chased out some suspicious workers that were near the fireball. Be on the lookout because they're heading your way."

"Roger that...Break." Garrison immediately signaled his men to prepare to intercept. "As soon as you neutralize your device, proceed up to Tunnel 23 and check for more fireballs. We have to clear the entire area."

"Roger, Iron Hawk. I'll report on the status."

Garrison glanced at the specialist disarming the unit. "Good luck, guys. Over and out."

Garrison moved down his arm containing the mic. "Okay, let's move. You guys head on up the conduit to intercept the suspects. James, you go with them. Alex and I will stay here."

"No," cried Alex, "I don't want James to go."

"Don't worry, Alex," said James. "I'll be all right."

"But it's dangerous," she insisted. "Stay here."

"They need the help. I have to go."

The soldiers checked their weapons and ammo and started to move out.

James hugged Alex tightly. "Use your gun if you have to. Okay?"

"Okay, but be careful!"

"I will."

He gave her one last look and then took off with the soldiers heading up to Tunnel 23.

Alex watched them slowly disappear. She didn't know what to think, but she had to concentrate and help with the nuke deactivation. It was a tense situation, but there was no time to think. A lot of lives depended on them.

[33]

Controlled Demolition

The men picked up their pace heading up the tunnel and had nearly made it up to Tunnel 22 when they heard footsteps and men talking in the passageway ahead of them. They immediately stopped, waiting for instructions. Agent Kelton, one of the CIA team members, directed them to hide their weapons but have them accessible when they were to pass by. They had to find out if they were real ITUS workers or the terrorists.

They continued walking slowly up the passageway, playing the part of a security force, when they spotted the men dressed in blue construction wear.

As they drew near, James noted they appeared nervous and uneasy.

Agent Kelton stopped. "Hey, guys. What's going on here? I don't recall ever seeing you in this area before."

One of the four men said, "Oh. We're helping out with a new communications line that's being installed in this area."

"Oh, really? We weren't notified of any equipment being installed here. I'm the security officer, and I don't know anything about it. Why don't you show me some ID and a work order?"

"Well, I'll have to check back with my superiors," the man said nervously. "I'm sure that we can straighten out this issue soon enough. Just let me get my phone and I'll call them right now."

Kelton tensed up as the man started to reach into his backpack. Then it hit him like a ton of bricks. James recognized that face and accent.

Eon Valstrand.

"Kelton!" James shouted. "That's Eon Valstrand. He works for Zepheron."

Kelton and his men immediately grabbed their weapons. Then all hell broke loose as the men in blue turned to run, firing off shots as they ran. The soldiers took cover and hit the floor, firing back at the assailants as they ran. James pulled out his pistol and looked around. When the coast was clear, the men jumped up and ran after them.

Kelton tossed his radio to James. "Notify Garrison and the other team."

James nodded and called it in as they ran.

"Disarm the nukes first, that's still our priority!" said Kelton. "If they get in the way, kill them."

As the service tunnel angled right, more shots were fired in front of them. Kelton took the radio back from James. "Tango Niner...we're at Tunnel 22 and taking fire."

"Roger, Iron Hawk, we'll send help your way. We located several more nukes up in Tunnel 25 and have disarmed them. Over."

"Good work, Tango Niner. Tunnel 19, what's going on there?"

Garrison answered, "We have the device neutralized. We're coming up to join you guys."

The shooting died down, and Kelton had their group advance. They ran quite a way up the passage before James called for them to stop.

"Look," he said, "The blue cable that's controlling the nukes makes a 'T' off here, right into this hallway."

"All right," said Kelton, "You guys go up to 23 and follow the blue cable up to there. Meet up with Tango Niner. James and I will check out the blue cable running this way."

"All right. Go!"

The men split up, and James and Kelton headed in the direction of the split-off passage to find out where it was heading. They moved quickly and traced it quite a ways in, where it made a few turns deeper into the complex. Then, unexpectedly, they entered a tunnel where the sound of construction equipment echoed in the distance.

They searched around for the cable, and at first they couldn't see it. The tunnel walls were not yet completed and the ground and walls were rocky and gravelly. After some probing, they found it again and followed it to the other side of the tunnel, where it went back into a passageway. As they entered, shots were fired. Luckily, neither of them were hit, and they took cover.

James shot off three rounds as he hugged the wall. Kelton blasted his compact machine gun, riddling the walls with bullets. After a minute of silence, they advanced, firing off shots as they moved up the shaft. They got close to the entryway where the cable went in and heard a voice cry, "You're too late, Sebring!"

It was Valstrand. He sounded desperate.

Kelton answered. "Give it up! Your plan isn't going to work."

"This entire complex is going to go up in a mushroom cloud and will fall into the ocean in about an hour. It can't be stopped."

More shots rang out, pinning them down. Kelton signaled for James to move to one side of the entrance. They'd storm the opening from there. James understood and stayed where he was while Kelton tried to get to the other side. He used the opportunity to reload. After Kelton dodged across, just missing some vicious fire, he gave James the signal. They both valiantly bolted into the entryway, blasting their weapons full force. It all seemed like a blur as bullets ricocheted off of everything.

One of Valstrand's men was killed while the other two continued to shoot back. Kelton took hits and fell to the floor but still managed to fire off a few rounds while he lay on the ground.

James dropped to the floor and rolled several times to avoid being hit. He just missed nasty volleys fired his way and then got off some significant shots with his pistol. He took out the man on the left, who took some direct rounds to his face and neck. Blood and tissue splattered all around. For a few seconds there was no shooting as each scrambled to find cover. James made it over to a large piece of equipment. Valstrand was hiding behind what appeared to be an electronics cabinet. Each was waiting for the other to make a move.

Kelton was moving on the ground, still alive. James had to distract Valstrand from seeing him; he'd kill him for sure. "Why are you doing this?" he yelled to Valstrand. "We know Namesbury's behind this, and it's not going to work!"

Valstrand hesitated and then said, "The world's changing, James! We're entering the age of peak oil. It's all going to be different in the future, and there's a lot of money to be made."

"You sound insane! Give yourself up, we have Navy SEALs and CIA agents disarming your bombs. They'll be here in minutes."

"No, they're not going to be able to get all of them. When this island breaks up into the Atlantic and creates a big tidal wave, the world's going to look a lot different!"

James looked around for what to do. He had to think of something, and quickly. They were in an isolated room of the tunnel system and backup could take a while.

Then he noticed Kelton's backpack on the ground near him with the thermite putty hanging out of it. He quickly snatched it, along with an igniter, and rolled it into a ball-like shape. He stuck the small igniter into the putty and flung it over the electronics cabinet at Valstrand. As it flew across the room, it exploded into a sizzling fireball.

Valstrand screamed. "GET IT OFF ME!"

James took a peek and saw Valstrand on fire, rolling around on the ground, trying to get the blazing material off his body. It was useless, as the thermite putty had created a white-hot plasma that within seconds was causing massive organ damage. James watched in horror as Valstrand's body thrashed on the ground. Smoke, steam and blood was everywhere, and the stench nearly made him gag. He covered his mouth and looked away.

James moved to Agent Kelton, who was still lying on the floor, obviously in a lot of pain. He got Kelton to his feet and they walked out of the room. As they turned the corner, men ran toward them with their guns drawn. He slumped with relief when he saw it was Agent Saveroff.

James wasted no time in relaying what had happened. "I think the master control device is in that room. You have to shut it down."

Several of the SEALs ran into the room while Agent Saveroff and another agent tended to Kelton's injuries.

James ran back into the room to see how the soldiers were making out with the disarming. They had taken apart the metal top to the controller, exposing an orange digital clock with a keypad. There was also a branch of colored electrical wires that entered an attached junction box where the infamous blue cable came out of. The clock was counting down, obviously indicating the time left before the bombs were to be detonated in a controlled sequence.

"What's going on?" asked James.

One of the men turned to him. "It doesn't look good. This clock is controlling all of the bombs in these tunnels in a programed sequence, and it's set to blow in sixty-two minutes."

"Did you disarm all of the nukes in the tunnels?"

"We disarmed five of them, but we think that there's another one or two left within the complex, and we're not sure where they are."

"What are we going to do?"

"We'll try to disarm this controller, but if we can't, we'll have to evacuate," he scowled.

The men worked frantically. They traced every wire going in and coming out and used an electronic scanning device, trying to discover a way to deactivate it. None of them had seen this type of controller. After several minutes of trying every possible solution, they realized that deactivation was not going to happen.

"We have to get out of here," one of them declared. "We can't disarm this timer safely without setting it off. Evacuate now!"

They all piled out of the room and sprinted in the direction of the main tunnel. One of the agents notified Garrison as he ran. They made it to Agent Saveroff, who was helping Kelton move up the tunnel. James took Kelton under his other arm. His head was spinning just thinking about the possibility of being trapped in the mountain when the bombs went off, but he shook it off. They had to focus on getting out. He had to get Alex to safety.

They eventually made it to their pick-up point outside of Tunnel 22. Emergency sirens blared, and a stream of ITUS workers were in a line for transport vehicles, several of which were already racing out of the tunnel. It was chaotic, hearing the sirens and seeing the rush of people. But they all were all relieved when they saw their transport vehicle waiting for them.

When they got to the entryway, the driver yelled, "Get in, we've got to go!"

Some of the agents helped shuffle Kelton into the vehicle, and the others quickly piled in. James was the last to get on board, and as he cleared the door, the vehicle sped off.

"Where is she?" he asked, craning his neck to look into the van. "Is she all right?" And then he heard her voice.

"James! James! I'm over here."

James searched for her voice and spotted her beside Garrison. He shoved his way around team members to get to her and they crushed each other in a hug. "God, I'm so glad to see you."

Alex smiled, but there was no hiding the stress on her face. "I was so worried about you being stuck in those damn tunnels. Thank God you made it out alive. Did they disarm all the bombs?"

James's face said it all. "No. They got most of them, but there's one or two left somewhere inside. Let's hope we make it out in time."

Alex squeezed his arm. "But what about all

the ITUS workers? My friends. My lab assistants."

James couldn't help but think they'd be lucky to die in a blast rather than a super tsunami, but he kept that to himself. "What would happen if only one or two of those nukes go off? Would it still cause a major tsunami?"

"Probably a smaller one. The tsunami generated would hit the east coast of the United States at night. There wouldn't be much of a warning. A few hours at most. That's just not enough time."

"Holy Christ," James said. Huge night waves, even smaller ones, hitting the coast of the United States would still potentially kill millions.

"The southern coast would get hit the worst. Maybe even your headquarters on Abaco. I'm sure they're being warned right now as we speak."

"Let's hope so," said James with an anxious frown.

Then unexpectedly their transport vehicle slowed to a crawl in a traffic jam just inside the main tunnel near the exit portal. Everyone inside became agitated as the line of vehicles inched slowly toward the tunnel opening. After a few minutes, the flow finally picked up, and they were outside of the complex. As they drove through the security checkpoint, they noticed a group of Spanish soldiers and police standing on both sides of the roadway, rifles in hand. The local authorities had been alerted and major countermeasures were being initiated.

The vehicle sped down the winding road, finally gaining miles away from the mountain. They started to feel some sense of relief that they were maybe going to make it. But the idea of a nuke going off inside the mountain was still too unpredictable.

Farther down the mountain, Garrison checked

the time—the devices were almost ready to go off.

Alex clenched her hand around James's knee. "James," she breathed, her voice quavering, "This is it!"

"I can't believe that this is happening. It seems like a bad dream."

As if as one, all on board anxiously turned to peer through the side windows, staring up at the mountain.

As they waited, time seemed to slow down as the minute mark came and went and nothing happened. They all waited tensely, and there was still no sign of an explosion. Light chatter among the team began, and James let out a breath. Alex's grip on his leg eased up.

Then, as some of the men started to celebrate, a deafening boom caused them all to cover their ears. They all looked up again, a collective groan of screams and anguish erupting in unison.

It all seemed to happen in slow motion. First, a large dust cloud plumed into the air, much like a volcano erupting. The dust cloud rose up and up and then started to fall back on itself, raining debris down the mountain.

The upper mountain seemed to cavitate and crawl like it was alive and moving. Then it happened. A deadly landslide began as a huge mass of terrain and dust slid down in a gigantic wave of energy and destruction that rolled and plowed until the devastating wave had disappeared from view, obscured by the hills.

It took some time for it all to sink into their minds as they all just stared at the path of annihilation and at each other. It was difficult to accept and put it into words, but Alex finally broke the silence. "It would have been ten times worse if all the bombs went off in a controlled demolition. At least we prevented the worst from happening."

James turned and caressed her hand against his face. "We did what we could. We'll have to see what happens. Let's just hope for the best."

***

When the enormous landslide hit the ocean, it created a huge tidal wave that later struck the islands surrounding La Palma, including the populated island of Tenerife. The impact generated a seventy-foot wave that smashed the seaside towns and harbors, killing hundreds. Hours later, the tsunami had radiated out in all directions, reaching Morocco and some western parts of Europe. There, it caused more destruction and some deaths, but because those landmasses were much farther away, its energy had dissipated, and the waves were noticeably diminished. By the time it touched the landmasses across the Atlantic Ocean some eight hours later, the monster tsunami had lost most of its deadly power. It still made an impact along the east coast of the United States, causing high flooding in many coastal areas. Florida got the brunt of its final phase, and the seaside communities of South Florida and the Keys noticed a major tidal surge and some fatalities.

News reports and warnings of the tsunami were broadcast to the public promptly by government agencies as it propagated from La Palma. This assisted in the preparation for its arrival and helped save many lives. The real cause of the landslide was not immediately reported. A full investigation of the deadly incident involving many government agencies was eventually released in a shielded form. No one wanted to let the public know how close the world had come to a super tsunami that could have killed millions of people worldwide.

[34]

A Celebration

Six months after the ITUS incident, James and Alex were finally able to set aside the memory of that chaotic event and their incredible involvement with it. They celebrated with a special trip to Cambridge, England, to visit Professor Aldridge. They gathered with the professor at the Peppermill, a local pub and restaurant located within the busy college town.

"I'm so glad that you both came up here to see me. This is wonderful," said the professor, smiling. He was a finely dressed elder gentleman, moderately tall and handsome for his age. He spoke eloquently in his distinguished British accent but had an easy and charming way in his conversations.

"Thanks for inviting us, Professor," said Alex, sipping a glass of fine Pinot Grigio. "It's always fun coming to Cambridge and touring the area. It has such a unique low-key vibe than the States. I love it here."

The pub was very quaint and had a distinguished, polished charm about it. It had a traditional wood interior with contrasting metallic wall decor and was where the elite of the famous university regularly came to hang out and chat about their collegiate happenings.

"Tell me, Alex, how do you like working for James?"

"I love it. I'm helping him out in research and development. It's a lot of fun, and I can be creative designing things."

"That's wonderful. You know, I remember when James was my student ages ago at Stony Brook and how he liked to design radical new forms of submarines and underwater drones. I'm sure you'll create some new fascinating designs on your own too."

She smiled. "Well, James is a natural at it, and I'm learning a lot from him. Right now, we're designing a new experimental submarine that'll be able to go deeper than the *Sagittarus*."

"Brilliant. You will have to show it to me when I come to Abaco. But I'm not sure I'll want to go down in it with you." He chuckled.

They laughed with him. "We'll show you the sub from sea level," said James, cheerfully sipping on his beer. "You don't have to go down with us if you don't want to." They were all having a great time.

The professor took a sip of his pint, then looked at James inquisitively. "James, I've been wanting to ask you about that ship that followed you to that secret location."

"Oh, that was the *Ososcelos*."

"I'm curious, did you ever find out why it followed you there?"

"It was a private mercenary ship owned by Callum Namesbury and his criminal organization. They had been using an ROV to examine the wreckage of the *Scorpion.* When they spotted our ship visiting the site, they were interested to see what we were doing there."

"Why were they so interested in the wreckage of the *Scorpion?*"

"We didn't understand that either until after the investigation team went through their records. They were planning to use special nuclear weapons to generate a killer tsunami. But they were inexperienced with building a tactical nuclear weapon. So they went to the *Scorpion* wreck to check out the design of the plutonium bombs that were aboard that submarine. As it turns out, they weren't able to get much information from the wreck because it was so deep and the hull of the ship was still relatively intact."

"So how were they able to build the nuclear weapons, then?"

"The investigators aren't sure yet. They think they got the design from another country. It's still an ongoing investigation."

"So, who was behind Namesbury, and why did they want to pull off this horrendous event?"

"They don't know that either, but they know for certain that Namesbury was part of an evil banking cartel that had run into financial problems. They had sold derivative investments all over the world to financial institutions, and those investments were worthless. So, to save themselves and to pocket billions, they were now placing new financial bets on a horrible financial panic that would happen if a super tsunami struck the world."

"Well, at least Namesbury and his criminals are locked up in prison, getting life sentences."

James snorted. "I'd like to see them get death sentences."

Alex frowned. "It's unbelievable to think that

an evil group would attempt such a massive inhuman incident just to make billions on the deaths of millions."

"It is, my dear," said Aldridge, "But that's certainly not the first time in history that evil individuals have attempted to pull off an event to make money on the deaths of people."

James nodded. "Just look what happened during World War II and at other times in history."

"You're right," she said. "I'm sure there are more wicked people hidden in the depths of our society, just waiting for an opportunity to commit mass genocide."

"They aren't all hidden," said James. "Governments are just as guilty, and they're in plain sight."

Aldridge nodded soberly. "It's always money. Lots of money."

Alex decided to change the direction of the conversation. "So when do we get to see the artifacts from that ancient wreckage?"

"Tomorrow, my dear," he said. "I have plans to take you to our archaeological restoration lab here at Cambridge to see those magnificent pieces."

"Fantastic. I can't wait to see them."

"Professor Willington, the director of the restoration lab, will give us all a personal tour. He's very eager to meet you two and chat with you about your discovery. He will show you the progress they made in restoring them and identifying their origins."

"Have they had any success in finding the date of the shipwreck and where it came from?"

"As of now, they are still not sure when the wreck went down. But they know for sure that it came from a time period well before the ancient Greeks." He leaned forward and lowered his voice. "And probably even before the Egyptians."

"The Egyptians?" asked Alex, stunned by his words.

He looked at them excitedly for a moment, a boyish look of glee on his face. "They are totally astounded by your discovery. This may rewrite the history of what we now know about ancient cultures."

"Will we get to see that metal device that you emailed me about?" James asked.

"Yes, indeed you will. Oh, and I happen to have brought you both a little pre-presentation for you to see."

He gave Alex a smile and reached into his jacket pocket and pulled out a small cloth bag.

Alex's eyes bulged as he carefully removed the items from the bag and placed them on the table before them.

"Here you go, Alex," he said, holding one up, "This one in particular I thought you'd be interested in."

Alex took the strange item and examined it slowly. "What is it?"

"They're not quite sure yet. It took some time to separate it out from the mass of concreation from the bottom, but they were able to clean it up relatively well."

Alex rolled it around in front of her eyes, trying to make sense of just what it could be. "It almost looks like a small feminine figurine."

"Yes, someone else noted that as well. Perhaps some sort of ritualistic goddess of worship? Or maybe a fertility symbol of some kind."

The three-inch-long greenish object appeared to be cut from a smooth gemstone and had a small corroded metallic band fastened around its neck. The face on the figurine appeared elongated but had clear feminine facial features.

"She's beautiful. Have they ever seen anything like this before?"

"No, not quite like this. Professor Willington told me that they have discovered ancient figurines similar to this from the Mediterranean region. But never of this type or style. It certainly has them mystified."

Then Aldridge turned to James and said, "And this here is for you, James. It's made of silver."

With heightened eyebrows, he accepted the small item and held it out in his hand to view. "An ancient coin."

James studied the small gray discolored flat metal piece, turning it over slowly, examining it. "I see some inscriptions here. Does that give a clue as to what region it's from?"

"Those appear similar to inscriptions found on ancient stone carvings from the island of Malta and southern Spain. But again, they have their own unique design characteristics."

"It's so exciting to think that some ancient ship from a time period well before the Egyptians was sailing those rough waters," said Alex with a gaze of wonderment, "Traveling to some mysterious destination. Who could they have been?"

"Yes, that is the question, isn't it? Some have speculated that there were civilizations living along the Atlantic coast of southern Europe before the end of the last Ice Age, many thousands of years ago. They were possibly trading with other civilizations across the European continent and the Atlantic Ocean and were thriving until the glacier ice sheets melted and flooded out their sea coast villages. Then the remnants of their civilizations scattered out across Europe, and maybe even the Atlantic, and blended into today's cultures."

"That's amazing to think," said James, holding his ancient coin in wonder. "Ancient civilizations traveling around the Atlantic, trading their goods and culture with unknown peoples."

The professor nodded. "What's also surprising

is there are remnants of an ancient civilization on the islands of the Azores that they are just now uncovering. That could be related to this ancient ship."

"Wow, we're going to have to check that out. What do you say, Alex? Would you like to visit the Azores sometime and go exploring?"

"Definitely," she said, "But let's go back to the ancient wreckage first and find out what else is down there."

James nodded. "Professor, would you like to join us when we go back?"

"That'd be smashing! I'd love to tag along and see what's there."

The professor grinned and raised his beer glass.

"To our joint quest in the spirit of adventure. Let's toast to our continued exploration of the mysterious ancient shipwreck that sank so many years ago. And to the many sailors who lost their lives there in that lonely spot. May God remember them and bless their lives forever."

They all drank from their glasses in celebration and continued to enjoy the evening, a celebration they would never forget. Memories were ephemeral, but the spirit of their adventure would live on forever.

[35]

Revisiting the Atlantic

Four months later, the *Aquatarus* was again out in the middle of the Atlantic Ocean, above the site of the ancient shipwreck. They had come back to search for any remaining artifacts and materials that still lay on the bottom, not far from the unfortunate wreck of the *Scorpion.*

It was a beautiful warm summer day, and the ocean was calm and reflected its magnificent deep-blue radiance to all those on board the ship. James had assembled a team of underwater explorers skilled in deep-water archaeological excavation. Some he had recruited from universities in England and others from the United States.

For five days, they had probed the site using submarines, including the *Sagittarus*, mapping the debris field. So far they had been unsuccessful in bringing up any substantial artifacts from the wreckage. But today they felt they were going to make a discovery and had a team excavating Zone 9 of the wreckage, using their best ROVs to rake the sea floor for booty.

James and Alex sped across the water in their Zodiac watercraft from the *Aquatarus*, heading toward the excavation barge that lay two hundred yards away in the open ocean.

"Do you have a strange feeling we're going to find something today?"

"Yeah, you feel it too?" He looked out at the water. "Can you imagine those crazy explorers who ventured out on the seas in small boats just to travel across the oceans?"

"What would happen to them if they hit rough seas?"

He laughed. "I wouldn't want to be in *this* thing in the middle of a storm where we are right now, I can tell you that."

When they reached the large rectangular excavation barge, one of the workers greeted them and helped Alex up the ladder. At first, James thought that it was one of the contractors, but it was Kent.

"Hey, welcome aboard, guys. Watch those ladder steps. They're a little tricky."

James pulled himself up the ten hazardous steps slowly behind Alex. After he caught his breath, he asked, "So how are we making out today?"

"It's going well. Here, let me show you guys what we have so far."

They walked over to a pile of bottom debris that had been deposited in the middle of the large barge.

"This is it. Our team was working all night surveying Zone 9, and they managed to bring this up."

"Oh, God, the smell," said Alex, covering her face with her hand. "How do you separate the haul from that black goo? What is that stuff?"

"Well, that's the way that most of the bottom of the oceans looks like. When plankton and marine life fall to the bottom, it piles up and forms a thick mud mat. We use high-pressure hoses to rinse it off and send it back into the ocean."

"So have you found anything yet?"

Kent smiled at them coyly, tantalizing them. "Over here."

He shuffled them over to some things separated from the main pile and pointed.

Alex bent down to examine the materials. "Holy crap! Look at *this*."

There was an assortment of broken clay pottery pieces of various sizes, including some that were almost entirely intact. There was also a piece of blemished green jewelry attached by a metallic wire. The jewelry appeared to be a beaded necklace but was in a dire need of a cleaning.

"My God, this is amazing."

"Yeah, everyone gets all geared up when we make a find. They have to be careful removing the material from the bottom so they don't damage it or disrupt the wreckage, so it takes a long time to do the excavation and record everything."

A loud sound from the nearby hoisting crane interrupted their conversation, and they all turned to watch as a large load of bottom material was deposited near the existing pile.

"Okay, let's move away," said Kent. "It's a little dangerous here."

They moved out of the way. As Alex walked toward the edge of the barge, she spotted the *Aquatarus* in the background and noticed two individuals in a Zodiac watercraft heading their way. Rebecca stood at the front.

"Hey, look, it's Nicki and Professor Aldridge coming."

James waved at them. "They're going to love this," said James.

"Yeah, and we already found some artifacts for them to see," said Alex, smiling.

As they turned back to the action on the barge, they noticed the new material had already been placed on deck and was actively being washed down. James took the time to enjoy the moment. After all, he was funding the project, and it was exciting to be there.

He clutched Alex's hand and grinned at her. "What do you think? Isn't this amazing for us to be here, above this ancient wreck, searching for its hidden secrets?"

"Aldridge is going to flip. I've always wanted to see a British professor squeal with glee."

James laughed.

Shouts rang out from the workers near the excavation pile. Confused, they turned and saw a commotion happening between workers wearing bright orange uniforms as they sorted through the excavated material.

"Think they found something?" asked Alex.

James squinted at the scene. "Maybe." Then he saw Kent headed in their direction, his face lit up like he was on fire.

"James! James! You guys have got to see this!"

They glanced at each other for a split second and then followed Kent over to the new material. As they drew near, they saw some objects peeking through a thin layer of black sediment.

Several workers were using specialized brushes and water pressure to clean away the muck from the objects. With more cleaning and washing, the hidden secrets of the discovery were slowly being exposed.

Alex walked up and peered around the crew. She put her hand over her mouth and gasped. "Unbelievable."

James was stunned when he spotted the exposed treasures. He looked up in the sky and with his hands up in the air, yelled, "Yeah!"

Their eyes focused on large metallic-looking objects that resembled pots or bowls. Their surface was corroded and tarnished, but their shape was obviously roundish and man-made.

"They're heavy, like they're made of iron," said the worker removing the black mud from the object.

Interspaced within other unidentifiable substrate were some items that resembled stone statues of various sizes, ranging from six to fourteen inches.

James moved closer to get a better look. He turned to a crew member and said, "Hey, can you wash off these pieces here?"

The worker agreed and brought his nozzle up to the statues and washed softly at first and then turned up the velocity so that the effectiveness of the high pressure would do the job. As the gooey-black layer was slowly washed away from the statues, they could start to see their details better.

Alex joined James, peering at the stone figurines, watching as their faces were revealed. Then the professor, Nicki, and Rebecca joined the gathering and announced themselves. James turned to see his guests.

"My God!" exclaimed Aldridge. "Already? What have you found?"

James laughed, glad the professor could be on board for this.

Nicki took out her phone. "I have to take a picture of this to show my kids." With her iPhone already in hand, she started snapping pictures.

After a few more minutes of sorting through the excavation, one of the crew pulled out something with an interesting shape even though it was still covered in muck. She used her hands to wipe it off as best she could and then employed a wash hose to clean it better. Slowly, it started to reveal itself. The black goo wore away, and a shiny gold color radiated from the partly exposed area.

This got everyone chattering. Then as it was entirely cleaned of the mud, she held it out for view. Then she smiled and handed it to James.

He gripped it with both his hands and turned it at different angles, observing it intently. "Professor, take a look at this and see what you think it could be."

Aldridge carefully examined the four-inch-long item. Intrigued, he turned it around and peered at it from the opposite side. After some time of examination, he said, "It's obviously a horse's head, made of gold by its weight. There's a beautiful engraving, both raised and etched, on the gold metal collar around the base of the head. It's in magnificent condition considering it's been on the bottom of the ocean for thousands of years."

"Where do you think it came from?" inquired James.

He thought for a few seconds. "You know this type of gold artifact reminds me of the famous Thracian gold items found in Bulgaria."

"The Thracian dynasty dated back to 4,000 BC, right?"

"Yes, but this appears different and unique from that dynasty. This could be even older than that by the looks of it."

"Wow."

Professor Aldridge smiled. "This is an exquisitely handcrafted artifact. The university would love to have a go at examining this."

Then someone within the excavation team called out excitedly, "Look! We found something else here."

They moved closer and watched as a small article lying on the deck of the barge was rinsed off. When the item was finally free of the sticky muck, they could make out its roundish shape. The employee stood up, holding it in her hand. "It's a gold medallion! Here, take a look, James."

James moved in to view it carefully. "This is beautiful."

Aldridge maneuvered to James's side and stared down in awe. It was a solid gold pendant adorned with the face of a woman. "Definitely not Greco-Roman, Egyptian, or Mediterranean."

Then his face lit up. He turned to James, looking like a little boy on Christmas morning. "Atlantis," he whispered.

James looked at him, startled.

Alex came in closer. James grinned and handed her the three-inch medallion. "This is for you, Alex," he said, winking. She hugged him, grinning widely.

She gazed at the beautiful item and then held it up in the air for all to see, turning it slowly. An applause broke out. They all felt proud and privileged to be part of the team that made the amazing discovery, taken by the gods of the sea so many ages ago.

***

Later that evening, James held a celebration for everyone. The finest food was served in a buffet-style banquet expertly crafted by Chef Hans and his professional staff.

The party went on well into the night, with piano music in the background. James and Alex mingled with everyone for hours, talking about the adventures they'd shared over the past few months and their amazing discovery.

At one point during the celebration, James interrupted the affair and offered up a speech to all involved with the project. "I want to thank you all for assisting us in this remarkable undersea discovery, and for all the expertise and effort that you bring to the excavation and recovery of the amazing items that we've found."

While holding up the ancient golden horse head in his hand, he continued. "It's because of you that we've been able to explore this wreck-age, map out the site, and bring up these treasures."

He looked around the room. "I especially want to thank my dedicated crew for all the adversity they've faced over the past several months on this voyage. You are the best crew that a profes-sional ocean engineering company could ever have."

Then James searched for Alex. "And, lastly, I want to thank my lovely Alex, who joined us on this cruise of adventure and ended up getting a little more excitement than any of us could ever have imagined."

A roar of laughter erupted from the attendees. Alex also chuckled, nearly spilling her cham-pagne on her dress.

"She's now a member of our team here at OECI and my beautiful soulmate. We're so lucky to have her here, and I'm so lucky to have her by my side."

Alex blushed as everyone clapped.

"Thank you, everyone, and enjoy your evening!"

Later on, while the guests partied on, James and Alex snuck out for a little nighttime stroll around the promenade. They held hands, walking to the starboard side overlooking the view of the ocean.

"The ocean looks so gorgeous tonight."

"It's really something to be able to see the moonlight reflect off the waves so far out at sea like this. It almost touches you inside."

She gazed at him, noticing the soft moonlight reflect off his eyes.

"Yes, it does, doesn't it? There's just so much energy in the water along with the cascading sound of the waves. It's so peaceful and hypnotic."

"So, tell me, how do you feel now that you've been on the ship this long? Has it changed you?"

She thought for a second. "It has. I feel like a different person now in some way. There's something about being here on the ocean for a long time like this."

He put his arm around her and looked in her eyes. "Isn't this amazing for you and me to be together here, out on the ocean, searching for its hidden secrets?"

"I'll remember this trip for as long as I live." She smiled at him lovingly. "But it's only memorable because I'm with you, James. This is what my life's all about. You and I will always be together. On the sea, you and me."

They drew near and kissed. Then they gazed out into the horizon, the ocean highlighted with the moon in the background. Sharing in the beautiful moment, thinking about the life ahead of them, traveling the world.

About the Author

Isidore (Izzy) Doroski was born and raised in New York, on eastern Long Island. After receiving his bachelors of science in biology at State University of New York at Cortland, Izzy attained certification as a Public Health Sanitarian. His early employment included a job as a research scientist in neurophysiology and as a wastewater treatment operation specialist. For most of his career, Izzy worked at an environmental agency as a senior environmental health scientist, protecting public health through environmental regulation enforcement.

Throughout his thirty-eight-year career, Izzy's profession took him to many fascinating locations, including several nuclear reactors, energy storage and production facilities, and many research and industrial manufacturing facilities. He also participated in emergency response situations and flew in the police helicopter. Some of the inspiration for this book comes from Izzy's time spent with the waters around eastern Long Island and his interest in SCUBA diving.

Izzy Doroski has always had a deep passion for science and has lectured at town halls, schools, and colleges on the subject of energy, alternate energy, and wastewater treatment. In his spare time, Izzy loves to hike, bike, and play guitar and electronic keyboards. He has recorded and published several music albums under his music name, Existence Wave, and has also written and published *The Inverted Mask*, his first science fiction novel. Izzy is a natural science fiction writer and totally enjoyed the writing experience with *Night Waves*. He is planning on writing several more sci-fi stories.

Made in the USA
San Bernardino, CA
14 January 2020